"Do you fear me?"

Mairi glanced sideways. "I just..." Her shoulders curved as furrows formed in her brow.

"Are you in pain? Did those brigands hurt—?"

"Nay. 'Tis just that everything happened so quickly." She turned her back and, burying her face in her palms, shook her shoulders. "Those men were—and then you— oh, heavenly Father!"

Dunn's heart twisted. Stepping nearer, he reached out his hand, but stopped before touching her. She wouldn't want that.

Instead, he tried to think of something to say to ease her suffering. "No refined woman should ever witness such brutality. My actions were carried out only to ensure your well-being, m'lady."

She spied him over her shoulder. "But you were so brutal. So savage. I've never seen anything like it...and there were *three* of them."

Dunn lowered his hands to his sides. She thought him a monster. And why not? He'd acted savagely—showed no mercy. "Three ruthless men with no moral virtue among them. Men capable of unspeakable acts. If I hadn't stopped them, you—"

"I ken." She nodded as she looked to her feet.

How could he assuage her fears? Did she think him a heartless tyrant? Is that why he was so unappealing to her? "I hope you do not fear me. I am here to protect you, m'lady. I will do so at any cost."

Her inhale faltered as she faced him, keeping her arms crossed. "I believe you," she whispered.

PRAISE FOR AMY JARECKI

THE HIGHLAND GUARDIAN

"Magnetic, sexy romance is at the heart of this novel, made complete with a cast of richly depicted characters, authentic historical detail, and a fast-moving plot."
—*Publishers Weekly*

"A true gem when it comes to compelling, dynamic characters.... With clever, enchanting writing, elements of life-or-death danger and a romance that takes both Reid and Audrey completely by surprise, *The Highland Guardian* is an historical romance so on point it'll leave readers awestruck."
—*BookPage*

THE HIGHLAND COMMANDER

"Readers craving history entwined with their romance (a la *Outlander*) will find everything they desire in Jarecki's latest. Scottish romance fans rejoice."
—*RT Book Reviews*

"Sizzles with romance...Jarecki brings the novel to life with vivid historical detail."
—*Publishers Weekly*

THE HIGHLAND DUKE

"Readers will admire plucky Akira, who, despite her poverty, is fiercely independent and is determined to be no man's mistress. The romance is scintillating and moving, enhanced by fast-paced suspense."

—Publishers Weekly

"This story was so much more than a romance, it was full of intrigue, excitement and drama...a fantastic read that I fully recommend."

—Buried Under Romance

THE HIGHLAND CHIEFTAIN

ALSO BY AMY JARECKI

Lords of the Highlands series
The Highland Duke
The Highland Commander
The Highland Guardian

THE HIGHLAND CHIEFTAIN

A Lords of the Highlands Novel

AMY JARECKI

FOREVER
New York Boston

Copyright © 2018 by Amy Jarecki
Preview of *The Highland Renegade* © 2018 by Amy Jarecki

Cover design by Elizabeth Turner Stokes
Cover illustration by Craig White
Cover copyright © 2018 by Hachette Book Group, Inc.

Forever
Hachette Book Group
1290 Avenue of the Americas, New York, NY 10104
forever-romance.com
twitter.com/foreverromance

First Edition: July 2018

Forever is an imprint of Grand Central Publishing. The Forever name and logo are trademarks of Hachette Book Group, Inc.

The publisher is not responsible for websites (or their content) that are not owned by the publisher.

The Hachette Speakers Bureau provides a wide range of authors for speaking events. To find out more, go to www.hachettespeakersbureau.com or call (866) 376-6591.

ISBN: 978-1-5387-2960-1 (mass market), 978-1-5387-2958-8 (ebook)

Printed in the United States of America

OPM

10 9 8 7 6 5 4 3 2 1

ATTENTION CORPORATIONS AND ORGANIZATIONS:
Most Hachette Book Group books are available at quantity discounts with bulk purchase for educational, business, or sales promotional use. For information, please call or write:

Special Markets Department, Hachette Book Group
1290 Avenue of the Americas, New York, NY 10104
Telephone: 1-800-222-6747 Fax: 1-800-477-5925

For my brother, PhD, MD, brilliant, and all things I am not. Growing up in your shadow, I learned to challenge myself, to reach higher, to persevere. Griffin, you will always be a shining star in my heart.

Acknowledgments

To all the amazing people who have helped with this novel, I am truly grateful. To my agent, **Elaine Spencer**, who shares my love of well-bred dogs and who is the only woman I know who can make miracles happen. To my fabulous editor, **Leah Hultenschmidt**, who is not only tactful, she is right most of the time. To the Grand Central Publishing Art Department, especially **Craig White** and **Elizabeth Turner Stokes**, for their brilliance in creating smoldering Highlander covers that ooze masculinity and foreboding. To **Estelle Hallick** for donning her armor and guiding my books through the tempestuous marketing maze, and to **Mari Okuda** and **Angelina Krahn** for their fastidious and diligent copyediting, without whom all my typing faux pas would be shamefully on display.

I would also like to thank the volunteers at the various museums, castles, and estates I have visited in Scotland, especially the **Highland Folk Museum** for giving me a realistic glimpse into Highland life in the eighteenth century and more.

Chapter One

En route to Urqhart Castle, midsummer 1711

*B*less it, you look worse than a rheumy-eyed ragamuffin." Mairi's father folded his gazette and slapped it on the bench beside him. "I've had enough of your moping. 'Tis time to sit straight and wipe away those confounding tears. There will be many influential men at the gathering, and I expect you to show the aristocracy of Scotland that the House of Cromartie is undaunted by your recent misfortune."

Her insides hollow and drained, Lady Mairi MacKenzie wiped a hand across her face, her gaze shifting to her father. They'd been riding in the coach for hours upon hours, yet the Earl of Cromartie looked as crisp as when they'd set out at dawn. His long, curled periwig framed the hard angles of his face, his lace neckerchief tied perfectly beneath his chin. Da expected her to be thus composed regardless of if she was disgraced, ruined, and too mortified to ever again be seen in society.

How can I possibly face everyone and pretend nothing is amiss?

She'd pleaded with her father to allow her to remain home at Castle Leod, but nay, Mairi was given no choice but to hold her chin high and behave as if all was well. In the past, she'd enjoyed attending Highland fetes—the food, the dancing, meeting old friends, especially those of the male variety. But today, she was merely doing her duty. She didn't want to laugh or dance or be sociable. She wanted to hide in her bedchamber with the shutters closed.

She could envision it now. As soon as she alighted from the coach, everyone would stare and the ladies would whisper behind their fans about her woeful state of affairs. Mairi could hear the gossip as well: *Redheads are the devil's spawn...Poor Cromartie, he'll be lumbered with a spinster for the rest of his days.*

All too soon, the coach rolled to a stop outside the crumbling gates of Urquhart Castle. Mairi closed the shutter, sat back, and crossed her arms.

Da reached over and tucked a curl under her bonnet. "Come, lass, 'tis time to put the past behind you. Square your shoulders, and hold your chin high."

Mairi gulped. She'd rather be facing a smithy with a pair of tongs and submit to a tooth extraction than show her face. "Must I? If the coach turned around right now, we'd arrive home by—"

"Absolutely out of the question." Da opened the door, climbed down the ladder, then thrust his hand inside. "Come, dearest, show the vultures you have a backbone of iron."

She stared at the outstretched palm and drew a stuttering breath. Now she knew how a caged lion must feel, wanting to pounce but powerless to do so. Indeed, creating a scene would double her humiliation. With no other choice, Mairi took Da's hand and climbed outside into the blinding sunlight. She swiftly opened her parasol, blinking rapidly.

Keeping her gaze downcast, she started for the drawbridge.

"Take heed!" a rider bellowed, reining a horse to a skidding stop as dirt and stones flew. The enormous black horse snorted and grunted, sidestepping. Mairi leaped out of the way while her parasol caught the wind, ripped from her hand, and flew to the ground.

"M'lady?" boomed the rider in a deep brogue—a familiar, rumbling voice that sent a shiver across the back of her neck.

Before she could stop herself, Mairi looked up. A tempest of butterflies swarmed in her stomach. Gooseflesh rose across her skin, making those tingles skitter down her spine. As far back as she remembered, Dunn MacRae had an unnerving effect on Mairi's insides. The laird was braw and rugged, his midnight-blue eyes arresting and haunting. When standing, he towered over everyone with shoulders as wide as a horse's hindquarter. He rarely smiled, and his shoulder-length hair was coarse and dark—just like the man. This day, he'd clubbed it back with a ribbon, but an errant strand hung to the side of his face, making him look dangerous and menacing.

But those eyes grew narrow and filled with bitterness. He bowed his head. "Are you well, m'lady?" he asked, his tone gruff.

"What were you thinking, MacRae?" demanded her father, collecting the parasol. "Did you not see the coach?"

"Forgive me, m'lord. My mind was elsewhere." He tipped his hat to Mairi. "Good day."

Mairi nodded, watching the backside of Laird MacRae's stallion disappear, tail swishing while horse and rider crossed the old drawbridge. Sighing, she took the parasol from Da and reassembled the shreds of her pride.

"Lady Mairi!" A happier voice came from the crowd. As she turned, Janet Cameron grasped her by the elbow. "'Tis so good to see you. I was afraid you mightn't come." A close friend, Janet had charming blue eyes and a delicate face framed with blonde curls.

Wishing she were still home in her bedchamber safely concealed from society, Mairi gave the lass a look of exasperation. *Everyone kens I've been cast aside and disgraced.*

Da stepped in and clasped Janet's hands. "It is good to see you as well, Miss Cameron. My daughter is in sore need of companionship. I trust you can impart some of your bountiful cheer."

"Oh my." Janet's eyes grew wide. "'Tis usually Her Ladyship who keeps me up all hours laughing."

Mairi forced a smile. "I'm afraid I've lost my ability to make merry for the rest of my days."

"Rubbish. If I ken your nature, m'lady, you'll be dancing reels afore the gathering's end." Janet pulled her away and toward the drawbridge. "They'll be serving the evening meal soon. Clan Grant have outdone themselves. Even my father was astonished."

Grateful for something new to talk about, Mairi arched

her eyebrows. "Is he not still feuding with the Grants? I'm surprised you are here."

"Me as well, but Da pushed aside his differences for the gathering." Janet leaned closer while she lowered her voice. "*The cause*, ye ken."

Mairi nodded. Presently she couldn't give a fig about the Jacobite cause or plans for the succession.

Janet didn't seem to notice as the lass stepped up the pace. "You absolutely must see the great hall. They've made it look so *medieval*, 'tis like traveling back in time two hundred years at least."

Twirling her parasol, Mairi rolled her eyes. "Do not tell me there are knights wearing full suits of armor."

Janet winked. "I haven't seen one as of yet, but there's still hope."

Mairi tried not to laugh, but stifled a snort before it blew through her nose.

"Is this the latest fashion?" asked Janet, flicking the scalloped brim of the parasol. "'Tis bonny."

"Aye, Da brought it from France—said all the ladies of the gentry are using them on the Continent."

"Your father dotes on you. I'm lucky if mine remembers my saint's day."

Mairi shook her head. Janet didn't know the half of it. "Mine is a little too overbearing, I'm afraid."

Once inside the curtain walls, noise came from the enormous hall on the shore of Loch Ness. Mairi had only been to Urquhart once, and Janet was right. It was a relic from ages past and it bore many a battle scar. The sound of boisterous laughter made her stop short and grasp her friend's arm. A hollow emptiness swelled in her chest. "I cannot go in there." Dear Lord, she might swoon.

"Oh my, you are melancholy, are you not?"

Blinking back sudden tears, Mairi drew her hand to her forehead. "Ever so much."

"Come, you must tell me everything afore the evening meal. I ken just the spot."

Janet pulled Mairi through the grounds to the abandoned dovecote. Inside it was cool and the light dim. After folding the parasol, Mairi sat on a stone shelf while Janet joined her. Exhausted by the journey preceded by days of crying, Mairi allowed her shoulders to droop. Quite possibly, Janet was the only soul at the fete to whom she could pour out her woes. "I'm ruined," she whispered as her throat constricted.

"Oh, my dearest, I hate seeing you so miserable." Janet patted Mairi's hand. "Please tell me what happened. Gossip is rife that the Earl of Seaforth married his ward."

"Ayeeee," Mairi cried, hiding her face in her hands, trying to keep her tears at bay. "I still cannot believe it."

"Good riddance, I say." Janet waved her hand through the air as if breaking an engagement was but a trifle.

"Good riddance?" Unable to believe her ears, Mairi's spine shot to rigid. "He's an earl, the man my family expected me to marry. Our fathers agreed to the betrothal when I was still in the cradle—a pact sealed by two great men."

"Over a dram of whisky, rumor has it."

"Curses to those scandalmongers!"

"I am truly sorry you have been hurt. It pains me to see you so melancholy."

"Thank you. Your concern means a great deal to me."

Taking Her Ladyship's hand, Janet rubbed the back of it soothingly. "As I recall, you once complained to me that the earl was never overly cordial toward you. Certainly, he was well mannered, but no more so toward you than anyone else."

Forcing herself to swallow against her urge to sob, Mairi dabbed her eyes. "I have no idea what I did wrong."

"The fault does not lie with you. Not in the slightest." Janet huffed. "Remember what you said last summer? You were worried about marrying Seaforth because you felt him distant. He was forever away and you scarcely had a chance to speak with him."

Shaking her head, Mairi refused to listen. "But Da always said the earl was acting like a typical bachelor—said he'd face his responsibility once he was ready to wed."

"Mm-hmm." Janet looked away.

Mairi's breath caught. Da's reasoning had always been so convincing, and she'd just blindly accepted it. Had Seaforth meant to rescind the agreement all along? Good Lord, she'd made a fool of herself time and again. "What must everyone think of me?"

"'Tis not you the clans are gossiping about. 'Tis Seaforth who must atone for *his* behavior. Everyone kens ye are a witty, bonny, and vivacious young woman who has limitless potential." Janet clapped her hands. "And I hear you've already shunned one suitor—a most braw Highlander at that."

"Duncan MacRae?" Mairi asked, using his given name rather than the moniker of Dunn, which everyone knew him by. "Och, the man offered for my hand hours after Seaforth took his nuptials—'twas merely an act of charity. My father avowed he only offered out of loyalty to the earl."

"I think not. He's a chieftain—one who can wield a mighty sword, with lands and riches of his own. MacRae has earned the respect of Clan Cameron for certain."

"Aye." Mairi heaved a sigh, her heart heavy. No matter how tempting MacRae's offer may have been, Da had already imparted her refusal, and there was no use harboring regrets. "The Highlander has always been rather imposing."

"Imposing? I'd say he looks like a gladiator—almost as handsome as Robert Grant."

"Almost?" Mairi might be melancholy, but she wasn't blind. Dunn MacRae was as handsome as he was braw— far more fetching than Grant.

"Mm-hmm." Janet's eyelashes fluttered.

Forming an O with her lips, Mairi gasped. "Are you smitten?"

"Never." The lass blushed clear up to her blonde tresses. "The Grants and the Camerons are always feuding about something. My admiration for Mr. Grant is simply a distant appreciation of a braw Highlander—his character is a different matter, however."

Mairi almost chuckled. Janet *was* smitten, whether she believed herself to be or nay. "What is your father feuding about now?"

"Another spat over lands."

"Aye, just like it has always been between men for the past two thousand years." Mairi stuffed her kerchief back into her sleeve. "Da says the feudal ways of the Highlands are doomed."

"That mightn't be such a bad thing." Janet sighed. "But it will not happen today. Come, why not cast aside your woes and bat your eyelashes at Mr. MacRae?"

She groaned, giving her friend a look of exasperation. "Because I have rejected him, that's why. Besides, Da insists he will not approve of my marriage to anyone less than a baron."

"Earls can be inordinately difficult."

"Tell me something I do not already ken. I've lived with an earl my entire life, and it hasn't been easy."

"You make living at Castle Leod sound like a great burden."

"And what about you? Achnacarry has opulence all its own."

"Aye, but my da leaves me be. He has my brothers to occupy his time."

"I see. So you do not believe he's scheming to arrange your marriage this very minute?"

Janet cringed. "He wouldn't dare—n-not without speaking to me about it first."

Mairi heaved a sigh and looked to the rounded ceiling of the dovecote. "Fathers. 'Tis a miracle they are not the death of us."

In the distance a bell sounded, announcing the evening meal. Janet grasped Mairi's hand. "We'd best not be late. Besides, I wouldn't miss tonight's meal for a dozen golden guineas."

"Just so you can ogle the lads?"

Janet gave a wink. "The *men*, mind you."

Mairi took in a deep breath and allowed her friend to pull her toward the rising voices of the crowd. Most often Mairi would be the flirty one eager to join the throng and Janet would be aghast. How circumstances had changed in a mere fortnight.

However, the trip to Urquhart was not a complete debacle. Thanks to her friend, the despair clawing at Mairi's heart had eased a bit...until they strode inside the hall.

Chapter Two

After crossing the drawbridge, Dunn, chieftain of Clan MacRae, glanced over his shoulder. Thank God Lady Mairi hadn't followed him across. He'd naturally assumed she'd send her apologies for this gathering and stay home. Late for a meeting with Robert Grant, he'd been riding at a brisk canter when the woman stepped in front of him without looking where she was headed. Dunn had almost run right over the lass.

Why Her Ladyship, and not any other woman in the Highlands?

Well, she was Cromartie's burden, and Dunn wouldn't give the lass another thought.

Robert Grant, laird of Glenmoriston, had planned a fine midsummer's gathering in the medieval remains of a once-formidable fortress. Presiding over the shores of Loch Ness, Urquhart Castle still commanded a sense of awe—even with the turret of the gatehouse upside down in the dry moat, having been ravaged by Cromwell's cannon during his invasion of Scotland sixty years prior.

A cool wind caressed his neck as he searched for Robert inside the grounds. Aye, air cleansed by the waters of the loch gave him a refreshing sense of freedom. There was nothing he enjoyed more than riding the Highlands with a dirk in his belt, a sword at his hip, and a flask of whisky in his sporran. Aye, Scotland pulsed through his blood with the rush of a roaring river.

Robert Grant bounded toward Dunn with a grin as wide as Black Rock Gorge—a grin as sincere as Highland hospitality. "You're late, MacRae."

"'Tis still Friday, is it not?" Dunn dismounted and passed his reins to a groom. "Give the big fella an extra ration of oats. Beastie's a Scottish-bred champion, none faster or stronger."

"Aye, sir." The lad smoothed his hand along the stallion's neck. "He's a beauty."

"That he is," said Grant, grasping Dunn's hand in a firm handshake.

"Och, 'tis good to see you this fine day." Dunn tossed the lad a coin before the boy led the horse into the stable. Then he squeezed his friend's arm, giving him a challenging grin. "Are ye favoring muskets in the games?"

Affecting an affronted grimace, Grant thwacked him on the shoulder. "I can give you a right royal thrashing in the wrestling arena any day, any time."

Dunn threw his head back and laughed. If ever he had heard a bold-faced lie, Robert Grant just spewed a gross fabrication. Too right, Dunn hadn't been bested since he'd achieved his majority, and everyone knew it well. "Forever the combatant, are you not?"

"Life wouldn't be nearly as fun without a healthy feud

to keep one amused." Grant, renowned for feuding with most of his neighbors, gestured toward the manse. "Come, allow me to treat you to a dram of whisky to wash away the dust from the trail afore the others arrive."

That brought a smile to Dunn's lips. He wasn't surprised he'd arrived first. And he'd hoped to catch up on the latest news with his old friend. "Words to warm a man's heart."

"And his gullet," added Grant.

Once inside the tower, Robert led the way to the old solar. "I've brought in a table and chairs for meetings during the gathering. 'Tis rustic, but will do in a pinch."

Dunn looked between the ancient stone walls while the heavy oak door closed behind them. "I think this is the perfect spot for the gathering. It will remind the Highland Defenders of their purpose—the reason why we're still at odds with the English. Tell me, when was Urquhart last occupied?"

"A Jacobite garrison in 1692. It's been falling into decay ever since. It would cost a king's fortune to make it livable again."

He looked to the rafters. "Well, at least she still has a roof."

Grant gestured to a high-backed chair before he moved to the sideboard and pulled the stopper out of a newfangled decanter. He poured two drams. "What trouble has the Earl of Seaforth encountered of late?"

Sitting, Dunn scratched the stubble on his jaw. He'd shaved that morn, but his unruly beard always made a showing in the afternoon, the damnable whiskers. "Now that His Lordship is married, it seems his strife has gone on holiday for the time being—but it has only been a fortnight."

Grant placed both glasses of whisky on the table. "I reckon that's a good thing. At least it affords you a chance to tend your own affairs."

"And 'tis about time, too. I've been watching Seaforth's back for so long, my rents haven't been collected in two years."

The shorter but solid chieftain took the chair opposite. "Good Lord, the crofters will never be able to meet the back payments."

Dunn raised his glass. "I do not aim to make them."

"What? Are you going soft in your old age?"

"Old age? I'm thirty." Dunn wasn't soft, either. The harvests for the past two years had been lean, and his kin needed respite. What kind of man was he if he did not give it?

"'Tis generous of you." The Grant laird gave him a once-over. "What other news? At thirty the chieftain of Clan MacRae ought to be thinking about settling down."

The whisky burned all the way to Dunn's gullet. Moreover, it burned with his friend's words. When was he supposed to find time to marry? Not that he wanted to marry anyone, especially after Lady Mairi's quick refusal. He looked at his glass and, rather than replying to his friend's probing question, took another healthy swig.

Grant stretched out his legs and crossed his ankles. "A tender subject, is it? I heard about your proposal to Mairi MacKenzie. But knowing you, I figured you'd brush it off, go out and wrestle a bull."

"Och, I was daft to think the lass might favor me," Dunn said with more of an edge to his voice than he'd intended. At every gathering he'd ever frequented where Lady Mairi had been in attendance, the lass had flirted with him mercilessly. And he'd done nothing but think back on all those encounters for the past several days. Had her favor been a figment of his imagination? All those smoldering looks, those coy glances across the many halls—her compliments and her light touches on his arm. Had she vexed him because she was promised and therefore unavailable? None of it made sense—but then Dunn had never met a woman who wasn't confounding.

"If you ask me," said Grant, "she has her head up her arse on account of being the daughter of an earl."

"But I always thought her amusing. I reckon her father has soured her—the bastard is hell-bent on marrying her off to a peer."

"Mairi MacKenzie?" A loud snort rumbled from Grant's nose. "It had best be a *Scottish* peer."

The sarcasm in his friend's voice made Dunn's entire body tense. "Why do you say that?"

"Because the wee lassie will be a handful, and I reckon she'd ride roughshod over any English nobleman. Sassenachs are just too damned soft."

Dunn chuckled and swirled the liquid in his glass. He wouldn't mind having Mairi MacKenzie ride roughshod over him—or try. It certainly would make for good sport. Then he scowled, internally admonishing himself. *I need to erase the woman from my memory.*

"What you need is a good romp with a sturdy Highland wench."

He raised his glass. "Now that's the most agreeable thing I've heard in days."

* * *

After Dunn and Robert enjoyed two drams of whisky, they moved to the hall and switched to ale. The festivities were just beginning. Clan chiefs were expected to lead the merriment, and Dunn never slighted his duty. A stalwart devotion to clan and kin had been ingrained in him by his father from the cradle. MacRae's lot wasn't only to protect his own, but to protect and serve the lofty MacKenzies. An oath of fealty had been pledged centuries past, and the two clans had held up their side of the bargain ever since. Though it did chap him a wee bit to always walk in the shadow of Seaforth, Dunn knew his purpose and he would never turn his back on it.

No matter how pleasurable it was to sit in the sanctity of the solar with Robert Grant and sip fine Scotch whisky, social duty called, and ale would have to suffice for the duration of the night. The hall was already filled with shouts and laughter rising above the fiddlers and drummers on the mezzanine. A serving wench swished in from the kitchens, her hips swaying with her every step. She had ample curves both top and bottom, and a saucy smile to boot. The woman's gaze shifted to Dunn, her expression growing bolder, looking as if she wanted to give him more than one of her frothing tankards of ale.

Possibly Grant was right. Dunn might enjoy a raucous toss in the hay with a buxom lass. God knew he needed it.

The corner of his mouth turned up as he assessed her from head to toe. She wore a corset atop her kirtle with a neckline scooping scandalously low. "I'll have one of those ales, lassie," he said, beckoning her nearer.

"I have a tankard for you, Laird MacRae." She stopped beside him and set all four on the table. Dunn reached for one while the other three disappeared into the hands of the gentlemen at the table.

"Ye ken the way to a man's heart," he said, taking a sip.

"Och, I ken the way to a great deal more than your heart, sir." She brazenly pulled away his tankard and set it down before she plopped onto his lap.

Across the table, Grant gave her a wink, the schemer. Doubtless he'd given the wench a bit of coin. Every man watched, amusement flickering in their eyes. Dunn's gut twisted with a warning, but he ignored it. Hell, it was midsummer and a gathering of clans. He lowered his hands to the lassie's waist. "Do you, now?"

"Aye." She leaned into him, the softness of her breast plying his chest. "You're a braw Highlander, MacRae." Her fingers gathered up the hem of his kilt. "And you're my choice to win the games."

Licking his lips, he grinned. The lass wasn't bad. Curvy—just what he liked. His hand slipped up and down her spine. "I reckon that's pretty brash talk, considering present company."

She rocked her hips from side to side, stirring his loins. Dunn clenched his teeth, willing himself not to roll his eyes and moan. Having a female in his lap reminded him how long he'd gone without one. She pressed her lips to his ear. "Aye, but you're bigger and stronger." Her hips rolled again with her wanton chuckle. "And my guess is you have the longest sword."

He considered a quick departure afore the meal was served. His men had erected his tent in the castle dry moat. It wouldn't take much to arrange a tryst beyond the gates. Hell, he was so ready, he ought to throw the wench over his shoulder and offer Grant his apologies on the way out.

Over the noise, a high-pitched gasp ripped Dunn from his fantasy. He shifted his gaze toward the sound, and a lump the size of a cannonball sank in his gut. Holy hell,

Lady Mairi stood at the far end of the hall staring directly at him, her hand covering her mouth.

Even from a distance, he could see the accusing glint in her sky-blue eyes. And from across the room, her disgust shamed him. The woman looked like a highborn queen, passing judgment without a trial. Though small, her presence was all-consuming. Voluminous red hair, a fair complexion, square shoulders, a tiny waist that fanned into folds and folds of plaid skirts. There she stood, the woman who'd shunned him, yet he was not impervious to her beauty. If anything, Mairi MacKenzie stood looking even bonnier than she had a mere fortnight ago.

In a blink, his throat thickened, his mouth went dry, and suddenly the wench on his lap became as enticing as a snorting sow. Sinking his fingers into her waist, he lifted and set the woman on her feet. "I'm sure you're being paid to provide a service," he said gruffly. "You'd best tend your duty."

Gaping, the lass moved her fists to her hips. "But—"

"Thanks for the ale, miss." Dunn picked up the tankard and guzzled it while the maid huffed and went on her way.

When he next looked across the hall, Mairi had moved to one of the high tables, where she sat with her back to him.

God bless it, Dunn shouldn't have acted so abruptly with the wench. He was a grown man, a chieftain of a well-respected clan. What did Lady Mairi care if he was about to head for his tent and give a buxom tart a crown for her favors? Her Ladyship had refused him. He was free to behave as he wished. There was nothing more to be said between them. The haughty lass was higher born and destined to marry a nobleman, as her father had so succinctly put it.

The Earl of Cromartie, seated at the far end of the high table, was a royalist in Highlander's clothes. And after his rebuttal, Dunn was convinced of it. The best thing for Dunn to do was to forget the Cromartie MacKenzies ever existed. Dunn might owe fealty to Reid MacKenzie, but he sure as hell didn't owe a farthing to Lord Gilroy MacKenzie and his heart-crushing, redheaded daughter.

Grant jabbed Dunn with an elbow. "You should see your face, MacRae."

"Aye, you look as if you're set to ride into battle." Ewen Cameron patted his dirk and scowled. "But you might affront our host this night. Come morn, I'll be more than happy to join you—take back those cattle Robert thieved from beneath my nose."

"You're talking shite," Grant growled, giving the laird across the table a scowl. "I've never thieved cattle."

Reid MacKenzie, the Earl of Seaforth, approached with his new bride on his arm. "At least not *Cameron* cattle, what say you, Grant?"

The tension in the air instantly eased. Highland gatherings were no place for petty feuds—even quibbles that had endured for centuries.

Grinning, Robert stood along with all the others on the dais. "'Tis good to see you as always, m'lord."

Dunn clasped his friend's hand, giving it a hearty shake. "Seaforth, you always had a knack for showing up at the most opportune time. We needed a diversion." He bowed to Her Ladyship. "'Tis a pleasure, Countess."

Lady Audrey curtsied. "Thank you, Dunn." She then regarded the men with a gracious smile. "I see this is the gentlemen's table. Perhaps I should join the wives."

"Not at all, my dear," Seaforth said, pulling out an empty chair.

As Her Ladyship sat, Dunn caught the stricken expression on Mairi MacKenzie's face. The poor lass blanched, clapping a hand to her chest. Beside her, Janet urged Mairi to turn back around. She did so, clutching her arms across her midriff while her shoulders shook. Janet looked back and cast a hateful glare at Seaforth, which, fortunately, His Lordship missed.

Months ago, Dunn had known Lady Mairi would be devastated when it was clear Seaforth had developed amorous feelings for Audrey. Dunn had tried on numerous occasions to remind the earl of his duty, but his words had fallen on deaf ears. And now Lady Mairi, the most vibrant young woman he'd ever met, sat in the midst of a happy gathering looking as miserable as a half-drowned puppy.

Dunn ground his molars. If only he could join the lass at her table, take Janet's place, and offer a consoling shoulder to cry upon. But she had rejected him. It was final. He needed to move on.

Jesus Saint Christopher Christ, I'm daft. I never should have offered for her hand so soon after Seaforth's hasty marriage.

"How are things at Eilean Donan?" asked Lady Audrey, smiling warmly. He could fault the countess for nothing. She'd risked her life to help Seaforth clear his name and deserved to be happy.

"It was good to visit clan and kin, thank you, m'lady." Dunn picked up his tankard. Finding it empty, he glanced to Mairi again. Her back was now ramrod straight. Aye, she was a survivor, that one, and Dunn had no doubt she'd eventually land on her feet. Her shrewd father would find her a suitable match in short order, and the fire would return to her eyes once again.

But that did nothing to help the roiling of Dunn's insides. He pushed back his chair and stood. "If you'll excuse me, I must step out for a wee bit of Highland air."

* * *

Mairi pursed her lips. *Curses to Janet!*

Once the meal was over, the Cameron lass fetched her brother Kennan, and now Mairi had no recourse but to dance with him. It only took one look at his face to know he'd rather be doing anything other than dancing, but Janet had practically shoved the pair of them onto the floor.

At least dancing provided a diversion, though there was nothing Mairi wanted to do more than steal away to the stables, saddle a horse, and gallop for home. She could practically feel Seaforth and his new bride watching her. Thank heavens the couple sat out this set. In fact, the earl and his countess had yet to take a turn.

And thank heavens the musicians were playing a country reel Mairi could perform in her sleep. Though she couldn't bring herself to paint on a smile, she executed the steps flawlessly, as one would expect from an earl's daughter. Janet's brother, on the other hand, obviously paid a fair bit more attention to sparring than to dancing lessons. Kennan had a reputation for his skill with a blade, but clomped around the dancefloor like an oversize workhorse.

None of it mattered. Da was still seated on the dais talking politics and, as long as Mairi held her head high, no one would fault her even though she didn't feel like dancing as she usually did. In fact, she usually laughed gaily and looked forward to dancing every set at these gatherings. A fortnight ago, she had not a care. It had all been so easy. Her life had been planned for her. All that was expected was that she live it.

But no more.

As she joined arms with Kennan, her attention was drawn to a lone figure who'd slipped inside the door. Tension radiated off the man, and Mairi knew who it was before her gaze locked with his. Her gaze was always managing to lock with that brooding Highlander. No matter how hard she tried, her accursed eyes insisted on straying his way.

And when they did, she was helpless to suppress the jitters spreading through her insides. Who wouldn't go a wee bit boneless when in the presence of such an imposing man? King's crosses, Dunn MacRae was as wild as the Highlands. Even his face was a work of brooding masculine ruggedness.

Holding her gaze, his midnight-blue eyes grew even darker as he took a step toward her. His thigh stretched the wool of his kilt, the flex of his calf powerful beneath the hose held in place by silk ribbons as all men wore. But ribbons seemed too genteel for this brawny Highlander.

The music ended and Janet's brother bowed.

Mairi hardly noticed.

Mr. MacRae swiftly closed the gap, heading directly for her. The fluttering of her insides increased ten-fold. No other man she'd ever met had drawn such an averse reaction from her soul. She clenched her fists behind her back. Dunn MacRae might wield the deadliest sword in the Highlands, but he was merely a laird, perhaps a member of the gentry, though not an aristocrat, as her father had put it. But Mairi wasn't as convinced. Mr. MacRae rode at the head of his army and was constable of the illustrious Eilean Donan Castle. Indeed, Dunn MacRae commanded respect from all corners of Scotland.

Though not a peer.

Mairi blinked, admonishing herself for staring.

He approached like a warrior fixated on his prey.

He's a rogue. My father wouldn't lie about that, would he?

"'Tis good to see you, Lady Mairi," MacRae said, dipping into a bow that was deeper and more reverent than necessary.

"And you." She curtsied hastily and started to turn. "If you'll excuse—"

He caught her arm. "I was hoping you would grace an old clan chief with a dance, m'lady."

"You're hardly old, sir." Good gracious, she made the mistake of looking up into his eyes. They were a smoldering shade of deep blue, and she imagined they harbored a lifetime of secrets and unseemly deeds.

"I'm older than you, lass," he said, his voice deep and gravelly.

Mairi knew exactly how old he was, but the nine-year difference in their ages did nothing to ease the heat making her skin flush. She flicked open her fan and cooled her face. "Is that so?"

The music started, *blast it.* Now she had no choice but to stay and dance lest she look like a simpering fool. They moved to their respective lines. He bowed. She curtsied, keeping her gaze lowered to avoid looking into those haunting eyes—eyes as dangerous as nightshade.

Nonetheless, she felt him watching her, the intensity of his stare boring into her, the silence between them unsettling.

Mairi stumbled with a gasp.

Mr. MacRae's fingers closed around her elbows. "Are you unwell, my lady?" He pulled her to the wall.

She looked at his hand—tanned, rough, flecked with white scars. *Unwell? Why did I not think of that?* Drawing her arm from his grasp, she rubbed away the sensation of his touch. "I-I'm afraid I must have eaten something that disagreed with me." She hastened for the door and away from prying eyes, but Mr. MacRae followed.

"Please allow me to escort you to your chamber. Are you staying in the tower?"

Dear Lord, must his voice rumble through her insides as well? "No." She pushed outside. "I mean, yes, I'm staying in the tower, but I am perfectly capable of making my way there without an escort." She mustn't be seen alone with him; it would be scandalous.

"Aye, but I'd be no kind of gentleman if I left you unaccompanied, especially with so many Highlanders milling about." He offered his elbow.

She didn't take it.

He leaned closer. "Come, Lady Mairi, I do not bite."

Curses. She squared her shoulders, her temper bubbling to the surface. Good heavens, a serving maid had been in his lap when she'd first entered the hall. That proved his suit of marriage had been a gesture of charity. How quickly he'd forgotten proclaiming his undying love to her father. "You mightn't bite, sir, but, as I've observed this eve, you are not above taking liberties." There. She outranked him. And as such, she must push aside her melancholy and assert herself. She was no waif to be taken advantage of. Mr. MacRae would not discombobulate her further.

His face looked stunned, guilty. "I—"

"Do you think I did not notice your *friendliness* with the serving wenches? I will have you know this instant, I am not to be trifled with."

"I...ah...I would never..." He dropped his arm with an edge to his jaw. Before he bowed, his eyes narrowed and filled with pain—the same torturous look she'd seen at the gate earlier in the day. "Good evening, m'lady."

Mairi suddenly found herself standing alone against the wall, dozens of people staring her way. Women whispered behind their fans, doubtless all gossiping. She knew this would happen, and now she was the laughingstock of the fete. Covering her mouth, she dashed from the hall, her eyes filling with tears.

How dare Dunn MacRae have asked her to dance. He had no business making butterflies swarm in her stomach. He had no business escorting her about the gathering or becoming familiar in any way. Not after she had refused his suit. Whatever friendship they'd once shared was now severed forever.

Da had an alliance to make with Mairi's hand. She was the firstborn daughter of an earl, a fact she'd best never forget. If only Seaforth had honored their agreement. All her life she'd been sure of her place. Everything had been neatly arranged—predestined. But now her world had crumbled. She was lost. She was hopeless.

Chapter Three

*B*efore the games started, a row arose between Ewen Cameron and Robert Grant. The two clans were always at odds, accusing each other of thievery, and nary a one was right. The Camerons left without breaking their fast. And if Dunn hadn't been friends with Grant, he would have ridden for home as well. But his reasons for wanting to leave were of a personal nature.

The chiding he'd received from Lady Mairi last eve had put him in a foul mood. Fortunately, heavy events were scheduled for the morn. Dunn needed something to work out the ire simmering under his skin. He'd thrown himself into the stone put as well as the four-stone weight over the bar. No one came close to besting him. And now if he won the caber toss, he'd take the heavy events as the undefeated champion.

His lieutenant, Ram, paced off the length of the caber. "Twenty feet, three inches by my calculation, sir."

Dunn used the blade of his dirk to gauge the thickness

of the log. It measured ten inches at the base. He eyed it critically. Every man would use the same length of tree. "I reckon she weighs a good eleven stone then."

"I'd say you're right," said Ram.

"Contestants for the caber toss, address the judges!" hollered the steward.

Dunn took the center spot in a line of twenty men facing the judges' tent. With three earls and the Duke of Gordon in attendance, the judging was almost as fierce as the competition. The nobility quibbled over every event, each man favoring his own contestants.

"All competitors will be allowed three throws of the caber. The entrant may take any length of run he wishes and may toss the caber from where he chooses, so long as it is within the judges' boundaries. The caber must be evaluated on its landing position, not the position to which it may bounce or roll. The winner shall be determined by the toss nearest to the twelve o'clock mark..."

Dunn stood at attention while the steward droned on, repeating rules he'd heard a hundred times. He tried his best to keep his eyes on the man, but by the time the oration was finished, his gaze had shifted to Lady Mairi.

She sat in the judges' tent behind her father with her hands folded. It was odd to see her so reserved and sad. He'd always known Lady Mairi to be full of laughter and joy. In previous years, she would watch with great enthusiasm, standing in the center of a circle of admiring friends.

Dunn growled under his breath as he clenched his teeth. Her Ladyship's plight was none of his concern.

Mairi peeked from under the brim of her fashionable straw hat. As if she'd known exactly where he was standing, her gaze immediately met Dunn's. His jaw twitched. His shoulders tightened. Hell, a great deal more than his shoulders tightened. He inhaled sharply.

I should smile.

But before the corners of his lips turned up, those lovely eyes shifted back to her hands.

Jesus Saint Christopher Christ, I have completely lost my mind.

Thankfully, the Duke of Gordon stood in all his royal finery. He drew his sword, and raised it over his head. "MacRae, you shall lead off the competition for the caber toss. And I wish good sport to all." The blade sliced through the air with a hiss followed by cheers from the crowd. They shouted words of encouragement to their champions, though Lady Mairi didn't even bother to look up.

Dejected, Dunn assumed his place, forcing himself to throw his shoulders back with a pretense of pride. There he stood, the champion of the morning, and the one person he wanted to cheer for him sat staring at her folded hands. Ballocks, he never should have come to this accursed gathering.

Removing his sword belt and resting it beside the starting line, Dunn readied himself for the task at hand. There was no time like the present to block Lady Mairi from his thoughts once and for all. No woman was worth the amount of time he'd spent thinking about her. How many times must he hear that she didn't like him? That she and her father didn't think he was good enough for the daughter of an earl? There were plenty of gentlewomen who would be happy to be seen on his arm, who would accept his suit of marriage. The chieftain of Clan MacRae never embarrassed himself by chasing after simpering lassies.

Robert Grant had been right. Dunn needed a woman. But not a serving wench. Dunn needed a well-bred, hearty Highland woman. In fact, as soon as this day's games were over he would set his sights on finding the lass of his dreams.

His men raised the caber to vertical while the judging tent remained clear in his periphery.

Lady Mairi looked up and drew her hands to her lips. Dunn's heart hammered out of rhythm.

Stop, blast you!

Bellowing like a prize bull, Dunn hefted the base of the caber into his cupped hands, ran like a possessed demon, and hurled the log as far as he'd ever thrown a caber in his life. The momentum made him stumble forward until he gained his balance by resting his hands on his bent knees. The twenty-foot log landed and stood upright for what seemed like an eternity.

Tip over, ye bastard.

As if a breeze picked up, the caber fell on a line to one minute past twelve and thundered to the earth. The crowd erupted in a raucous applause. Hell, even Dunn couldn't help but take in a deep breath and puff out his chest. He'd thrown countless cabers in his life and nary a one had landed so close to the mark.

As his men collected the log, Dunn glanced to the damned judges' tent again. Ignoring him, Lady Mairi stood and whispered in her father's ear, then slipped away.

He grasped the caber for his next turn and looked to the skies. It was probably best if the lass weren't watching. Her Ladyship was too distracting.

The second throw was good, but nothing would beat the first.

Before the third throw, he spotted Mairi. She was heading straight for the wood. Alone.

Damnation! As soon as the toss was finished he'd have a word with her about wandering off alone, whether she liked it or not. She could go ahead and berate him all she liked; she wasn't going to walk off unescorted under his nose.

Horses thundered in from the west.

Dunn shifted his gaze toward the approaching company. *Blast.* Redcoats—an entire company of them.

What the bloody hell do they want?

Led by a captain wearing a tricorn hat over a periwig, they headed straight for the judges' tent while the soldiers encircled the crowd. Dunn moved in slowly.

The Duke of Gordon was the first to stand. "To what do we owe the *pleasure* of your presence? Have you come to enjoy the games?"

"Aye, I reckon the troops might learn a thing or two." Seaforth moved in beside him, resting his hand on the hilt of his sword.

"This is an unlawful gathering," said the captain, not bothering to dismount.

Dunn moved his hand to his sword, but grasped nothing. Blast, his weapons were still on the ground at the starting line. He cast a backward glance and spied his sword belt and dirk while three mounted dragoons heading for the wood caught his attention. He shifted his gaze to Seaforth, then inclined his head in the direction of the soldiers, indicating his intent. The earl knit his brows, giving a wee shake of his head.

Dunn took a step closer to his weapons.

"You there, stay where you are," a lieutenant barked, his eyes trained on Dunn.

He froze, his gaze shifting back to the wood. Birds flitted above the trees, squawking a warning. Dunn's heartbeat raced. It was only a matter of moments before the soldiers would happen upon Lady Mairi.

"Do you realize whom you are addressing, sir?" asked the duke.

"It matters not who you are, Your Grace," said the captain. "I have it on good order that this is a Jacobite meeting, and must be disbanded immediately."

"You are sorely misinformed." Cromartie stood. "This is a friendly gathering of clans meant to foster kinship and goodwill."

The captain drew his saber and pointed it at the duke. With a scraping of blade against scabbard, every Highlander in attendance unsheathed his weapon. Horses skittered while soldiers raised muskets to shoulders. A peaceful gathering was on the verge of turning into a bloody battle, and Her Ladyship was taking an afternoon stroll alone.

The captain flicked his wrist, sweeping his blade across the scene. "Tell them to gather their things and head for home, else I shall command my men to open fire."

"'Tis of no consequence to us," Dunn shouted, marching toward the captain, making sure the nobles had his attention. They might not know his motives, but they all trusted his judgment. "Our celebrations are nearly at an end."

"Laird MacRae is right," said Seaforth. "There's nothing unlawful going on here."

The captain pulled a flintlock pistol from his belt and pointed it at Seaforth. "I beg to differ. Tell your men to stand down."

Dunn closed in, focusing on the weapon.

At the far side of the field, a horse whinnied. Women screamed. A musket fired with a thundering crack.

In a blink, the entire dry moat of Urquhart Castle erupted in pandemonium. The captain's mare stutter-stepped while the man took aim. Sprinting, Dunn rushed for the pistol and batted the flintlock skyward just as it fired.

"I'll kill you for that!" The captain swung with a back-hand aimed at Dunn's face.

In a heartbeat, he caught the arm and used the down-ward force to pull the bastard from the horse. As the man fell, Dunn slammed his fist into the base of the varlet's neck—not a lethal strike, but a vicious one. Grunting, the captain dropped face-first to the dirt. His body fell limp and didn't move.

Wasting no time, Dunn mounted the horse and gal-loped to his weapons. Taking his weight on the left stir-rup, he grabbed a fist of mane, swept downward, and clamped his fingers around his sword belt.

In the judges' tent, Seaforth and Gordon fought like badgers while Cromartie and Sutherland cowered behind them. Bellowing his battle cry, Robert Grant and a mob of Highlanders broke through the redcoats' line and rushed to the aid of the nobles. The battle raged with flashing blades and the screams from fleeing women and children while Dunn kicked his heels, racing for the wood.

Hold fast m'lady. No scoundrel will lay hands on you this day!

Chapter Four

*M*airi could watch no longer—or listen. Everyone at the gathering continually hollered, "MacRae!" as if the chieftain were the champion of all Christendom. Further, the laird managed to be in the center of every event. No one for miles would mistake him. He stood nearly six inches above everyone else, his shoulders wider, his arms as big around as a man's thigh, and his legs... well, she'd already established that his legs were enormous. MacRae had earned his reputation because of his behemoth size and his skill on the battlefield. He was a warrior who ran into the face of danger when others were tucking their tails and fleeing.

And he completely disarmed her.

Having MacRae present only made her torture worse. No, she couldn't deny she harbored some sort of feelings for the man—awkward, unnerving, heart palpitating—all of them able to be summed up in one word: nervousness.

If only Da hadn't made her attend this accursed gathering. He could have allowed her to remain at Castle Leod, but he thought being around people would make her feel better. Da was wrong. And now that Janet had left for Achnacarry with her kin, it made things all the more difficult to bear.

Mumbling an excuse to her father, she'd fled the crowd at the games and now strolled along a well-used path in the forest, keeping the loch on her left. For the first time in her life, being alone infused her with a sense of calm, a sense of empowerment.

She didn't expect to see a soul, so the sound of horses from the direction of the castle startled her. Mairi stepped off the path to allow the riders to pass.

Then her heart nearly leaped out of her chest.

Bright scarlet flickered through the trees.

Dragoons!

Gasping, she broke into a run, frantically racing for cover behind a fallen tree.

Her skirts caught on a broken branch as she dived for shelter. Stopping a cry in her throat, she reached back to free herself, but the riders were already upon her. Heart racing, Mairi looked both ways. Curses! No place to flee. Before she straightened, she reached inside her sleeve, pulled out a wee dagger, and hid it behind her back.

"What do we have here?" asked a soldier, his lips stretched in a sneer.

"Ha ha. It looks like a tasty morsel for all of us to share."

Mairi slashed an arc with her knife. "Stay back!"

One of the men dismounted. "A feisty redheaded wench, are you?"

She squared her shoulders and addressed them. "I am Lady Mairi MacKenzie, and if you dare lay one finger on me, you will face the entire army of the Earl of Cromartie."

The other two dragoons slid to their feet and sauntered forward.

"Do you believe that, mate?" one said.

"Not at all. No noblewoman would be wandering the forest without a chaperone."

Mairi gulped and shook the dagger. "Go on your way. Leave me be."

"Oh no, we're not about to let a bit o' fun pass. And if your father is the Earl of Cromartie, he's in more hot water with the queen on account of presiding over a Jacobite gathering."

"Aye," said another. "I reckon the captain will be taking captives and throwing them into the castle's pit while we await orders from London."

A musket cracked, coming from the castle grounds. Mairi pressed herself against the tree, clutching the dagger with both her hands. "You are mistaken. This is no Jacobite gathering."

"We received a report just this morn stating the contrary."

"You are *sorely* mistaken, sir. This is but a gathering of Highland clans." Her mind raced—how could she convince these men otherwise? "Tell me. Who dared to speak out against these kind Highland folk?"

One of the dragoons puffed out his chest with importance. "It was a MacKay man, one of the Earl of Sutherland's own."

The hackles on her neck stood on end. Sutherland was a backstabber? She knew the earl to be a royalist, but the gentry often waffled between their loyalties to Queen Anne and Her Majesty's outcast brother, James.

But Mairi couldn't worry about posturing now. The ugly grins on the encroaching dragoons' faces made her toes curl. Her dagger shook in her hands. One beast grabbed for her shoulder. She swiped the blade at his fingers. "Stay back, I said!"

Another reached for her and, before she swung her knife his way, he seized her arm. Mairi jolted and shrieked. "Remove your hands this instant!"

The blackguard's grip tightened. "You think a wee dagger can stop us?"

"You men will swing from the gallows unless you leave me be this very trice." Mairi's words came out high-pitched and rapid, betraying her fear.

A dragoon snatched her other arm, twisting her wrist downward until the knife dropped from her hands.

"Help!" she screamed as he pulled her back against his smelly body, crushing her throat in the crook of his arm while her hat fell to the ground.

The vile beast pressed his lips against her ear. "We're finished with chatting, wench."

"That's right, you need to pay," sneered the third as he tugged up the hem of her gown.

All three attacked at once, grappling for her skirts. Kicking her legs, Mairi fought. "Release me!" She thrashed her head back and forth. Her arms flailed while her mind raced.

"Help, help, help!"

This couldn't be happening. Fabric tore as her kick connected with a thud.

A dragoon grunted.

Hands released.

"You bloody rutting bastards," a deep voice growled. *MacRae!*

Fists swung in every direction as Mairi twisted free from the last captor with such jolting force, she fell and scraped her head on the broken branch.

Rolling away, she clutched her fists beneath her chin, watching Mr. MacRae savagely wield his dirk until all three soldiers lay dead.

Blood dripped from his blade. He spun and looked her from head to toe, his eyes round and wild like a madman's. "Have you been harmed?" he demanded, wiping his blade on a dead man's coat, then shoving the weapon into its scabbard.

Mairi's mouth went dry, her entire being shaking like a leaf in the wind. Was she hurt? Too numb to feel anything, she replied, "I-I-I think I am well."

"We have no time to spare." Lunging toward her, he thrust out his hand. "*Jesu*, you're bleeding."

She touched her fingers to her temple and hissed. "I f-fell."

He stooped and tore off a strip from her petticoat.

Mairi scooted away, tucking her legs beneath her. "Sir!"

Grabbing her arm, he held her steady. "I just want to swab the blood, lass. Hold still." Gracious, his voice was softer and deeper than she'd ever heard it.

Too frightened to fight, Mairi did as he said. She clenched her teeth, expecting it to hurt, but his touch was so much gentler than she expected.

He handed her the cloth. "Hold this against your head."

"Is it bad?"

"I've seen worse, but we've no time to tarry. I must spirit you back to your father's men."

The sound of fighting echoed from the castle grounds. "What's happening?"

"The troops claimed the gathering unlawful—and some arse decided to fire his musket. That's when all hell broke loose." MacRae narrowed his gaze, looking like the devil incarnate. "Someone betrayed us—lied to the queen's dragoons about a Jacobite gathering."

Mairi gasped with her nod. "I-it was a Sutherland man—th-those awful soldiers said so."

"Och, I should have known. Sutherland is a backbiter of the worst sort." He offered his hand. "Come now, I'll help you mount."

She spied the bay hackney—something wasn't right. "That's not your horse—you have a big stallion. I've seen him."

"I'll fetch Beastie once I've seen you safely to your da."

She nodded, allowing him to pull her to her feet. She glanced to the dead dragoons, choking back her urge to vomit. "What are you going to do with them?"

"One thing at a time, m'lady. We must make haste." He stooped and threaded his fingers together, making a step for her to mount. "I'll give you a leg up."

Grasping the saddle with trembling hands, Mairi planted her foot in his palms and helped to pull herself up while the chieftain hoisted her into the saddle. Keeping her legs to one side like a lady, she shifted her knee over the pommel for balance. Then he mounted behind her. Her head grew dizzy as he reached around her and gathered the reins. Clapping a hand to her chest, she took a deep breath. Goodness, she must be overcome with shock.

In an effort to control her tremors, Mairi pointed. "The soldiers' horses are down by the loch." But the tremors and the spinning of her head refused to stop.

"I see them." The laird slapped the reins. "I'll have my men fetch them later." Though gruff, his words brought a shower of relief, as did the arms surrounding her.

Mairi glanced down to the strong fingers clutching the reins and gratefully leaned against his chest. Mr. MacRae's arms felt fiercely, unquestionably secure after meeting with those vile dragoons. "Has the fighting stopped?" she asked.

"Sounds like it may have."

By the saints, Mairi had been so fixated on the struggle around her, she hadn't listened for anything else. Shouts roared from beyond the wood. The ground thundered with horses as well.

Mr. MacRae urged the mare ahead slowly.

Flashes of redcoats flickered through the forest, just as they'd done before the dragoons attacked. Mairi's heart hammered so fast, she swooned again.

The brush stirred.

A rider leaped a horse over a clump of broom, aiming a musket directly at them. "There are more here!" he bellowed.

Mairi shrieked.

Growling curses under his breath, Dunn spun the mare in a half-turn and slapped the reins.

Crack!

Mairi winced. But as the musket fired, Dunn bent over her, protecting her with his body while he kicked his heels. "Faster, ye beast!" His words were low and intense.

Snorting, the hackney picked up speed, careening through the forest. Running like a pursued fox, she galloped away from Urquhart Castle—galloped away from Da.

Near the loch, the fallen dragoons' riderless mounts

whinnied and started to run as well. Crashing through the scrub, they fell in step with Mairi and Dunn. They bounded forward like wild horses trained to follow the herd's lead mare.

Leaning forward, Dunn ferociously wielded the reins like a whip, demanding more speed. Curled down to the horse's withers, Mairi gritted her teeth and threaded her fingers through its mane, holding on for dear life. She flopped up and down, side to side, her hands and arms burning from the strength it took not to fall off. All the while, her heart continued to thunder with the force of a reverberating smithy's hammer.

"Relax your seat, lass," Dunn's deep voice rumbled in her ear. "I'll never let ye fall."

Chapter Five

The skirmish ended almost as quickly as it began. The Duke of Gordon's army had fired a cannon from the ramparts. The booming blast stopped the fight and, as the Earl of Cromartie and Lord Advocate to Her Majesty, Gilroy MacKenzie immediately addressed the army captain, who had come to and was being restrained by the point of Seaforth's dirk. "You, sir, shall be stripped of your rank and imprisoned for your irresponsible and malicious conduct." Gilroy gestured to his guard. "Lock him in irons and send his men back to their garrison."

The Cromartie lieutenant held up a set of manacles. "Just the captain, m'lord?"

"Aye, we shan't be responsible for feeding and transporting an entire company of Her Majesty's dragoons." Having asserted his authority, Gilroy turned full circle, sickly bile rising in his gut. "Where on earth is my daughter?"

"I saw Lady Mairi heading for the forest, m'lord," a man shouted from the rear of the crowd. "Alone."

"Och." Seaforth returned his dirk to its scabbard. "That's what MacRae was trying to tell me."

"Why in God's name was Lady Mairi heading for the forest?" Gilroy shifted an accusing gaze to Robert Grant. "We are here at your invitation, sir. Explain why your men would allow the daughter of an earl to enter a forest unescorted."

"Ah…" The young laird's shoulders inched up to his ears. "I'll have my men investigate, m'lord."

"You had best do that or I'll have your hide." Gilroy whipped around to his nephew. "Come at once, Seaforth, and let Robert pray nothing untoward has happened to Mairi."

A commoner pushed through the crowd. "Beg your pardon, m'lord. Not long after Her Ladyship entered the forest, dragoons followed. I saw it all. That's when Mr. MacRae took the captain's horse and chased after them like he was hunting Satan himself."

"Good God, it grows worse." Growling under his breath, Cromartie grasped Seaforth by the elbow and strode for the wood. "Why couldn't anyone have ridden to Lady Mairi's rescue aside from Dunn MacRae?"

Reid's lips formed a thin line as he strode ahead on long legs. "If I had my pick of any fighting men in the Highlands, Dunn would be my choice to go after the lass. I ken of no one who can match him in a fight."

Cromartie scowled. "And I might have had her married off by now…if you had thought with anything aside from your cock."

"My debt with you has been settled, and I expect you to honor it." Seaforth shot him a leer. "Know this: Mairi may be a delightful gel, but she was never for me. I'm afraid you'd be in the exact same predicament—"

Gilroy sliced his hand through the air. "No, I would not, you arse. My daughter would have been flitting through the crowd like a queen bee rather than moping like a shunned courtier."

"I would remember to whom you are speaking, Uncle. I may be your grandnephew, but the House of Seaforth occupies the clan seat, not Cromartie."

Bile burned Gilroy's throat. He hated playing second fiddle to Seaforth. Unlike his nephew, Gilroy had earned his title through service to Britain and to the queen. It was no secret that Seaforth had Jacobite leanings, though by virtue of his good looks, he managed to capture the queen's favor. Regardless, the Earl of Cromartie would hold his cards close to his chest when the time for the succession came, and he would not be on the wrong side of the argument. Blast Seaforth's loyalty to the Stuart line.

Followed into the forest by their lieutenants and countless others, the smell of pine wafted through the air. Birds flitted about as if all was amiable and peaceful on this midsummer's day. The forest floor absorbed the sound of their footsteps, enhancing the call of the birds. It didn't take long to find three dead dragoons.

Something shiny flashed. Gilroy recognized the knife straightaway. "Good God, 'tis Mairi's dagger."

Seaforth stooped to retrieve it. "Then why did they not return to the castle grounds?"

Robert Grant examined the assorted prints. "They were chased. See?"

"Stay back," ordered Seaforth, holding up his palm to prevent the men from trampling the tracks.

Grant pointed as he made his way around the prints, reading the story. "They mounted here and started heading back. By the depth of the prints, there were two on one mount." He pointed. "There's where a horse jumped through the brush—then MacRae's mount dipped its hindquarters and spun."

"And it looks like at least four dragoons made chase," added Seaforth, studying the clues a few paces along the trail.

"Exactly." Grant trotted ahead while the others followed. About fifty yards up, he stopped. "New tracks here, and they're not as deep."

"That's because they had no riders. I'd wager a hundred pounds these are from the horses of those sorry dragoons lying dead back there," said Gilroy. He wasn't about to be made to look a fool. "And my daughter remains in the clutches of a man whose interest in her has been expressed most clearly. This is an abomination. Worse, Mairi is running from a mob of government soldiers because of a wretched misunderstanding."

Grant slammed his fist into his palm. "Bloody Ewen Cameron. He's behind this. He's the only one who left the games this morning. Full of threats he was, the bastard."

"Damnation," cursed Seaforth. "I never in my life thought Cameron would have stooped so low. He's a Highlander through to the bone."

Grant scowled. "He's a cattle thief and a thorn in my side."

"I don't give a rat's arse about Cameron. Dunn MacRae has abducted my daughter! Everyone kens I denied his suit, and now the blackguard has taken her." Raising his voice, Gilroy addressed the crowd. "Fifty guineas to the man who seizes MacRae and returns Lady

Mairi to Castle Leod. Unscathed, and if it means running a dirk across that bastard's throat, then so be it!"

* * *

After galloping for the hills, Dunn slowed the hackney to a fast walk, a pace the animal could sustain for hours. Still in full military tack, the stray horses continued to follow their lead mare. Dunn knew exactly where to go. He knew the Highlands like he knew his own soul. And if he didn't want to be found, God save anyone who tried.

Now with the precious cargo riding in front of him, he'd be even more vigilant. Christ, he'd nearly turned into a madman back there when he'd found those three scoundrels with their hands on Lady Mairi. He could have torn the limbs from each rutting bastard one at a time, and even that wouldn't have been punishment enough.

To shelter her between his arms made him feel more like a man than winning a hundred caber tosses. With her hat gone, mussed locks of luminous red hair had come unpinned and lightly brushed Dunn's face. Leaning forward, Dunn inhaled her scent. The fragrance was heavenly and ethereal, and reminded him of magnolias in full bloom. Her bonny perfume made something in his heart twist. Aye, he would protect the lass with his dying breath if need be. Perhaps it was because she was a MacKenzie, a daughter of the clan that Dunn and his forefathers had vowed to protect for centuries past. True, he fancied the lass. He couldn't deny his affection went deeper than lust. Lady Mairi was meant to be put on a pedestal and adored.

He steered the horse through the forest and up a rocky crag, one high enough to have a clear view across the glen carved through the eons by the waters of Loch Ness. At the top, they rode in a complete circle until he spied their pursuers. "Look." He pointed. "The dragoons have turned north. They've lost our trail."

"Thank heavens." With her deep sigh, Mairi's shoulders relaxed a bit.

"Aye, but mark me, they'll double back. With the extra horses in our wake, I'm afraid we've left quite a trail."

"What can we do?"

"We must keep moving. Keep them guessing. Do not worry, lass. I'll not let them find us." He dismounted and reached for her. "Before we travel any farther, I should have a look at your wound."

Placing her hands on his shoulders, Mairi trembled as she allowed him to help her down. Dunn's palms closed around her waist, so small, his fingertips touched. He held her aloft a moment longer than necessary, savoring her—everything about her, from her bonny blue eyes to the creamy texture of her skin, the bow shape of her lips, and the hint of freckles across the bridge of her dainty nose. She was featherlight, and he held her like a precious artifact that needed the utmost care. And as she exhaled, she blew life into his limbs.

Ever so gradually, he lowered her toward the earth, watching those sky-blue eyes. Innocent, they had rings of navy blue around the outer edge of her irises, making her stare all the more intense. Why had he not noticed the rings before?

"Fascinating."

"I beg your pardon?" she asked.

He blinked. "Did I say something?"

"'Fascinating.' You said 'fascinating.'"

Och, he needed to hold his tongue. "Forgive me, m'lady, but your eyes are mesmerizing."

Biting her lip, she squeezed his shoulders and looked downward. "Though I feel safe in your arms, Mr. MacRae," she said as if his compliment hadn't been uttered, "I do believe I am able to stand on my own two feet."

Good Lord, he hadn't yet set her down? "Ah." Though he might have stood there for an hour without tiring, it was unforgivably forward of him to linger. He set the maid on her feet and then stepped away and bowed. "M'lady."

She, too, took a step back, putting more distance between them, then rubbed her outer arms.

"Are you cold?" he asked.

"Nay."

"Do you fear me?"

She glanced sideways. "I just..." Her shoulders curved as furrows formed in her brow.

"Are you in pain? Did those brigands hurt—?"

"Nay. 'Tis just that everything happened so quickly." She turned her back and, burying her face in her palms, shook her shoulders. "Those men were—and then you—and then we—oh, heavenly Father!"

Dunn's heart twisted. Good God, he'd ridden into battle and had seen horrors this lass could never imagine. And there he'd stood like a lovesick dastard, holding forth about Her Ladyship's fascinating eyes. Stepping nearer, he reached out his hand, but stopped before touching her. She wouldn't want that.

Instead, he pressed praying fingers to his lips, desperately trying to think of something to say to ease her suffering. "No refined woman should ever witness such brutality. Ah..." He looked skyward. "My actions were carried out only to ensure your well-being, m'lady."

She spied him over her shoulder. "But you were so brutal. So savage. I've never seen anything like it...and there were *three* of them."

Dunn lowered his hands to his sides. She thought him a monster. And why not? He'd acted savagely—showed no mercy. "Three ruthless men with no virtue among them. Men capable of unspeakable acts. If I hadn't stopped them, you—"

"I ken." She nodded as she looked to her feet.

How could he assuage her fears? Did she think him a heartless tyrant? Is that why he was so unappealing to her? "I hope you do not fear me. I am here to protect you, m'lady. I will do so at any cost."

Her inhale faltered as she faced him, keeping her arms crossed. "I believe you," she whispered, looking like a queen, crusted blood at her temple and all.

If only he had leave to draw the lass into his embrace and tell her everything would be all right.

But she'd refused him.

She wasn't his to have and to hold.

The air between them felt like a wall of stone.

"What are we to do?" she asked, her expression growing forlorn.

"I aim to take you back to Castle Leod." He looked to the sky. "But 'tis a full day's ride from dawn to dusk, and we only have a few hours of daylight remaining."

Holding out her palms, she glanced from side to side. "Where can we go?"

"Somewhere the dragoons will not set upon us," he said, knowing where to take her but unsure whether she would accept it. "Not far from here, there's a hiding place used only by my kin. 'Tis rough, but we can build a fire, and I promise you will sleep in comfort."

"Rough? Is it a shieling?"

He shook his head. "A cave—a place no one outside Clan MacRae kens exists."

"Good heavens," she said, drawing a hand over her mouth. "Is there no inn?"

"None where we will not be recognized." He bowed his head. "I firmly believe it is where you will be safest, else I would not have suggested it."

"Your fealty to the MacKenzie goes without question. I will trust your judgment."

"Thank you, m'lady." He beckoned her forward. "With Your Ladyship's approval, I'd like to check the wound on your head."

Taking a step in, she cringed. "I must look a fright."

"Not at all." He held up his hand. "May I?"

She nodded and he carefully pushed aside her hair, pressing his fingers around the bruising. "Does this hurt?"

"A little. Do I need leeches?"

"I've never been fond of leeches. Mayhap there's a salve in the captain's saddlebags." Dunn found a jar of ointment right where he would have expected it. Pulling off the cork, he sniffed. "It bears a strong scent of house-leek."

"The healer in Strathpeffer uses houseleek for everything."

"Then let's give it a go, shall we?"

"If you promise it won't hurt."

"I hope it will not, but I trust Your Ladyship can endure a wee sting. We do not want such a head wound to turn putrid." He scooped a bit with a finger. "Here. Let us try a small amount." As he dabbed it on ever so carefully, Mairi stood without flinching.

"Better?" he asked.

"It didn't hurt at all."

"That's a good sign."

The three horses that had followed had stopped down below to graze. Dunn grasped the reins of the mare he and Mairi had been riding. "If you'll stay here and hold this filly, I'll bring up the others."

"What do you aim to do with them all?"

"Take them along so they won't fall into the wrong hands. Besides, you need a mount."

Disappointment flashed across Mairi's face so fast, Dunn might have imagined it. Shaking his head, he berated himself for the mere thought. They needed to keep moving, and he could ill afford to lose sight of his task to ensure Her Ladyship's safety and return her to Cromartie with haste.

Chapter Six

*T*wilight fell, fingering shadows through the trees. Mairi rode one of the hackneys behind Mr. MacRae, blindly following him across hills and glens she'd never seen before. The horses moved slowly, hindered by the thick foliage, and she was forever batting away branches to prevent them from hitting her face.

To keep the strays on their path, MacRae had tied them together with a lead line. They ambled along, grabbing bites of grass along the way. They'd been climbing for near to an hour when he turned left, leading them over a massive formation of solid rock. As they crossed into the open, Mairi glanced down. *Good heavens!* In a blink, her heart flew to her throat while the reins slipped in her palms. The downward drop seemed infinite. Darkness swallowed the earth below. She shuddered to her toes. A fall would end in an abyss of death. Before she reined her mount to a stop, the accursed horse followed Mr. MacRae out onto the shelf no wider than a plank.

Mairi's breath caught in her chest. Her skirts scraped along the rock wall to her right, but she was too frightened to tug them away. Every muscle in her body tensed. Her horse snorted and shook his head. She grappled for his mane. "Easy!" she squeaked.

"Breathe, m'lady. We'll be across in no time," Mr. MacRae barked over his shoulder, his voice always sounding inordinately gruff and doing nothing to ease her terror.

She closed her eyes and tried to force herself to relax her seat. A practiced horsewoman knew her mount sensed the tension from its rider. If Mairi was tense, the hackney would be ten times tenser. No matter how hard she tried, fear gripped every fiber of her body. The horse jounced. Her stomach dropped. Just as she sent up prayers for her soul, the hackney's movement grew smooth, as if walking on a cloud.

"'Tis all right to open your eyes, m'lady," said the boorish Highlander. How dare he lead her out onto a narrow shelf? It was a miracle she hadn't fallen to her death.

"I thought you said…" Mairi's jaw dropped as she opened her eyes. Through the shadows of dusk, she beheld a sight of pure beauty. Ahead, the mouth of a cave was concealed by moss and vines, rustling softly with the breeze. To the left, the forest opened to a mountain lagoon, fed by a waterfall that tumbled over the rocks in tiers. "What is this place?"

He rode toward the loch, then reined his horse to a stop. "My kin call it Cavern of the Fairies."

"Do magical folk live here?" She stopped beside him.

"None that I've seen, but I wouldn't be surprised if they do." He dismounted. "'Tis enchanted." It sounded odd to hear such a rugged man speak of fairy folk.

"Why enchanted?" she asked while he helped her down. This time his action was more efficient, and as soon as her feet touched the ground he released his grip.

"Up here a man can ease his guard a wee bit—ponder his existence and feel the awe-inspiring gifts of our Mother Nature."

Scraping her teeth across her bottom lip, Mairi studied the man. Yes, she'd known Mr. MacRae forever but had never drawn so much of a conversation from him. Indeed, there was a greater depth to the laird than she'd imagined.

He met her gaze, but only for an instant. Then, looking aside as if feeling awkward, he gestured to the horses. "Once I hobble these nags, I'll see to your comfort."

She watched him make quick work of tying loose ropes to the front legs of each horse and removing their tack. Plenty of mountain grass grew about the clearing for them to eat. He tossed the soldiers' saddlebags over his shoulder and offered his hand. "Allow me to escort you inside, m'lady."

Mairi placed her fingers in his calloused palm while he led her over the uneven ground and pulled aside the vines. "Inside I've rigged a comfortable seat lined with furs."

"Do you stay here often?"

"A sennight or two in summer mostly. This place is usually ten feet deep in snow during the winter months."

The cave was dark and musty, but true to Dunn's word, a fur-lined chair sat waiting for someone to occupy it.

"It will take a moment to give the furs a good shake."

Mairi stood while he hastened outside, shook the pelts, and dutifully returned, smoothing them over the natural stone chair. He seemed oddly endearing as he worked. A gruff man, so concerned with tending to her comfort. When she finally sat, Mairi sank into pure luxury. "Is this where you usually sit?" she asked, looking from wall to wall. The cave wasn't large. It had a dry dirt floor, a fire pit, and along one side, a row of tidy bedrolls.

"Aye," he said, using a customary monosyllabic response.

Reclining in the coziness, she sighed while she watched as he lit an oil lamp and set to starting a fire. Mr. MacRae was a quandary. His movements were precise and swift. He focused on his tasks without engaging in idle chatter. Yet his presence was dominant.

Perhaps 'tis his rugged looks.

Stubble from his beard had grown in since the morn, leaving a dark shadow on his face. Most of his thick hair had come loose from its ribbon and shrouded his eyes. The lines on his face were deep for a man of thirty, making him look all the more dangerous. He even had a spiderweb etching the corners of his eyes with white streaks emphasized by his darker, tanned skin.

He must spend a great deal of time out of doors.

Once the fire was crackling, Mairi held out her hands to warm them. "Thank you."

He glanced up from placing a stick of wood in the flame, his expression piercing. "M'lady?"

"Thank you for riding to my aid. Had you not arrived when you did, things could have..." Though her voice trailed off, she was unable to look away.

His eyes grew intense as he froze, making her incredibly aware. But the moment passed with his severe nod as he reached for a saddlebag and pulled out a leather parcel. "I'll wager there's a wee morsel in here," he said, as if saving her life was but a trifle. Sitting beside her, he pulled the thong and unwrapped it. "Look here. Dried meat and oatcakes."

Saliva swirled in her mouth, suddenly reminding her that she hadn't eaten since she broke her fast. "It sounds like a feast."

"Nothing similar to your usual fare, m'lady." He held out the opened parcel. "But it will keep you from going hungry."

When she selected a piece of meat, she inadvertently brushed the rough pads of his fingertips. The friction made her gasp. Shrugging it off, she chuckled and took a nibble. "'Tis salty."

"Preserved with brine." He tore off a bite with healthy white teeth, watching her as he chewed.

The firelight danced across his dark features, making him appear more menacing than he did in daylight. A shiver coursed over Mairi's skin. No, she wasn't afraid of him, but his looks stirred her insides with a tempest she didn't understand. Mr. MacRae was bewildering, though a man she wanted on her side. It was no wonder Seaforth had put so much trust in the laird. If she were an earl or a clan chieftain, she would do the same.

After shoving the rest of the strip of meat into his mouth, he rummaged through the saddlebags and found a flask. Shaking it, his eyebrows arched. He almost smiled. "'Tis full." He pulled off the stopper and sniffed. After taking a hearty swig, he sighed and wiped his lips. "Who would have thought a scoundrel like the captain would develop good taste in whisky?"

"All men drink it, do they not?"

"The English generally prefer brandy and rum." He held out the flask. "Beg your pardon, I'm not being mannerly. Would you care for a tot? It might make the wee bump on your head feel better, as long as you only take a sip."

Mairi pursed her lips. "Ladies must not allow their lips to touch the spirit of Satan."

"Suit yourself. Though I ken a great many noble-women who do not mind a dram."

"Aye? Who, may I ask?"

"The Baroness of Sleat, for starters." He took another drink, followed by an awkward pause. "Um...how?"

"Hmm?"

"I was just admiring how well you've learned the intricacies of ladies' etiquette. It must have been difficult losing your mother at such a young age. Nonetheless, you turned into a fine young woman, if you'll allow me to be so bold, m'lady."

Mairi's mother had passed away shortly after she was born. Sadly, she had no recollection of her, though people oft remarked on how much they looked alike. "Thank you. Fortunately, I had an efficient governess."

"Whom you often evaded, as I recall."

"Ye ken about that?"

"Och, our paths have crossed many times over the years."

She nodded. Truth be told, Mr. MacRae had seen her when she was a spirited teen. Good heavens, she'd been difficult for her father—difficult for anyone. Yet, after all her sauciness, Mr. MacRae still seemed to like her. Bless it, for the first time in sennights, a wee spark of daring flickered in her breast. She reached for the flask. "Perhaps I will have a wee tot."

The corner of his mouth turned up while he handed the drink across the fire. "For medicinal purposes."

"Aye." She eyed him as she sipped. "I trust you will not tell my father, but I slipped into his study a time or two and helped myself."

"You didn't."

"With Alasdair, mind you."

"Do not tell me your elder brother led you astray."

"He did, and now he hasn't bothered to return my letters, he's so absorbed by his duties serving the queen's army on the Continent." Mairi sipped again, the spirit already making her head swim. She cleared her throat. "This must be potent."

Mr. MacRae reached for the flask. "Pure spirit."

She reclined into the furs and watched him drink. Why had such a man offered for her hand? Of course, Mairi couldn't ask. It would be uncouth to bring it up. Besides, she knew why—he'd done it to make her feel better. In her observation, through the man's gruff exterior lay a kind heart.

She reflected for a moment, then smiled to herself. She didn't understand why, but since they'd raced away from the redcoats, Mairi actually felt more herself. Perhaps being in the midst of life-threatening danger reset her priorities. "I think I like being away from people. At least for a time."

He stirred the fire with a stick. "Spending time alone revives the soul."

"Truly? I usually prefer crowds to solitude."

"Indeed you do," he said as if her preferences were well-known throughout the Highlands.

"So, what do you like to do with the time you spend alone reviving your soul?"

He shrugged, tossing the stick onto the fire. "'Tis not often I am able to wander off by myself. I'm usually charged with carrying out the earl's bidding. He is quite good at delegating tasks."

"Aye, but when Seaforth is otherwise occupied, what do you do?"

"I suppose I mostly tend to my clan and kin." He scratched the stubble along his jaw. "But when I can steal precious time alone, I hunt. If there's time, I come up here."

"To your magical place?"

He gave a nod—almost grinned. "A man could live out his days in these hills. The pool's spring fed. There's wildlife aplenty."

"Do you think you'd be satisfied up here all alone for days on end?"

"Satisfied? Aye. But 'tis a fanciful dream. The chieftain of a clan is much like an earl. I have the souls of my kin to protect. There are always barns to raise, roofs to repair, and mouths to feed, rents to collect and—"

"You have Seaforth's affairs to dispatch between it all," she finished.

"I do."

"Why—?" She stopped herself from asking why he hadn't married. *I'm such a dolt.* Perhaps the whisky had loosed her tongue too much.

"Why?" he pressed.

"Nothing. 'Tis not for me to ask."

Pursing his lips, he looked away as if he knew what she'd been thinking. "The hour is late and we have a long ride ahead of us on the morrow."

* * *

Once Dunn ensured Her Ladyship was resting comfortably on a bed of furs, he stoked the fire and placed his sword beside his bedroll and his dirk by his head, where he always kept it when sleeping. He gave the cave a once-over before lying down. His gaze stopped at Lady Mairi.

Resting on her side with her back to him, she looked like a goddess incarnate. A mane of long red tresses sprawled in every direction. His fingers twitched as his eyes meandered along the curve from her shoulder to her waist, then her rounded hip. Never in his life had he beheld a woman who stirred his blood like Mairi MacKenzie.

Earlier, the fire had danced across her fair skin, making it luminous. A bit of mischief had returned to her enormous eyes. He'd been ever so aware as she'd watched him. She asked innocent questions, making simple talk, completely oblivious to how much he enjoyed her attention. If only the eve could have lasted forever. He liked having her eyes on him. Liked being alone with her, listening to the sweet lull of her voice, watching her blush at the slightest distraction.

He climbed between the furs and lay on his back. The fire danced across the cave's ceiling in a prismatic display of amber. He pictured Mairi through the movement. Who wouldn't? With impeccable manners, Her Ladyship had selected a piece of dried meat and carefully bit into it, chewing delicately. And then it had been priceless when she sipped the whisky, however it didn't surprise him that her elder brother had introduced her to it. Alasdair had been a ruffian as a lad, though the heir to the Cromartie earldom was making a name for himself in the wars.

But Dunn's mood soured when her father's words came to mind. *Nay. I cannot consider your proposal, sir. I've a grand alliance to make with Mairi's hand, and the only place I will find a suitor equal to Seaforth is at court.*

Court. The mere word soured his stomach. Lady Mairi didn't belong among the queen's vultures. No, Dunn couldn't picture Her Ladyship cloistered with the nobles at court, watched by noblewomen who preyed on innocent Highland maids. Mairi needed to be free, to allow her spirit to soar, to laugh and dance without critical eyes judging her every act.

Draping his arm over his eyes, Dunn let out a deep breath. He'd brought Her Ladyship to the Cavern of the Fairies to keep her safe from the soldiers, but it didn't take a seer to know Cromartie would be angry. The sooner Dunn returned Lady Mairi to Castle Leod, the better chance there was to keep relations amicable between Clan MacRae and Clan MacKenzie.

Had there been another way, or were my actions selfish?

True, he'd started out doing the right thing by taking her back to Urquhart Castle grounds, but the dragoons had made chase. If Dunn had tried to face them—or even reason with them, there was every chance Lady Mairi would have been in even greater danger. If Dunn hadn't acted swiftly, they both might be lying dead beside those rutting bastards who had tried to force the lass.

Dunn groaned.

Blast Cromartie. If he calls me out, then so be it. I acted in the lady's best interest. Soldiers made chase. I had no option but to run.

And no matter how much he wanted to rise from his pallet and cradle Lady Mairi in his arms, he would remain in his place and carry out his duty for the MacKenzie, just as his family had done for centuries. Her Ladyship was kin to Reid Seaforth and therefore under the protection of his sword.

Honor. I will act honorably toward Her Ladyship and I will see her home safely. I vow it on my father's grave.

Chapter Seven

Lady Mairi slept soundly, her breathing barely audible as Dunn stood over her. He hated to wake the lass, but they had a long day's ride ahead. He also loathed leaving the Cavern of the Fairies, but no matter how much he wanted to keep Her Ladyship with him, it was time to take her back to her father. She wasn't Dunn's woman and never would be. He needed to go back down the mountains and face his lot. Up in the Highlands, it was too easy to lose sight of reality.

Dunn clenched his fists at his sides. "M'lady," he said with authority. "'Tis time we set out."

She stretched with a wee moan and then opened her eyes. "My heavens!" Startled, she clutched the blanket under her chin. "Do you always loom over people when you wake them?"

Blast it all, he'd spent the better part of a half hour trying to think of how best to rouse the woman. God forbid if he'd bent down and touched her shoulder. But then again, he was a large man, perhaps a bit beastly looking, especially with the beard that had grown in overnight. He moved toward the mouth of the cave. "I've left some oatcakes and a flagon of water near the fire. Once you've seen to your...ah...needs, we'd best set out on our journey."

She gave a nod, still watching him from beneath the bedclothes—rough as they may be. The daughter of an earl should not be sleeping on a pallet in a cave, of all places. Dunn strode toward the horses, admonishing himself for not finding an inn.

But that would have been perilous.

He tightened the girth on the lead mare's saddle.

Perilous for me or her?

Unsure, he moved to the gelding he'd chosen for Mairi to ride. There were too many unanswered questions, and the only way to learn about the outcome of the skirmish at Urquhart Castle was to go down to the glens and ask. Had the government dragoons been victorious? Surely their captain had been informed by someone who wanted to cause a stir—possibly smear the name of the nobles present. There were Jacobites and royalists alike at the games. The soldier had told Mairi the Earl of Sutherland's man had informed the garrison of a Jacobite gathering.

Why? Who's feuding with Sutherland?

Perhaps Sutherland held everyone in low esteem. He was a flaming royalist. The earl made clear his politics at every gathering—which is why Dunn steered clear of the man.

Nonetheless, when they rode down to the glens this day, he would need to be vigilant, especially with Her Ladyship in his care.

By the time Dunn had the horses saddled and the

remaining food packed and stowed in the saddlebags, he was in more of a quandary than he'd been when he started. Things between royalists and Jacobites had been relatively amicable since Queen Anne's ascension to the throne. Though not the true male heir, Her Majesty was still born from the Stuart line. But with her declining health and failure to produce an heir, tensions between the two factions were growing, and Dunn had no doubt they would come to a head upon the queen's death. Nobles like Cromartie who played the fence would soon be forced to choose a side.

And Dunn feared civil war. Honestly, he preferred the company of nobles like Seaforth who were sound in their politics, who didn't change with the whims of whoever assumed rule in London.

With the horses saddled and ready to ride, Dunn paced outside the cave. And paced. Just when he was about to head back inside to offer assistance, Mairi made an appearance. She'd braided her hair and smoothed out her skirts, and carried her head high. Heaven help him, she looked like a princess.

He smiled to himself. If anything, this mishap had reignited the fire in her breast. She'd appeared so melancholy at the gathering, Dunn had worried. He'd prayed Seaforth hadn't extinguished her spirited nature for good—Dunn never should have doubted. Lady Mairi had a spine of steel. She would bounce back from any adversity. It was just a matter of time.

"You look lovely this morn, m'lady."

She patted her hair. "And you are very good at stretching the truth, Mr. MacRae." Blessing him with a smile, she continued, "If my father were here, he would be aghast at the state of my gown and my disheveled locks."

Then thank God the earl isn't present.

Dunn stooped to help her mount.

Taking in a sharp breath, she placed her hand on his shoulder. "Would...?"

"Are you troubled?" he asked, straightening.

"No." She covered her mouth. "Aye...ah..." Blushing, she cringed.

Oh, how the rose in her cheeks made his heart flutter. "Do you not like this mount?"

"'Tisn't that." Gulping, she looked toward the path. "Must we ride out along that *dangerous* cliff?"

Dunn frowned to prevent himself from smiling. The lass was afraid of heights. "Och, some of the toughest of men grow a bit anxious when riding along the ledge." He swiped his hand across his mouth. "Would you feel more content making the crossing with me? I'm as steady as an iron rod." Now he was probably turning red, as an entirely different picture filled his mind. *Jesu.*

After he mounted behind her and took up the reins, his mind totally ran amok. Having the crescent of Lady Mairi's hip nestled against his loins made his blood thrum while he studied the woman's delicate, slender, undeniably kissable neck.

Good Lord, as they ambled along, the woman's fragrance alone drove him mad—sweet, floral, and sensual. Every eager part of his body touched her. Strands of hair that had come loose from her braid danced around his face. Her back nestled into the cradle he made by reaching around and holding the reins. His arm rested in the arc of her waist and, though she sat aside like a lady, her shapely buttock rubbed him in the most sinful place of all. Dunn ground his teeth, recited sums in his head, tried to remember the twenty-third psalm, but nothing stopped the surge of desire making him hard, making him want her with every fiber of his being.

She shifted her seat, and a tortured moan came through Dunn's throat.

Turning her face toward him, she looked up with the purest, most ethereal blues he'd ever had the pleasure of gazing upon. "Are you uncomfortable?"

Aye. I'm bloody well losing my mind. He cleared his throat. "Not at all."

If he dipped his chin a mere six inches, he'd be able to capture that bow-shaped mouth with a kiss. A bone-melting, fire-igniting, passionate kiss. A kiss that could lead to so much more. Hands touching, caressing. The discarding of clothes. The erotic sensation of flesh against flesh, of taut nipples, of heady, steamy, wet—

"Mr. MacRae?"

He blinked. "Aye," he said, his voice sounding like the lowest note from a pipe organ.

She gestured to the path. "We've crossed the perilous shelf. Would you be more comfortable if I shifted to my own mount?"

Again, he regarded her eyes, though this time too many inappropriate words came to his lips. Licking them, he pondered. "It is not my comfort that is in question, m'lady. But I am sure you will appreciate the freedom of commanding your own reins."

'Tis confirmed. I have gone completely mad.

For the second time since they had started out on their journey, a hint of disappointment flashed across her face, though she looked away before Dunn could be sure. Regardless, his musings had been entirely inappropriate. Her Ladyship needed to shift to the other mount simply for his sanity. Besides, by dusk they would part ways, and it might be eons until he saw the lass again. In fact, Cromartie could have her married off to a duke or a foreign prince by then.

Curse him to Hades.

Having plunged into a foul mood, Dunn reined the mare to a stop.

* * *

They'd been riding for at least two hours when Mr. MacRae took a detour up another crag. The man knew of more lookouts than a hawk. At least he was being careful and, if Mairi's luck hadn't run its course, it would be dark before they reached Castle Leod. She sincerely hoped there would be a cave filled with comfortable furs nearby. Mairi was still unable to believe she had spent an entire night alone in a cave with a man. Not just any man, but the champion of the Highlands. A laird. The great and powerful chieftain of Clan MacRae.

How scandalously delicious.

The wee scandal was almost juicy enough to make her forget being cast aside by Seaforth. In fact, she'd managed not to feel sorry for herself for an entire day. Who cared what the gossips might say? By the queen's knees, Da would be irate, even though nothing untoward had happened. As Mairi expected, Mr. MacRae had behaved as a gentleman ought. That rough, rugged man who looked like a dastardly scoundrel had protected her virtue and saved her from ruination by those vulgar dragoons. He'd fought for her and fed her, and had provided her with a comfortable night's sleep—and in a cave, atop a pallet with a fire crackling at her back.

The past day had been akin to living in a fairy tale.

If only it didn't have to end. She sighed. *How can I set Da's mind at ease?* He would never understand how gracious Mr. MacRae had been. Her father might even go so far as to hold an inquisition.

"Blast," Mr. MacRae cursed, cuing his horse to a halt.

"What is it?" Mairi trotted her horse beside him.

"A blockade of government troops—right at the river confluence, the bastards." He pointed down the slope, then cringed. "Pardon my language, m'lady. I reckon they're looking for us."

"Do you think they mean to do us harm?"

"Do *me* harm, aye." He glanced her way. "Most likely not you."

"They certainly tried to harm me just one day past."

He gestured east to a crofter working a scythe in a paddock around the river bend from the soldiers. "Perhaps the farmer can tell us what the dragoons are up to."

Though the crofter looked to be miles away, once they arrived at the bottom of the hill, it didn't take long to reach him.

"Hello, friend," called Mr. MacRae. "We saw a blockade at the crossing. Do ye ken for what the dragoons are searching?"

The man leaned on the handle of his scythe and squinted at them with a severe expression. "They're looking for hellions from yesterday's gathering at Urquhart." His lips pulled back in a semblance of a smile, revealing two missing front teeth. "I reckon they're leading the bastards straight to the gallows, beg your pardon, miss."

Mairi pursed her lips. The crofter was vile.

Mr. MacRae pulled a coin from his sporran and held it up. "Are they searching for anyone in particular?"

"You'll need a lot more than a half crown." The man's

fingers tightened around his scythe. "There's a purse of fifty guineas on the head of the MacRae laird."

Mairi's jaw dropped. "That is absolutely absurd."

"Ye ken MacRae?" the man asked, his gaze narrowing and darting back and forth between them. "You're Lady Mairi, are you not? Aye. They said the lass has red hair— and you." He pointed to her savior. "Ye look like the rogue they described."

"You are mistaken," Mr. MacRae said as he sidled his horse closer to Mairi. Good Lord, he had a murderous glint in his eye.

Snarling, the man lunged toward the chieftain, raising the scythe. "And I reckon you're the bloody bastard!"

Dunn's horse reared. Dodging the weapon, he pulled the mare's head around. "You're mad!"

"Soldiers," the crofter shouted, running for the river. "I found him. I won the fifty guineas! He's here!"

"Damn him to hell." Snatching Mairi's bridle, MacRae slammed his heels into his mare's barrel. "Gallop for the hills!"

Mairi's heartbeat raced while she kicked with all her might and slapped her horse's rump. She was a skilled horsewoman, but Dunn rode like a man possessed. His mount gained ground as they galloped for the shelter of the forest.

Crack! A musket fired from the rear.

Mairi flattened her body over the horse's mane. "Help!"

The big chieftain glanced back. "Jesus Saint Christopher Christ!" With a flick of his reins, the horse spun in a half turn. He circled in beside her. "Kick," he bellowed, reaching for the bridle.

"I am." Mairi bore down and rapped her heel while using her reins as a whip. "I cannot ride as fast as you. Not when my legs are aside."

Crack! Another musket fired—farther away this time.

Together they plunged into the concealment of the wood while Dunn demanded more speed. About a mile in, he released his grip on her bridle. "Can you handle your mount from here?"

She glanced back, listening for muskets and shouting. When she heard none, she gave a nod. "Aye."

"Keep pace. If you fall behind, give a shout."

"Where are we heading?" A clap of thunder boomed above, making her blood run cold. Holy Moses, they were on the run from dragoons and now the heavens decided to open?

"The only place the English will not find us."

Unable to help herself, Mairi grinned while her heart fluttered. They might be caught in a storm. There might be an entire army making chase, but she was still with Dunn MacRae. And if anyone could evade disaster, be it man or weather, it was the big Highlander. Rain began to pelt her face, and yet she remained in high spirits. Och aye, Mairi trusted this man to her very bones.

Chapter Eight

By the time they arrived at the dreaded shear-faced crossing, Mairi was soaked through. It seemed as if they'd been riding in circles for ages. Worse, she was completely lost—didn't even know north from south. That was until she spied the cliff face. Her teeth chattered as she pulled her mount to a halt. "Surely y-you don't mean to cross in this horrible squall," she said, blinking rain from her eyes.

Mr. MacRae shot a dark-eyed look over his shoulder, one she was growing accustomed to. "It will be fine. Besides, we must reach shelter. You'll catch your death if we do not stoke the fire and dry your gown."

She didn't care if it started snowing. Mairi wasn't about to ride across a narrow shelf in the pouring rain. "I *hate* that there's no other path to the cave. Please, I can't make that crossing again."

He turned his horse to face her and rested his arms on the mare's withers. "We can climb up and around, but 'tis an hour's ride."

She ran a hand over her face. Goodness, she was cold, but being miserable for an hour trumped tumbling into the black abyss. Not even a wildcat could keep its footing on that narrow shelf in the rain. "Why did you not tell me that in the first place?"

"Because taking that route makes no sense at all."

"Well, it makes sense to me. Not falling off the cliff to my death is a very good reason."

With a grumble, he led her into the thick wood along a route that was no more than a game trail. True to his word, the ride around took a good hour. All the while the storm grew worse with rain pelting down in sheets. It poured so hard, Mairi was scarcely able to see Mr. MacRae in front of her, and God forbid she lose sight of him. She would be lost forever.

When they finally descended the wee hill by the waterfall, a chill cut through Mairi's flesh all the way to the bone. Barely able to grip the reins, her entire body shook. Her teeth rattled with incessant chattering.

As soon as they stopped, Mr. MacRae dismounted and strode straight to her side. "I kent it wasn't a good idea to ride around. Look at you, m'lady. You'll be lucky not to catch your death."

"I-I'll be right," she said through freezing lips while he pulled her into his arms. "F-f-fire."

"We'll see you warmed in no time. I just hope 'tis not too late."

Mairi curled into Dunn's warmth. Goodness, he was as drenched as she, yet he felt warm as a brazier.

Cradling her as if she weighed nothing, he hastened inside the cave and set her on the seat of fur. "'Tis a good thing we have dry wood to burn." He stirred the coals, coaxing up a wee flame, then added a stick of wood and blew like a bellows until the fire leaped across the timber.

Mairi rubbed her hands. "It feels warm already."

"Och, you ought to be reunited with your da by now," he said gruffly, looking angry. "I should have thought back at the river. If I'd left you with the soldiers—"

"I beg your pardon?" she interrupted. "It was soldiers who attacked me in the forest just one day ago. Vile, *corrupt* dragoons."

"Jesu. I ken, but I do not reckon the soldiers at the roadblock would have behaved so improperly." He stacked more wood on the fire.

"You think not? The crofter said there were fifty guineas on your head. What would they have done if they'd caught me? Beat me until I showed them how to find this cave?" She shook her head vehemently. "I would have followed *you*. Not them."

"But you should be home with your father, not holed up in a lair with the likes of me. Your reputation might be ruined because of my thoughtlessness."

"My reputation?" She guffawed. "Seaforth saw to it my reputation was soiled. It may as well weather a bit more bruising."

"Seaforth's blunder was his error to bear alone. It did nothing to diminish your virtue." He looked up, the intensity of his stare bringing on a shiver starting in her breast and rattling her teeth. "But disappearing into the Highlands with a man is something different altogether."

Letting out a deep breath, Mr. MacRae rocked onto his haunches and looked away. Then he picked up a fur and moved beside her. "Put this over your shoulders, m'lady."

"My thanks." She reached out to take it, but he leaned

over and tucked the fur around her. She closed her eyes as his warm fingers brushed her cheek.

"I must send word to Cromartie. Let your father ken you are well. The lookouts might be searching for me, but I'll wager one of Grant's men will have no problem traveling through the barricade with a missive."

Mairi pulled the edges of the fur closed around her. "I suppose Da would be less likely to do something rash if he knew I was unharmed."

"Indeed." He returned to his seat across the fire.

As her shivering subsided, Mairi's insides warmed. "To be honest, I'm glad the soldiers blocked the road," she whispered, wanting him to hear, but hoping he didn't. What would Mr. MacRae think of her if he knew she wasn't ready to go home? Was she behaving like a harlot?

He glanced up—those haunting eyes were too disarming. Aye, he'd heard her for certain. The man didn't need to ask why; the expression on his face was clear enough to read his question, though he allowed her to volunteer the reason.

"I-I'm not ready to return home as of yet," she admitted, throwing caution aside. Let him think what he may. At least she was being plainspoken.

The faintest of smiles turned up his lips...right before he frowned.

Mairi's insides twisted. Was he upset with her? Goodness, she hadn't thought of the inconvenience she posed to him. And with a purse of fifty guineas on MacRae's head, her father had obviously assumed the worst. Of course, MacRae was angry with her. She must be a burden to an important chieftain. He had a clan to look after, and Seaforth's affairs to manage, and Lord knew what else.

"I was..." Her cheeks burned. He undoubtedly didn't

give a farthing about her feelings or how she'd found herself again, if only for a short while.

Moving around the fire, he pulled over another fur and sat beside her. "You were what, m'lady?"

Groaning, she rolled her eyes. "I should not have bothered you with my woes."

He shrugged. "'Tis raining outside. There are countless dragoons chasing us, and we've naught to do but stay here. You may as well tell me what's gnawing at you, m'lady."

Taking in a deep breath, she brushed a strand of hair from her face. "After Seaforth broke off the engagement, I felt quite sorry for myself. In fact, I was so gripped by melancholy, I wanted to hide for the rest of my days."

"That isn't like you."

"Not at all."

"Hiding your bonny face from the world would be a travesty. I certainly would have missed you a great deal. I deeply regret how Seaforth's stupidity must have cut you to the quick."

"You are kind, sir." She scraped her teeth over her bottom lip. "But I kent it all along, no matter what Da told me. I only lied to myself—convinced myself the earl would open his eyes and see me as worthy of his..."

"Love?"

Mairi nodded, the old anguish threatening to grip her heart.

"Och, Seaforth did not deserve you. Never did, if you ask me."

A sad smile turned up the corners of her mouth. "Do ye ken he eluded me at every gathering we ever attended? I swear, over the years I've probably danced more with you than Reid MacKenzie."

"That so?" Dunn scratched his beard. "Well then, I reckon he did you a favor."

"Why do you say that?"

"'Cause now you can find a better man. One who puts you on a pedestal where you deserve to be. One who might grow jealous if any other man asked you to dance."

"That's very kind of you to say, Mr. MacRae."

"I reckon when we're alone together, there's no reason why you shouldn't call me Dunn."

"Not Duncan?"

He shook his head. "No one ever called me Duncan. It sounds awkward to my ears."

"Very well. Dunn it is." However, the shortened name didn't sound respectful enough to her. Mairi would need to think on his request before she completely relented.

He pulled the flask from his sporran and shook it beside his ear. "This is empty."

"There's not much remaining in the saddlebags, either."

"Then that settles it. I must slip down to Glenmoriston tonight and gather supplies—find out what's going on as well." He reached for his musket. "Do ye ken how to shoot one of these?"

She shook her head. "Da only allowed me to learn archery."

"I ken you cannot wield a dirk."

"Oh?"

"Do you not recall? I saw you at the loch with the soldiers."

"Curses." Her shoulders fell with her huff. "I'm afraid I am not much of a warrior woman."

"Mayhap we can remedy that when I return. In the meantime, if you hear a sound, you'd best climb into the alcove behind the curtain and hide."

She craned her neck and peered around him. "There's an alcove?"

"Aye,'tis a secret I only share with my closest friends."

"But why can I not go with you? It will be frightening to be tucked away in this dark cavern alone."

"You'll be fine. Believe me, lass. It will be safer for you to remain here—not to mention warmer. And I'm no healer, mark me. If you fall ill, only God can save us."

Mairi opened her eyes wide. "What do you mean by *us*?"

He eyed her like he did when he wasn't about to withstand a rebuttal. "'Cause you'll be knocking on death's door and I'll be skewered by the pointy end of your father's dirk."

* * *

In all honesty, Dunn would have preferred to bring Mairi along, but she'd slow him down. Aye, she was an accomplished horsewoman, though she rode aside—not to mention her fear of the cliff. And to be forthright, he knew of no highborn lady able to negotiate treacherous cliffs and wet conditions without both legs firmly straddling her horse's back. The lass was safer in the cave where her clothes would dry and she'd be toasty warm by the fire. He wouldn't be distracted by those enormous blue eyes constantly staring at him from a visage of pure beauty. If nothing else, he needed a respite from the painful twisting of his heart.

With the low cloud cover overhead, it was darker than a mire and the going wasn't easy. But he made it to Grant's manse in Glenmoriston. Given the late hour and not being one for formalities, Dunn climbed the trellis to the laird's bedchamber and slipped in through the window.

Robert crouched near the hearth with a sword in his hand, snarling like he was ready to fight to the death. But as soon as Dunn flashed a grin, his friend lowered his weapon. "Good God, MacRae. Do you not ken there's a door?"

Dunn moved into the room with a swagger, noting his friend was sleeping alone this eve. "Seeing there's fifty guineas offered for my head, I thought I ought to be less conspicuous to your servants." He stopped at the sideboard and pulled the stopper off the whisky decanter. "Fancy a dram?"

"Please." After sheathing his weapon, Grant walked to the window and peered out. "Where is Lady Mairi?"

"Where nary a man can touch her." Dunn poured two glasses and set one on the side table beside the laird's chair.

"Had that mongrel Ewen Cameron not informed the garrison that we were plotting a Jacobite rebellion, none of this would have happened. The pox on Cameron and his spawn," Robert spat. "He's a thorn in my side. Always has been."

"What the blazes are you going on about?" Dunn chopped his hand through the air. "The bleeding red-coats boasted to Lady Mairi it was a Sutherland spy who informed on us, albeit falsely. That, however, I can believe."

"Sutherland?" Grant spewed the name with distaste. "If you ask me, they're *both* backbiters. Though I swear the Earl of Sutherland licks his lips every time he thinks he can cause a stir. I'll wager he's colluding with Cameron."

"I disagree. Cameron is Highland folk clear to the bone. I'd fight beside Ewen any day."

"Well, you can have him and his shifty sons." Grant raised his glass and drank.

Dunn followed suit and drank thoughtfully. There was no use telling Robert Grant he was wrong about the Camerons. Feuds between their clans were always either on or off, and Dunn had stopped trying to keep track. "I tried to take Mairi home to Castle Leod today and we ended up chased by a mob of bloody dragoons. They've set up a blockade at the confluence of the River Conon and the Black Water."

The younger laird wiped his mouth with his sleeve. "Christ, if anyone has a way of finding trouble, 'tis you. Troops are searching for you everywhere. Ye ken they're burning crofts, behaving like a mob of riotous hellions."

"Good God, 'tis worse than I thought." Dunn paced in front of the fire. "What news of Eilean Donan Castle? Are my kin safe?"

Grant retreated to his chair. "'Twas the first place searched."

"Have the dragoons posted guards?"

"Of course."

"Ballocks." Dunn took a healthy swig of whisky, then strode to the writing table and took up the quill. "I must send word to Cromartie that Lady Mairi is safe and well. Can your runner deliver a missive?"

"Aye, but the earl will not like it. He's the one footing the fifty guineas—the bastard wants your head. He thinks you stole away with the lass."

"I thought he may have been behind the reward, but bloody hell, stealing away? With three dead dragoons in

my wake? Can the news grow worse? I was saving Her
Ladyship from harm, dammit. Did he not see those rutting soldiers?"

"He saw them all right, and drew the wrong conclusion. I'll have my man deliver your letter, but in the
meantime, you must remain hidden until things settle."
Grant picked up his glass and joined MacRae at the writing table. "Cromartie didn't specify whether you were to
be delivered alive or dead."

"Bastard," Dunn growled, the quill jerking with the
movement of his hand.

"You're not wrong there. He's as much a snake as
Sutherland."

MacRae wrote furiously, read his prose, and sanded
the parchment. Once satisfied, he rested the quill in its
stand. "Jesus Saint Christopher Christ, If I hadn't intervened, Lady Mairi would have been pillaged and ruined
for life."

"And what now? You have her hidden somewhere in
the Highlands? Do you believe the gossip isn't running
rampant?"

"It may be, but Lady Mairi's reputation ought to
weather such a storm. I'm Seaforth's protector. That
alone should explain my actions—as well as ensure Her
Ladyship's virtue remains unscathed."

"So say you."

"Aye, I do say, and I do stand by my word." Shooting
Robert an angry glare, Dunn dipped the quill, signed the
letter, and folded and sealed it. "May I impose upon you
for stores?"

"My larder is yours for the picking."

Dunn offered his hand. "My thanks, friend. And let no
one speak ill of my intentions. I will deliver Lady Mairi

to Castle Leod as soon as the earl retracts his offer for my head—a point I clearly expressed in my missive."

"I shall send word of the earl's reply—to where?"

"Send it to my lieutenant at Eilean Donan. Ram will ken where to find me." To be honest, the only man Dunn would trust with his whereabouts at a time like this was Ram.

After Dunn collected supplies, he hastened back to the Cavern of the Fairies where, by God's grace, he found Mairi wrapped in furs and sound asleep. He stoked the fire and watched her slumber for a time. Facing the flames, she looked like a fairy come to life, complete with wings and stardust sparkling about her ruby locks. To watch Her Ladyship at rest was akin to enjoying a dram of fine whisky—one aged for a century—one that slid down his gullet like silk.

With a sleeping beauty like the lass, Dunn needed no spirit to help him slumber. He only needed more of her. If only he could touch her, pull her into his arms and cradle her.

I will protect her with my life until...

He slammed his fist into his palm.

Until bloody Cromartie marries her to some dimwitted arse.

Sighing, he made himself a pallet and waited until sleep took away the pain of having his love trampled by the nobility of the lands he'd pledged his sword to protect.

Chapter Nine

*D*irectly onto Dunn's face, an unwelcome ray of light shone through the vines hanging over the cave entrance. His body craved another hour of sleep, but the bright light was too overbearing even with his eyes closed. As he stretched, his aching bones punished him from sleeping on the rocky cavern floor. Mornings in the wild reminded him that age had a way of creeping up on a man. Bloody oath, when he was a lad, he didn't need a fur to sleep upon, and now at thirty, one fur wasn't enough.

He stretched again and rolled to his side, shading his face with his hand.

I'm growing soft.

The thought vanished when he blinked. Something was off.

Dunn jolted awake.

He pushed up and stared across the coals. A shot of alarm surged through his blood. Mairi's pallet was empty.

Casting the fur aside, he leaped to his feet. "Lady Mairi?" he croaked, his voice filled with morning gravel.

Hastening to the rear of the cavern, he checked the alcove. Blast, she wasn't there, either.

A shrill scream came from outside.

Dunn's heart flew to his throat. He swooped down and grabbed his dirk. Breaking into a run, he charged through the archway, forgetting to duck. Stopped by immobile and craggy rock crashing into his head, he stumbled, fighting to keep his balance. With no time to lose Dunn gave his head a shake and forced himself to ignore the pain. Ducking this time, he bounded outside while he clapped his hand to his forehead. Warm blood oozed through his fingers. Blast it all, he wasn't about to worry about a wee knock on the head when a woman was in peril. Gritting his teeth, he raced across the stones in bare feet. "Mairi!"

Near the waterfall, the lass floundered in the lagoon, her hands splashing erratically.

"Hold on, I'll save you!" he bellowed. Sprinting, Dunn raced for the shore and dived. Frigid water attacked like prickling needles as he paddled through the pond with forceful strokes, swimming on a path directly for Her Ladyship. The cold all but froze his muscles solid, but Dunn powered through. He would walk across the snows of Ben Nevis barefoot in winter to ensure Lady Mairi's safety. He sucked in one more deep breath and kicked with all his might until he reached her. In the blink of an eye, he wrapped her in his arms. "I have you, m'lady!"

"You do not—" Mairi's head went under, garbling the sound. Dunn swiftly raised her up while she thrashed and kicked. Once he had her firmly secured, he swam with powerful strokes, hauling her toward land.

But she still fought him. "I—"

"Save your breath," he growled. "We're nearly to dry ground." Once he found his feet, he cradled her in his arms, carrying her through the water until he could set her down on soft grass. Odd, the lagoon seemed shallower than he'd remembered, though he hadn't taken a dip in her icy water since he was a lad.

As soon as he placed the lass on her feet, Her Ladyship gave him a solid push. Her face was as angry as a wild-cat's. "I cannot believe you interrupted a lady's bath, you boorish oaf! I had merely dropped the soap. I am quite an accomplished swimmer, mind you." She jammed her fists into her hips. "And the water wasn't even over my head."

Dunn stood dumbfounded—staring. Hardly able to speak. "Soap?" he managed.

"Aye. I found a cake in one of the saddlebags. Bless it, I've had dirt in my hair and grime under my nails since being attacked by the dragoons."

MacRae was too stunned to form words. The wind blew, making his wet clothes feel like ice sticking to flesh, but he stood motionless. Dumbstruck. Unable to form a rational thought in his thick, bull-brained head. Aye, Mairi wore a linen chemise, but the woman might as well have been totally nude. If he'd been lovelorn before, no one in all of Christendom could save him now. The holland clung to every curve, every feminine detail. The thrum of her pulse beat at the base of her neck. Ample breasts, gloriously round and too large even for his palms, curved toward him as if presenting an invitation to be fondled. Taut nipples pointed at him—hard pebbles that demanded to be licked and suckled and worshipped. But the beauty of her breasts was only the prelude.

Heaven help him, Mairi's waist was tiny, curving de-lightfully as if she did not need constricting stays. Dunn's loins tightened as his gaze moved lower to widely flared hips—women's hips. Hips that announced this was one feisty lady not to be trifled with, but to be idolized. As the lass stood nearly naked before him, Dunn beheld the curves he'd admired so often when watching Her Ladyship dance. But the most blessed gift of all was the shadow at her apex—dark, but he knew her treasure was concealed by curls as red as the soaking wet tresses falling about her shoulders.

"Mr. MacRae, did you hear a word I said?" she shouted, stamping her foot.

He gulped and made himself swipe a hand over his eyes. "You dropped the soap?" he asked, snapping to his senses, but without a clue whether she'd said anything else while his mind was in paradise. He couldn't let on that he'd just stood there like a simpleton, ogling the lass. "Jesus Saint Christopher Christ," he barked with a scowl. "From the sound of your shriek, I thought you were drowning."

She looked as if she were about to deliver an angry retort but, as she drew in a breath, concern filled her eyes. "Good heavens, Mr. MacRae, your head is bleeding."

He touched the tender spot where he'd hit his noggin, and let out a wee hiss. "Och, when I heard you scream, I ran out of the cave so fast, I forgot to stoop." He looked at his fingers, and they came back covered with blood.

"Daft Highlander, now you're the one who needs tending." She grasped his arm and led him to the lagoon, as if oblivious to the fact that her chemise was wet and sheer as glass.

"Pay no mind to me," he groused. "You'd best go inside and remove your wet garment—put on some dry clothes afore the cold chills you to the bone."

"And what about you? I can hear your teeth chattering, sir." She tugged his arm. "Now kneel down so I can have a look at your head."

"*Bloody, bleeding hell.* If you insist, m'lady." Feeling like a clod, he dropped to one knee and leaned forward.

"'Tis difficult to believe you can sustain such an injury, as hardheaded as you are." Mairi stood over him and examined his head. She tore a bit of cloth from her hem and leaned close, swabbing the blood. The neckline of her chemise dropped open, giving him a much undeserved eyeful of creamy swells. Dunn moaned aloud.

"Am I hurting you?"

Jesu, how could a man feel pain when presented with such beauty? "Nay," he said, rubbing his fingertips together, sensing the petal softness. "But I reckon you'd best heed me and don your kirtle, Mairi." His voice was deep and soft and filled with want, and he'd called her her familiar name for a reason. "You may not ken, but you're tempting me something fierce. I've sworn to protect you and your clan, but I'm still a man, flesh and blood, and the damp chemise clinging to your—*ah*—clinging to *so very much* of you is driving me to the brink of insanity."

Mairi's hand stilled. Straightening, she took a step away. Looking down and back up, her eyes filled with shock. She dropped the cloth. A gasp squeaked from her throat as she quickly snapped her arms across her chest.

Dunn dropped to his arse as he watched her dash back to the cave, a knot the size of his fist spreading in his chest. He balled the cloth and pressed it against his skull. *Christ, when it comes to Lady Mairi, why must I always shove my goddamned boot in my mouth?*

* * *

Mortified, Mairi dashed into the cave, grabbed a fur, and pulled it tightly around her shoulders. Of course she didn't make a practice of bathing in her chemise, but it was what she wore when she swam in the loch at home—though never in the company of men. *Curses*. At least she was wearing *something*. She'd even thought it a prudent precaution.

And why had he awakened? The man should have been fast asleep. It had been nearly dawn when he'd returned. By all rights, he should still be slumbering wrapped in deer hide. Besides, Mairi would have finished bathing before he'd run to her rescue if it weren't for the slippery soap.

My daft butterfingers.

The bar had flown from her hands like a frog leaping from a lily pad into the water.

I shouldn't have cried out. That's what woke him, no doubt.

Mairi didn't mean to scream, the noise just blurted from her throat.

And now Mr. MacRae thinks me a harlot.

She bit her knuckle and paced around the fire. How could she ever face him again? How could she look him in the eye?

And why did he not say something sooner?

He was looking straight through her chemise the whole time she tended his head wound. No wonder he appeared so out of sorts. He was too busy staring.

And then I was too daft to notice.

She looked outside.

I hope he's all right.

It was odd that while she'd been pacing in the cave, she hadn't heard him mulling about…or cursing. Mr.

MacRae had proved quite adept at cursing. Should she head back out to the loch?

A shudder coursed across her skin. She'd tempted him, for heaven's sake. She absolutely should not go outside until she was good and dry.

After fanning the hem of her chemise over the fire, she sat in the chair and pulled the fur tighter around her shoulders. Mairi needed to think—needed to sort out the hundreds of thoughts swirling around in her head, and there was nothing more soothing than staring at a fire while one tried to piece her feelings together.

She wished she could run home—hop on a horse and gallop for Castle Leod, but then she'd have to cross the terrifying rock shelf with the mortifying drop. If lucky enough to make it over without falling to her death, she'd then have to face at least one barricade of dragoons, possibly more—vile, disrespectful ravagers of helpless maids. Nay, running was not an option.

Mairi would need to swallow her pride—pretend nothing had happened. As the daughter of an earl, she could play the part of an aloof noblewoman. She'd been bred to it. All she needed to do was follow her father's example and the whole debacle would be forgotten. Truly.

No doubt Mr. MacRae would be a gentleman and not mention it again.

Mairi cringed and looked out through the vines. Even if she pretended to be aloof, she knew. He knew. And the whole incident was humiliating.

The flames danced while she conjured his face in her mind's eye—the one filled with pain when he said, *I'm still a man, flesh and blood.* And that she was *driving him to the brink of insanity.*

Him? Gruff Mr. MacRae with the brooding eyes is affected by me?

All this time, Mairi had believed he had taken pity on her and offered his hand in marriage because of Seaforth's actions. Never once did she think he *liked* her. Heavens, he always looked at her with a scowl. If anything, she assumed he *disliked* her. Come to think of it, he always looked serious, no matter to whom he was speaking.

Mairi drummed her fingers on her lips. Mr. MacRae was rather attractive in a rugged sort of way. His hawkish eyes never missed a thing. Always shifting, watching, calculating. Midnight blue, so dark they were almost gray. His heavy eyebrows made his appearance all the more menacing.

Deep in his heart, I believe he's kind.

Suddenly, Mairi clapped a hand over her mouth to stifle a laugh. Poor Mr. MacRae had looked so bewildered when she'd insisted she wasn't drowning. The look on his face was delightfully amusing, though she'd never admit the fact to him.

"Mairi?" She jolted as his deep burr rumbled from outside.

Chapter Ten

I wish you would allow me to take another look at your head. You might need leeches," Lady Mairi said as she followed Dunn on a brisk walk through the forest. They'd soon need more food, and they weren't going to find any game splashing around in the lagoon.

"I don't need bloody leeches," Dunn groused.

Och aye, the last thing he could tolerate was having Her Ladyship hover over him again. He doubted he'd ever be able to withstand her being so near without going mad while he tried not to look into those shiny blue eyes. Tried not to inhale too deeply lest he breathe in her intoxicating fragrance, a scent that made his hands itch to touch her, to pull her into his body and devour her with kisses.

Kissing. The mere thought made his knees buckle.

God bless it, Lady Mairi is not for the likes of me!

Dunn surged ahead, pushing branches out of the way and holding them so they wouldn't whip back and smack the lass in the face.

"But the healer says—"

"I don't give a rat's arse what the healer says. And you ought to stop worrying about me and pay attention to the task at hand."

"Hunting?"

"Aye—we're setting a snare." He glanced over his shoulder. Mairi's hair was mussed with a wee twig sticking out the side. Even then, she was as adorable as a pixie. "Have you ever set a snare, m'lady?"

"I cannot say that I have."

He didn't think so. "How on earth have you survived one and twenty years without learning? 'Tis a basic skill for survival."

"Oh?" she asked shrilly. "Oddly, I have never seen a snare in the halls of Castle Leod."

"My oath, you have been cosseted, have you not?" he asked, watching her out of the corner of his eye.

"I suppose." She stopped, her voice filling with hurt. "Why wouldn't I be? Ye ken my da. You've been to my home. What on earth do you expect of me?"

Dunn stopped and ran his knuckles across the itchy stubble on his face. It wasn't the lassie's fault she was protected from the ways of the world. He'd seen it time and again. Highborn ladies were bred for a life of privilege and not taught a damned thing about how to care for themselves. Aye, they could read, sew, and embroider. Some were good at archery—when shooting at a target. But he'd never met a noblewoman who knew how to prepare oatcakes over a fire, gut a fish, set a snare, or wash clothes in a river. Not that he expected Lady Mairi to do any of those things, but it would behoove her to know how.

Still, he'd been abrupt with her. He knew it. He was always abrupt when it came to Her Ladyship. If he behaved in any other way and let his true feelings come through, she might laugh at him—shun him again. Grousing, he softened his tone. "Forgive me, m'lady. There aren't many things you need to concern yourself with, but I believe that it is important for anyone to ken how to survive in the wild. What if you were riding in a coach that threw a wheel, and you had no food and were subsequently forced to sleep in the open?"

She moved her hands to her hips. "Believe it or not, that did happen once on the way to Inverness."

"And what did you eat?"

"Well, Cook had packed a basket." Mairi dropped her hands to her sides. "But by the time we reached Inverness there was nothing left and I was hungry."

"You see? Snare setting is a skill everyone should learn. You ran out of food, and if you hadn't reached Inverness, you would have needed sustenance. Just like now—the morsels remaining from those I brought back from Mr. Grant's larder will not last."

"Like defending oneself from attack?"

"Indeed." That was another thing he'd promised Her Ladyship—teaching her to defend herself from a knife attack. How could he manage such a task without touching the lass?

Moving along, he spied a rabbit warren with plenty of fresh droppings to indicate wee bunnies must be milling about. "Look there." He pointed. "What do you see?"

She bent down. "Holes...rabbit holes for certain."

"You are correct."

She turned in a circle. "Is this where we set the snare?"

"Nearby." He led her into the scrub a few paces, pulled a leather thong from his sporran, and handed it to Mairi. "Hold this."

He found a sapling, bendable enough for the spring. He found two sticks, carved notches in both, and made a spike out of the end of the thickest one. Using the butt of his dirk, he drove the spike into the ground. "Now hand me the thong," he said, reaching for it.

"What will you do with it?" she asked.

He tied a knot around the second stick while he gestured to the sapling with his head. "See the wee tree?"

"Aye."

"It will act as our whip." Grabbing it about five feet up, he tied the thong around the trunk, then pulled the strip down and secured the notches of the two sticks. Once sure the trigger would hold in place, he gestured to the remaining length of leather. "Make a slipknot at the end."

"I can do that." Mairi smiled as if thrilled to be of help—aye, no matter how much Dunn wanted to believe it, the lass was not an unbending noblewoman. When finished, she held up her handiwork. "There."

"Perfect."

"Truly?"

"Aye, m'lady. I never say anything I do not mean." He grinned. "Now pull the cord through the slipknot you made and make a circle about eight inches in diameter."

Biting her bottom lip, she quickly complied.

"All right then." Dunn gingerly released his fingers from the trigger. "Let us see if it works."

Mairi clapped her hands. "How?"

He picked up another stick and handed it to her. "Tap the inside of the circle ever so slightly."

When she did, the sapling snapped up so fast, the lass must have jumped five feet. She gaped at him with eyes as round as silver sovereigns—eyes as bonny as a midsummer sky. "It worked!"

His damned heart fluttered. "Did you doubt me, lass?"

She glanced at the stick in her hand. "Nay . . . I, well, *I* might have done something wrong."

"Not at all." Hiding his smile, Dunn busied himself by resetting the snare and picking a handful of dandelion leaves, which he placed inside the ring. "Rabbits cannot resist these."

"You are knowledgeable in a great many things, Mr. MacRae."

He'd asked her to call him Dunn, but given the incident at the lagoon, it was best that she continued to address him formally. "Perhaps," he said. "Though the older I grow, it seems the more I realize how much there is I have yet to learn."

One thing Dunn did know was how to behave like a gentleman. After all, he was a laird and educated at the University of Edinburgh. He owned lands and sea galleys. His kin operated the largest herring and haddock business west of Inverness, and Eilean Donan Castle had been in his family's care for centuries.

A wee voice in his head told Dunn to do the gentlemanly thing and take a step back, but before he moved, she brushed her fingers along his jaw.

"Your beard is so thick."

Taking in a sharp breath, Dunn tried to steady his thumping heart. "Aye, and it grows in faster than weeds in a wheat field."

She raised her other hand and caressed the second cheek. "'Tis softer than I'd imagined."

Good God, strike me down now and take me to heaven. She's making it bloody difficult for me to keep my hands to myself. "If only I had a mirror, I'd shave my whiskers, so I wouldn't be so unsightly."

She sighed and lowered her hands, but didn't step away, nor did she lower her gaze. Did the woman have any idea how bold she appeared? An unmarried maid alone in the wood with a man, albeit a man sworn to protect her—but a man all the same, who only that morn had clearly expressed his inappropriate yearnings. "I do not think you unappealing, sir."

Dunn spun on his heel, his heart thumping so fast, he was certain Mairi could hear it. "Mayhap we should go. If we stand here, we'll never catch a rabbit."

She hastened along behind. "I have a splendid idea," she said far too cheerfully.

"What's that?"

"*I* shall shave your beard."

* * *

Goodness gracious, convincing Mr. MacRae that she was completely competent to use a razor had all but taken an act of God. Of course Mairi had used a razor before— *once*. She'd shaved her brother Alasdair's face. She'd been twelve at the time and he seventeen, but she hadn't nicked him. Not even once.

While the Highlander sat on a log by the lagoon, she expertly lathered his face with another cake of soap she'd found in the saddlebags. "At least it hasn't rained today," she said, trying to sound exuberant. Mr. MacRae was always so serious; he needed to be surrounded by cheerful people—at least that was Mairi's conclusion. Besides, she was feeling much better about her own lot as of late— mayhap because she'd put it out of her mind. Her spirits were a hundred times more pleasant than the creeping, evil, horrible melancholy she'd endured only days past.

"Agreed," he said. "Though I don't expect the fine weather to last."

"Whyever not?"

He raised his eyelashes and met her gaze, making Mairi's insides flit about like moths to a flame. She leaned in to study his lashes more closely. Dark brown, they were thicker than hers and longer. Perhaps they were what made his eyes always look so intense. With a shift of his expression, he glared at her, arching his bold brows. "Are you planning to use that blade, or just stare at my bonny face?"

"Ah." Snapping her gaze away, she tapped her fingers to her lips. "I was just noticing your eyelashes."

"What about them?" he asked, sounding gruff, but Mairi discounted acrimony. In fact, she was quite certain he was not as coarse as he let on.

"They're lovelier than mine." She raised the razor.

He frowned, making a deep crease between his eyebrows.

After taking a clean swipe, she wiped away the foam on a cloth. "Why do you always frown after I pay you a compliment?"

"I don't frown."

"You just did."

"No, m'lady. I did not frown."

Pursing her lips, she took another swipe, this one faster and harder. "I beg your pardon, but when I said your eyelashes were bonnier than mine, you frowned whether you realize it or not... and you have done it many, many times in the past." Mairi thought back. "You did the same when I said I wasn't ready to return home as of yet."

"Hogwash."

His response made heat flash across the back of her

neck. He was deliberately denying his own expressions. Why? Why would he do that? Furiously, she shaved his face with quick flicks of her wrist.

He always spoke the truth about other matters. She knew this to be true by reputation and by experience, but something was preventing him from being honest with himself. If only they did have a mirror. The next time the corners of his mouth pulled down and those eyes grew dark as coal she would shove it in front of his face and show him exactly what he looked like.

Sighing, she stood back and examined her handiwork. "I need to push up your nose to reach your mustache."

He nodded. "Very well."

"How is the knock on your head?" she asked, gently nudging up the end of his nose.

"Barely ken 'tis there." He winked. "With a head as hard as mine, it is difficult for a man like me to notice such things." Now he was feeding her chaff.

She giggled. Truly, she'd behaved badly. Though he had as well. "I'm glad you're not afflicted with a megrim."

He thumped his skull. "She'll come good in a day or two, mark me."

Finished with shaving, Mairi set the razor down and examined the wound, now starting to scab over. "There's a knot and a purple bruise."

"I reckoned there would be." He grabbed the cloth and wiped his face. "How do I look? Passable for a visit to court?"

"Aye, you are." She eyed him. "Are you planning a trip to London?"

"Not anytime soon. Never again if it were up to me."

"Then why go at all?"

He tossed the cloth aside. "Sooner or later Seaforth will call upon me and I'll have no recourse but to ride alongside him and ensure he eludes trouble."

"Does His Lordship find trouble often?"

"Aye, he does. And he never seems to mind having me clean up the messes he leaves behind."

Numb tingling spread across Mairi's skin. Within the blink of an eye, the horrors from the day Seaforth broke their engagement returned full force. Tears welled in her eyes as she shook her head and backed away. That's right. Mr. MacRae cleaned up the Earl of Seaforth's blunders, just as he'd attempted to do by offering for her hand. She drew her palm over her mouth to stifle a sob. "You may try, sir. But you cannot always make up for Seaforth's indiscretions." Before she crumpled into a weeping heap, Mairi spun on her heel and ran for the cave.

Curses, why had she been so dimwitted to think the laird might actually care for her? Why did she allow herself to feel happiness? Every time her heart fluttered with a modicum of joy, she ended up humiliating herself. For the love of God, the man frowned all the time. He groused all the time. The only reason MacRae had saved her was because it was his sworn duty to protect MacKenzie kin.

She was such a fool to think otherwise. Da was right. Her father needed to make an alliance with a noble family. That's what she'd been bred for. She may as well face it. If she ever married, which was growing more doubtful by the day, it would be to a man of her father's choosing. A man who would further her family's interests. A nobleman who had connections in London, who wore fine silk and velvet doublets and couldn't grow a full beard in two days if his life depended upon it.

She plopped onto the fur chair and buried her face in her hands. Her future husband would never consider hiding out in the Highlands in a cave. A man as refined as he would carry a sword only for show. His army would do all the fighting for him.

"Mairi," Dunn whispered right beside her, though she hadn't heard him come inside.

She turned away. "Leave me be."

"I cannot do that." He kneeled, raised his hand and, after a moment's hesitation, caressed her hair.

Holy Mother, his touch felt so undeniably soothing, Mairi craved for his hand to linger. If only he cared for her, for Mairi MacKenzie, the redheaded lass whom he'd rescued from the grip of dastards. "Please. I cannot bear to have you touch me when you are *not* truly fond of me."

"What did you say?"

She looked up through bleary eyes. "You heard me. You said yourself, you clean up Seaforth's blunders." She thumped her chest. Hard. "Well, I'm his latest mistake, am I not? He all but left me standing alone at the altar."

"Good heavens, Mairi, you are not *his* blunder. Have I not been clear on that?" Reaching over, he pulled her to his breast and cradled her head against his powerful chest. His heart beat a strong rhythm while he smoothed a big gentle hand up and down her spine.

The wonderfulness of his succor was almost too painful to bear.

"You're the bonniest, most vibrant rose in the Highlands, Mairi MacKenzie."

"I'm not."

"You are, and do ye ken what else?"

She shook her head while her daft sobs turned to hiccups.

"You're right. I do frown when you pay me a compliment."

"You see? Why do you do it?"

His hand stilled against her back, his body tensed. "Because I'm afraid you'll reject me once more. Such a rejection I could never again bear."

Chapter Eleven

*R*eason told Dunn to keep his mouth shut, but the torture of seeing Mairi weeping and miserable twisted his heart into a hundred knots. How could he continue to hold his tongue? The lass needed to know the truth—needed to know he had not been impervious to her refusal. "Now can you understand why I am sympathetic to your plight? I, too, have been rejected by someone I care for very deeply."

Mairi gasped and broke away from his embrace. "But Da said..."

"What did your father say?" he asked while his gut churned.

She drew her hand over her mouth as if she were afraid to speak further. But Dunn didn't need to probe. He knew Cromartie to be a snake. The earl cared nothing about Mairi's happiness. The man's only concern was the advancement of his holdings—to gain favor at court and acquire lands and riches. Of course, he would use Mairi as a pawn in his scheme. Many noblemen thought of their alliances before they considered the wishes of their off-spring.

And now Dunn had opened his mouth. He'd revealed his hand. Scooting away, he placed a stick of wood atop the coals. They both sat in silence for a time while the fire crackled. Another few days and he'd attempt to take her home again. No doubt the government troops would soon abandon their blockades for duties more critical to the crown. And when the Earl of Cromartie received the missive, he ought to rescind the price on Dunn's head. In fact, it wouldn't be a surprise if at any time Ram rode into camp with news that all had been forgiven and the roads were clear.

"Forgive my reticence," Mairi finally said in a soft tone. "I am overwhelmed with confusion."

"There is no need to explain." What was done was done, and MacRae had no intention of cutting open old wounds. Lady Mairi's father had tied her hands. She could no sooner pledge undying love than change her birthright.

But at least now she knew Dunn's offer of marriage hadn't been an act of pity.

"I wonder . . . ," she said, glancing his way for a moment.

"Hm?" He cracked his thumbs. "Ye ken you can speak freely, m'lady. Anything you say in confidence will nay be repeated by these lips."

She smiled thoughtfully. "I was just going to ask what duties are mounting whilst you hide away with me."

Not exactly the question he was expecting, but he welcomed the change of subject. "As I mentioned afore, being the chieftain of a clan is not so different from being an earl—at least what I've witnessed from years of following Seaforth around. There are lands to manage and let to crofters. Livestock must be bred, branded, and taken to market. Decisions are made, rents are collected and, at times, discipline must be enforced."

"Aye, that does sound similar, except you left out the part about increasing your wealth."

He snorted. "Make no bones about it, lass, all men see to increase their fortunes in one way or another."

She heaved a long sigh, then her gaze slid his way—a very wise expression for one so young. "Ye ken what I mean."

"I do, and I reckon if I had a daughter, I would be seeking to make a good alliance with her hand."

"Would you consider her wishes, or would your word be law?"

He pursed his lips and tapped them with his pointer finger. "I'm not certain I can answer that fairly, given I have sired no children."

"But what if you had? Imagine yourself with a daughter of marriageable age. She's bright, she loves and respects you, she's bonny and good-natured..."

"Does she have red hair?"

Mairi held up a dainty finger. "This is merely theoretical, mind you."

"Apologies. I was simply adding detail to my imaginary daughter's rendering."

"Very well. You can choose her hair color."

"Brown."

Mairi's brow furrowed. "Why brown?"

"Because I have brown hair."

"Ah. That does make perfect sense."

Dunn smirked. At least this whole exercise made sense to someone.

"Now close your eyes," she said.

The least he could do was humor her. "All right. They're closed."

"Imagine your daughter with long, flowing brown locks. When she was a wee one, she'd sit on your lap and make you laugh with her antics. You taught her how to ride a horse and how to jump logs and pursue a fox on a hunt. You watched her grow from a wee bairn to a saucy youth and then to a woman full grown. Your daughter is part of you, would do anything for you. She watches you with admiration in her eyes." Mairi paused for a moment. "Now tell me, when it came time for this daughter to wed, would you consider her wishes?"

It didn't take Dunn long to respond. "Of course, I would consider her wishes because a daughter like that would have my heartstrings wound tightly around her wee finger." He shook his head. "But I doubt there would be a man in all of Britain whom I would consider worthy enough for her hand. It would be very difficult indeed to approve of anyone and see her leave my home, venturing out on her own to a life of which I ken will be difficult."

"Difficult?"

"Aye, life always brings difficulty, lass, especially for women. Childbearing and child rearing are not easy tasks, and many a woman has fallen prey to its perils."

She gulped. "When you put it like that, it doesn't sound romantic at all."

"I'm speaking from a father's point of view, mind you."

"Perhaps we built too vivid a rendering."

"Nay. I believe it was just enough to stir up my protective instincts." He slapped his thigh, wishing to give her shoulder an encouraging pat, but things had grown oddly formal between them. "You may have noticed when I set my mind to safeguard anything, I take my responsibility most seriously."

* * *

The mouthwatering smell of bacon wafted around her. It crackled on the cast-iron griddle. Mairi rolled to her side and slid deeper beneath the fur blanket. She wasn't ready to wake. It had been so hard to sleep last eve after all Mr. MacRae said. Though she appreciated his candor, she didn't know what to make of it. The one thought that continually needled her mind was that Mr. MacRae hadn't proposed marriage out of pity. That fact shocked her to her very core. It took so much time to ponder the significance of his admission. Da had told her that Mr. MacRae would benefit greatly from an alliance with the house of Cromartie and that Mr. MacRae was nothing but a fortune-seeking Highlander. Da had gone on to insist he would make an alliance with Mairi's hand, one that would ensure the earls of Cromartie grew in power and remained strong influences throughout Scotland as well as England.

Over the years Da spent a great deal of time in London feathering his nest. Of course, all noblemen sought wealth and power. Even Dunn admitted to the fact. But what about happiness? What about love? There hadn't been much happiness and love at Castle Leod while Mairi was growing up. Most often Da was away, and her brother, Alasdair, rarely paid her any mind. She didn't remember her mother. In truth, it was the governess who had raised her, a spinster and the seventh daughter of the chieftain of Clan Gunn. The woman was homely with an inordinately large nose. Though strict and unbending, she had provided the nurturing Mairi needed through her formative years. Once Mairi had reached her majority, the governess had accepted another position with the Sinclair family.

After that, Mairi traveled with her father. She sailed to London and attended balls, though her favorite were the gatherings in Scotland with her fellow Highlanders. Often Seaforth visited the same events as her father. Mr. MacRae would be there, too, with his brooding stare. Had he fancied her all along?

Who was to know? Mr. MacRae would never express his true feelings if it meant conflicting with the Earl of Seaforth. In fact, though he wasn't a peer, the brooding chieftain happened to be the most gentlemanly of the gentlemen Mairi had ever met. And now all was ruined. She had refused him. Such a refusal was final. A lady didn't turn down a proposal of marriage and turn around and change her mind. Even if she did change her mind, it would be highly improper to return to the suitor and apologize.

Not only improper, but impossible.

A refusal was absolute. The end. In no way would it be proper for her to raise the subject with him.

"Lady Mairi, are you awake, lass?" Dunn's deep burr rolled through the air and hung there like sweet molasses syrup.

She said nothing for a time, wanting to fall back to sleep where she wasn't plagued by her thoughts. But he hovered. Unable to keep her eyes closed, she rolled to her back and looked up. "Aye, I am awake." She covered her mouth and emitted a wee cough.

Dunn leaned nearer like a worried old hen. "Och, are you ill?"

Mairi shook her head. "Not at all. Just tired."

The crease between his brows eased with his nod. "I've cooked up the last of the bacon and put it on a trencher with some oatcakes. I'll leave you to eat and attend to your needs. And then I reckon 'tis time to teach you how to fend off an attack."

"Truly?" She thought he may have forgotten. "Do you think I can hold my own against three dastardly dragoons?"

"I think you might be able to purchase time to enable yourself to run away." He bowed. "I'll see you outside."

Mairi clutched the fur still up about her neck. "Have you checked the snare we set?"

"Nay, I thought you might want to come along to have a look."

Mairi waited until Dunn left the cave before she rose. She made quick work of tending to her morning needs, then she ate the food he had prepared, braided her hair, and set out for a lesson in which she had no idea what to expect. The nicest thing? Mr. MacRae would be the teacher.

Chapter Twelve

Standing in the clearing, Mairi stared at the flintlock pistol in Mr. MacRae's hand. "How am I expected to carry a weapon of any size on my person? Women do not roam about wearing scabbards of any sort."

"You're jumping ahead." He held up the pistol, then drew his sword and held it aloft as well. "Which do you consider the better weapon?"

"A sword." She pointed. "A musket has only one shot, and if you miss, about all you can use it for is to club someone over the head—unless you have a bayonet affixed like the soldiers do."

"Very good. I am impressed." He rested both weapons on a big rock he used as a table. "And you were correct; a woman cannot easily carry or conceal a sword or a musket of any kind—besides, muskets need black powder and balls of lead, and those things are not easy to tote around."

Mairi crossed her arms and suppressed a smile. The great chieftain of Clan MacRae was quite entertaining when it came to talking about weapons. Even a spark flashed in his eyes.

He drew his dirk from its scabbard. "The best weapon for a lass is a dirk or dagger."

"But I had a dagger in my hands when the dragoons attacked." She shook her finger. "And that wee knife didn't scare them in the least."

"That's 'cause ye did not ken how to use it."

She pursed her lips and nodded. Mr. MacRae was right. The blasted dagger had trembled in her hand like it was about to be blown away by the wind. She rolled her hand through the air. "Carry on then."

He set the dirk beside the other weapons, then moved his fists to his hips. He faced her with the same serious expression she'd seen for days now. Though she no longer feared him. His hair hung loose about his shoulders, and the face she'd shaved clean the day before sported a dark shadow. His shirt clung to the solid male beneath, snugly fitting his muscular chest. His kilt was belted low across his hips and, as with all Highlanders, a long length of tartan draped over his shoulder, secured in place by an enormous clan brooch. He wore hose to his knees, secured in place by red ribbon, adorning massively sturdy and powerful legs.

While she stared, he said something indiscernible, followed by an awkward pause. "Are you listening, lass?"

Mairi blinked.

Dunn was definitely not smiling now.

Weapons training was no time to be ogling the master. "Sorry. What was that?"

"I said, your first defense should always be evasion. Do not put yourself in a situation where you might become a victim."

"But—"

"I ken, 'tisn't always possible, but you must think that way. Had you taken an escort into the wood at Urquhart Castle, you would have been safer."

She nodded.

"Your next option is to run or hide. Remove yourself from the situation."

"But—"

"You mustn't keep interrupting me, m'lady. I'm only giving you hypothetical situations. The first lesson of warfare is that you must realize you have options as to how you react. Trust your insides."

She knit her brows. "I beg your pardon?"

"Have you ever felt a queasiness in your stomach telling you something bad was about to happen?"

"Aye—I did when those soldiers came into the wood."

"That feeling doesn't happen for naught. 'Tis an early warning telling you that you must act quickly. Understood?"

"Aye."

"Right. Then, in the face of danger, never show fear."

"How—?"

He held up his finger. "Square your shoulders, hold your head high, and above all, make eye contact. You are the daughter of an earl and you will not be trifled with." He gestured at her with his palm. "Say it."

"I am the daughter of an earl and I will not be trifled with."

"I'm not convinced." He moved in closer, looming as if to slay her with those blasted, piercing dark eyes. "Say it again."

"I-I—!"

"Say it again," he bellowed loud enough to be heard in the next county.

This time she squared her shoulders and gave him a stern glare. "I *am* the daughter of an earl and I *will not* be trifled with."

"Better." He stepped back while Mairi released an enormous breath she hadn't realized she'd been holding. "Am I frightening you?" he asked.

"Aye."

"Good. Because you need to be able to act even when frightened. Standing frozen with your eyes wide will do ye no good at all."

She gave a tsk of her tongue. "I'll keep that in mind the next time I am accosted."

He resumed his foot-planted, fists-on-the-hips stance. A posture that made him look like the king of the Highlands. "Search for the opportunity to surprise. Strike with speed, then retreat. Do not remain in harm's way any longer than you absolutely must."

"Do you do that?"

"If I'm attacked in the wood by a mob of highwaymen, then aye. Though most anyone who has ever made the mistake of trying it is no longer breathing."

Tapping her fingers to her lips, Mairi sniggered. "I would have thought no less."

He held up a finger. "Bleating bloody murder is a good tactic as well, especially if there are people nearby."

"I'm quite good at that."

"Most lassies are." He gestured to the dirk. "Now, show me how to hold a knife."

She picked it up and, holding it firmly in her hand, pointed straight at his chest.

"Well then, come at me."

She lowered her hand to her side and shook her head. "I cannot."

"You can and you will." He beckoned with his fingers. "Come, lass. Do not go easy on me."

Gnashing her teeth, she lunged. Mr. MacRae stepped to the side, grabbed the hilt above her fingers, and twisted the knife right out of her hand. Mairi's jaw dropped. "How did you do that?"

"Simple mechanics." Turning sideways, he raised the dirk and demonstrated. "You held the knife like most everyone else, with the blade coming out the top of your fist. Your thumb is the weakest part of your grip. I merely grasped the hilt and bent it toward your thumb."

After he showed her exactly how his maneuver worked, he had Mairi do the same as he held the dirk in his beefy fist. Determined, she took hold of the exposed hilt, shoved it against his thumb with all her might. His grip broke. Astonished, she examined the dirk in front of her nose. "Did I really take it from you?"

His eyebrows shot up with a hint of laughter in those midnight-blue eyes. "'Tis in your hand, is it not?"

Mairi couldn't help but smile. Truly, she wasn't daft enough to think the big laird hadn't allowed her to succeed, but she'd disarmed him all the same. Perhaps lassies weren't completely helpless. After she disarmed him five more times, he took the dirk and turned it around so that the blade pointed downward when he held his fist straight out.

"Try to disarm me now." He didn't even bring the weapon into his body, he just stood there holding it out. Mairi attacked like she had before, and the hilt wouldn't budge a fraction.

"Why can I not disarm you?" She shuffled away and crossed her arms.

"This is a stronger grip. And remember what I said about striking swiftly and with surprise?"

"Aye."

"Always grasp your hilt like this." He swung it across his body, close and tight. "One slice to the neck, and it is all over."

Mairi mirrored the strike. "Goodness, that even looks deadly without a weapon in my hand."

"That's 'cause 'tis the same motion as a jab across the jaw."

She held out her hand. "May I give it a try?"

He turned the dirk around and presented her with the hilt. "Grow accustomed to the feel of the grip in your hand, the weight of your weapon, and allow it to become an extension of your arm."

Mairi took the weapon and shifted it backward, forward, up and down. In her hands it felt savage and primal, and so much more secure than the grip she'd been using.

Mr. MacRae moved to a tree with an exposed trunk—one with so many slashes through its bark, the oak looked as if it had been on the receiving end of a year's worth of duels and lost. "Take a few jabs. Imagine your opponent's neck or his belly. Feel the power in your arm."

Mairi's first few swings were rather unimpressive, though MacRae said nothing, just looked on with his fists on his hips. Clearly, he missed nothing and, no doubt, watched with a critical eye. Och, it would be but a matter of time before he launched into a litany of her errors. Her shoulders tense and throat dry, she lunged and took another swing, slicing an anemic line through the bark. She stopped and dropped her arms. "You're making me nervous."

"You are doing well. One doesn't pick up a weapon and immediately become proficient with it. Mastery takes time and hours upon hours of practice."

Lunging, Mairi took another swing at the tree, this time making a pronounced gouge.

"See? You're improving already."

She glanced over her shoulder. "I'll wager you wouldn't want me to come at you when holding the blade like this."

He leveled his stare and a dark-eyed challenge. "You could give it a go...if you dare."

A dare? How impossible to resist.

However, Mairi didn't want to cause any damage. She studied him out of the corner of her eye. "A glancing blow?"

"Give it your best, lass."

"But I might hurt you."

"We haven't all day."

She gulped. If she aimed for his flank, at least she wouldn't kill him. Her decision made, she planted her foot, whipped around, and struck with a forceful swing of her arm.

Everything blurred.

Instead of suffering her glancing blow, Mr. MacRae moved like lightning. He seized her wrist and bent it down so her arm seared with unbearable pain. The knife dropped from her grasp as his grip strengthened. The pain blinded her. Continuing to control her wrist, he levered Mairi's arm up her back while she spun into a headlock. Her back arched and pressed flush against his chest— a hard unyielding wall of a chest. Unable to move, she rose up on her toes to relieve the crushing pressure on her throat.

Gasping, she bore down and jolted her entire body in a futile attempt to break free. "Release me, you brute!"

He moved his lips to her ear, his hot breath making a shiver course down her spine. "Where are my weak points? Even a wee lassie like you can overcome me."

She struggled again. "Weak points? You're as hard as granite. There's not a place on your body not hewn from stone."

"That's where you're wrong," he growled in her ear—a menacing, thrilling, bone-melting growl. "Stomp on my arch, use your elbows—you have one free arm. Ball your fist and take a swing at my cods—the softest, most vulnerable part of any man."

Mairi stopped struggling while gooseflesh spread across her skin. His grip eased ever so slightly. "I beg your pardon, but did you just instruct me to strike your nether parts?"

"I did."

"That is barbaric."

"Fighting is barbaric. Skill is important, but the most savage and determined man wins. If you engage in a fight, you must commit to seeing it through to the end."

Licking her lips, she clenched her fist and shifted her gaze downward. "If I try to strike, you'll counter, will you not?"

"I'll admit, I will avoid such a strike at all costs."

"All costs?"

"Aye."

Her mind rifling through options, she turned her head toward his face—toward those full lips whispering in her ear. Panning her gaze up further, she met his stare. Good Lord, she'd never been this close to his face. True, his eyes were a deep blue, but flecks sparkled through them like crystals—mysterious and fathomless pools met her eyes with a challenge, waiting like a predator for her next move.

There's only one thing that will arrest him.

She did step on his foot, but she didn't stomp. She used it to gain height. Rising, she pursed her lips and kissed him—planted a smooch right on those menacing, pouty lips—those lips that sneered and frowned and seldom smiled. Lips that made her blood stir and race through her heart like a raging torrent.

Before she drew away, he'd released his hold, grasped her shoulders, and pulled her into him. A powerful embrace surrounded her while her knees turned boneless. Ever so gently, the Goliath holding her in his arms cradled her head while the softest, most delicious lips imaginable plied hers.

Floating, Mairi never wanted the kiss to end, wished to remain wrapped in those brawny arms forever. Her breasts pressed flush against Duncan MacRae's masculine chest, craving something more, more touching, more closeness, more of this man who confused and discombobulated her and, right at this very moment, had her wrapped in his tangled web.

Her eyes flashed open when he brushed the parting of her lips with his tongue. She tried to pull away, but his hand held her firmly. A soft moan rumbled in his chest, making her breasts swell all the more. And then it happened again. His tongue brushed her lips, making a flood of need pulse through her body—a need so intense, she feared she might swoon. Timidly, Mairi opened her lips, praying this was what he wanted, hoping her actions were not too bold.

Dear God, what if he pushes me away?

But as soon as the question formed in her mind, his tongue swept into her mouth. Boldly entered and brushed her tongue. Swooning? Och aye, Mairi had surpassed swooning. Her entire body soared as if carried away on a summer's breeze.

She let him lead while together they danced, their mouths joined in the most intimate kiss imaginable.

And then her feet touched ground. His hands moved to her shoulders as he drew his head away. Deep concern filled his eyes and etched in the furrow between his eyebrows. "I-I am sorry, m'lady. I lost my head." His Adam's apple bobbed.

She gaped at him, unable to form words. He was sorry? For kissing her?

"'Twas a mistake." He bowed. "It will not happen again."

Tears blurred her eyes. A mistake? Never again? She drew her hand over her mouth.

A refusal was absolute and as final as death. How could she forget? Holy Moses, she would regret turning down this braw man's offer of marriage for the rest of her days.

"I must check the trap." Unable to face him any longer, she started for the trail.

He fell in step behind her. "Aye, we must."

She turned and thrust out her palm. "No, sir. I will go alone."

"But—"

"I am the daughter of the Earl of Cromartie, and thus you will obey my wishes. There is no other human soul for miles who might wish to do me harm and I *will* check the snare without your assistance!"

She turned and ran before a tear streamed down her

cheek. That boorish oaf of a man. How dare he turn her into a melting, swooning, floating mess? And then apologize for it? Did he not realize no man had ever kissed her thus before? Did he think because she rejected him, he had the right to take her heart and squash it in his gigantic hands?

Lightning flashed above followed by an earsplitting boom. Clouds opened with a deluge, the wind picking up to a gale. But Mairi kept running while icy droplets of water soaked through her kirtle. How could she face him again?

Does that brute feel nothing?

Chapter Thirteen

*D*unn stood clenching his fists while Mairi disappeared into the wood. Why on earth, when it came to her, did he always end up acting like a complete and utter fool? Why the hell couldn't he keep his hands to himself? He knew better than to challenge her—to draw her in so close, their bodies touched.

Jesus Saint Christopher Christ, as soon as her lush curves had molded into his body, he was lost—a rogue on the prowl, ready to conquer his quarry.

What the hell was I thinking?

He'd behaved contemptibly. How dare he allow himself a moment of weakness. He was Lady Mairi's sworn protector. Responsibility to clan and kin was his creed. As soon as he'd pulled her into an armlock, his smoldering desire had boiled to the surface and overtaken the sensibilities he always tried so hard to keep in check. He should never—not ever—show his emotions to Her Ladyship and, furthermore, last eve he should not have indicated how deeply her refusal had injured him. Regardless of her recent disappointment, Lady Mairi would learn soon enough how desirable she was to men.

Dunn groaned. Aye, it went against every fiber in his body not to chase after Her Ladyship, but doing so might only serve to make her angrier. And she was right. There wasn't another living soul for miles—especially in the direction she was traveling. She could walk for five days and not meet up with another human.

She'll check the traps and be back in no time.

Thunder rumbled overhead, bringing with it a squall. He looked toward the wood, the tightness in his chest returning tenfold. They'd set the snare only a few dozen yards in. She should have been back by now. *I must go after her.* Half out of his mind, he started down the path, but stopped himself. *Dammit, I have no choice but to give her some time alone—time for her ire to cool.* She had pulled rank and ordered him to obey her wishes. Besides, a few drops of rain never hurt a soul.

He stared through the trees, searching for movement. *She will not linger in the rain for certain.*

Returning to the clearing, Dunn busied himself with gathering wood for the fire and stacked it in the cave while it was still dry enough to burn. All the while, a hollow chasm of pain spread in his chest. When they'd run into the barricade of dragoons and were forced to return to the Cavern of the Fairies, he'd secretly been overjoyed—relieved to have an excuse to spend a sennight or more with Her Ladyship. But in truth an entire sennight might kill him. Hell, it had only been three days and she'd already driven him to the brink of madness.

No. His damned feelings had led him to ignore his better judgment. Only he was to blame. Lady Mairi had done nothing wrong. She had been a victim—time and again.

Outside the cave, the rain poured down in sheets.

Dunn watched the water drip from the vines and willed her to appear.

Where are you, my dear lady?

* * *

The rabbit in the snare was dead. Aye, Mairi had seen many a dead animal, but something about looking at the small creature twisted her heart all the more. The weather fit her mood ideally. After the cloudburst, instead of subsiding, the rain poured down harder. She was soaked through, her teeth chattering. For pity's sake, it was August and yet felt cold enough to snow. Wet, freezing, and miserable, Mairi sat staring at a dead rabbit. How had she ended up in such a befuddled mess? The daughter of an earl was hiding out in a cave because vile dragoons had attacked her. Where was the justice in that? And why had her father been so daft as to put a price on Mr. MacRae's head—the one man who had raced to her rescue? Da should be rewarding the laird, not accusing him.

Duncan MacRae, the hero of the Highlands.

Why did she have to like him so much? And how had they ended up kissing? She'd only meant to give him a wee peck. Certainly, as soon as they rode down from the mountain, Dunn would resume his vast responsibilities and forget about the kiss they'd just shared.

But Mairi would never forget.

She hid her face in her palms. "Arrgh!" *I'm so confused.*

If only she had someone with whom to talk—another

woman who was wiser in the ways of men. Why had
Mr. MacRae kissed her so passionately? And then he'd
pushed her away—apologized as if he'd committed a
mortal sin. Heaven help her, she wanted more. And yet
she knew that wanting more would lead nowhere good.

Sooner or later she would have to return to Castle Leod
and face her father... What if she told Da she had recon-
sidered Mr. MacRae's proposal?

He'd lock me in my chamber for a fortnight.

But a fortnight of solitude would be little price to pay.
If only.

Mairi sneezed. Goodness gracious, there wasn't a dry
fiber on her body. Resolutely, she picked up the rabbit and
trudged back along the trail, her skirts heavy and wet. Her
nose ran, her throat started to burn, and as she walked, the
black abyss of melancholy spread through her chest like
an evil spirit. She had no choice but to go back and face
MacRae. Once again, she must pretend nothing had happened between them, play the role of noblewoman and sit
with her back erect.

Before entering the cave, she took a deep breath.

*I am Lady Mairi MacKenzie and I shall hold my head
high. I have nothing to be ashamed of. That wee kiss will
never be mentioned again.*

Sneezing, she stepped inside and held out the rabbit.
"A wee beastie for our evening meal, sir."

Concern filled his eyes as he snatched the rabbit from
her hand. The big man stood back and gulped, looking
her from head to toe. "You're soaked to the bone, m'lady."

Shivers coursed across her flesh as she nodded, unable
to control the chattering of her teeth.

"Come." He reached for her shoulder, but stopped himself before he touched her. Turning up his palm, he ges-

tured toward the chair. "Please. Sit by the fire whilst I prepare the rabbit."

She pulled the wet kerchief from her sleeve and wiped her nose while she stumbled for the chair. "I'm so c-cold."

"I ken. We'll see you warmed straightaway."

After she sat, he draped a fur across her shoulders, then stoked the fire. "It will be toasty warm in here in no time." He reached for another pelt and held it up. "May I place this across your lap?"

"Thank you."

"I should not have allowed you to fetch the rabbit. This is all my blasted doing. Why did you stay out in the rain so long?"

"I—" What should she say? *I couldn't look you in the face? You tore out my heart when you insisted our kiss was a mistake?* Did he know that no man had ever held her in his arms so tenderly? Did he know no man had ever kissed her so passionately? She coughed, making her throat burn. "I like the rain," she said feebly.

He pursed his lips, narrowing those dark eyes. "Let us pray your fondness for the weather doesn't result in illness."

Nothing else was said while he set to preparing the rabbit. Mairi's shivers eased, but the tickle in the back of her throat brought on another fit of coughing. She swallowed hard. "May I have some whisky, please?"

He looked up. "Ah...aye." Setting his work aside, he wiped his hands on a cloth and pulled the flask from his sporran. "This ought to warm your insides."

She took a healthy swig, but the fiery liquid slid down her throat like a burning stream. Slapping her chest, her eyes watered while she tried not to cough. "Water!" she squeaked.

Dunn snatched a flagon and handed it to her. "Och. Whisky is a potent brew."

Unable to speak, she guzzled the water, her eyes tearing. Then she wiped her mouth while he hovered. "That's better," she finally said, looking up and making herself smile. He reached for the flagon, but she tightened her grip. "I think I'll keep it for a bit."

"Very well."

Taking sips of water, Mairi managed to control her cough, though even with the furs covering her, she shivered. The flames danced across the cave walls, making them come alive. Across the fire, Mr. MacRae worked swiftly, cleaning the rabbit and removing the pelt. Though his fingers were thick and strong, they were deft as well.

Mairi watched him thoughtfully, keeping her observations to herself. Dunn MacRae was a man of many talents. He could be brutally savage and incredibly opinionated, though he often withheld his opinions. What surprised her the most was his capacity to be unutterably passionate. A man as coarse and rugged as this braw Highlander expressed more emotion in a wee kiss than she'd ever seen from Seaforth—or anyone else for that matter. Not that she had a great deal of experience with men, but Mairi considered herself a good judge of character, and Mr. MacRae topped the list for the most passionate.

Her tongued slipped to the corner of her mouth. *Who would have guessed?*

He glanced up, bringing on a new bout of shivers. But this time they weren't caused by the cold. Mairi held his gaze, filled with deep, unspoken emotion. Only yesterday she'd thought those eyes were brooding, but she was wrong. They smoldered. They posed as windows into the complex thoughts and mechanics of a man with a great deal of responsibility. A good man who not only protected his clan and kin, but wielded his sword for Clan MacKenzie as well. She'd only just begun to understand the depth of Mr. MacRae's character, and God save her, she wanted to learn more.

Chapter Fourteen

*T*he sound of raucous coughing stirred Dunn awake. He rose on his elbow and peered across the fire. "Lady Mairi?" he asked softly.

A soft moan slipped through her lips. He leaned closer for a better look. Her eyes were closed, and a sheen of sweat glistened on her face.

"Lady Mairi?" he asked again. Louder this time.

"Mm-hmm," she mumbled.

Sitting up, he stared at her. Something was wrong. Should he try to rouse the lass? But what of propriety?

She moaned again.

He pushed to his feet. Bless it, if it were Seaforth across the fire lying in a pool of sweat, coughing and moaning, Dunn wouldn't hesitate to rush to his side.

Ballocks.

Resolutely, he marched around the fire and kneeled beside her. "Lady Mairi." He placed his hand on her shoulder and gave her a nudge. "Are you ill?"

She coughed, but didn't open her eyes.

He pressed the back of his hand to Her Ladyship's forehead.

Good Lord, she's hotter than a griddle.

"Lady Mairi, you're fevered," he said more urgently, patting her hand repeatedly.

She opened her eyes. "My throat hurts." With a cringe, she closed her eyes. "My head feels like it has been bludgeoned."

He fished in his sporran for his pocket watch, then turned the face toward the fire.

Midnight.

Leaving the sanctity of the cave bore such a risk. Swiping a hand across his mouth, he looked to Mairi while his heart ached. *I am no healer. And remaining here for another moment bears more risk than facing a mob of dragoons.*

If he headed out now, with luck they might be able to slip into Eilean Donan Castle without being detected by the government scouts.

Making a decision, he moved quickly to collect their things and saddle one of the horses. Once ready to ride, he again kneeled at Mairi's side. "'Tis time to go."

"Go?" She barely opened her eyes.

"I'm taking you home, m'lady." *Where I should have taken her all along.* Bless it, if he had to summon all of Clan MacRae to make a stand, he would do so. The Earl of Cromartie had no grounds upon which to declare Dunn an outlaw. It was time to take matters in hand. Good Lord, he'd ridden beside Seaforth for so long, perhaps it was time to call in a well-earned mark.

Dunn was always the man who solved problems. He'd fought and cajoled for the MacKenzie. Aye, he alone had helped Seaforth out of more situations than he could count. For the love of God, Dunn and his men had risked their necks creating a ruse to break Seaforth out of Durham Gaol. They'd run for their lives for days, fleeing to Scotland.

Well, Dunn happened to be the one in trouble for a change, and it was high time the earl came to *his* aid.

Once he had Her Ladyship wrapped in a pelt, Dunn climbed aboard the mare and headed out. A heavy mist shrouded the mountains as he cradled Mairi in one arm while guiding the horse through the byways at a steady walk. The rain had subsided, but the mist made visibility near impossible. Though Dunn knew these hills like the halls of Eilean Donan, the going was perilous. On the other hand, the fog gave them the cover they needed to move without being spotted.

Following the wee burn, he rode down the mountain and turned northwest at the River Shiel. At the bridge, he found Jimmy MacGowan's skiff right where the crofter kept it, thank God. Gingerly, Dunn slid down from the hackney, holding Her Ladyship firmly in his arms. He rested her in the hull of the skiff. Seeing to her comfort, he smoothed his hand over her hair—soft as silk.

"Where are we?" Lady Mairi mumbled.

"Nearly there, m'lady," he whispered, wishing he were the one fevered and not she. "How are you feeling?"

"Throat. Sore."

In payment for the skiff, he hobbled the horse and left the mare where the beast could feed and drink until Jimmy discovered her.

Now entering MacRae lands, the chances of being spotted grew tenfold. The mist in the mountains had cleared a few miles back, but it was still dark, and the thick cloud cover overhead made the river look inky.

Dunn pushed the boat, wading through the water until it grew too deep to walk as it opened into Loch Duich. He was so close to home, he could taste it. Resisting the urge to hop into the skiff and row, he swam beside the boat where he'd be hidden by the hull. With Lady Mairi sleeping on the deck, anyone who might happen to be awake would be far less apt to suspect an empty skiff.

The cold water made his teeth chatter, but Dunn had weathered worse. From a young age, he'd been trained by his father to steel his mind against pain and suffering, and swimming the waves of Loch Duich was not foreign to him. Da had even pushed Dunn to swim in winter—to turn his mind to achieving his goal—to believe in his ability to conquer any adversity and win.

Sitting between peaks called the Five Sisters of Kintail, the loch was long and narrow like most Highland waters. Eilean Donan stood at the confluence of Loch Duich and Loch Alsh—a strategic stronghold for centuries. For countless generations, Dunn's kin had held and safeguarded the castle for the MacKenzie barons and the earls who had followed.

On and on Dunn swam, ignoring the fatigue of his muscles and the cold threatening to sap his strength. He noted each landmark on the loch as he passed. The wee village of Inverinate and the Toad's Croak Alehouse, and finally when he passed the schoolhouse nestled in the wood along the shore, he looked ahead for the dark outline reflecting the rigid lines of his beloved home.

Braziers flickered in two corners her battlements, though Dunn knew four were lit. The other two were not visible from the loch. As he neared, he heard the guards' voices shouting orders. The skiff had been spotted for certain.

He ground his teeth, willing his men to quiet. Their excitement may alert any government scouts who might have a spyglass trained on the castle.

He navigated the boat to the sea gate. As soon as his feet touched, he crouched low, pulling the skiff through the shallows onto the shore. Two guardsmen slipped out the gate, their muskets at the ready. "Who goes there?"

"*Sgurr Uaran.*" Dunn growled the MacRae battle cry as well as the name of the tallest of the five peaks surrounding Loch Duich. "'Tis your laird and master."

"MacRae?" one asked.

"Keep your voice down and hide this skiff." Dunn lifted Mairi into his arms. "Where's Ram?"

"He has been summoned, sir. He'll be here anon."

Dunn hastened through the gate and up the incline into the courtyard.

Ram, his lieutenant, strode from the keep while fastening his belt. "Good God, MacRae, is that Lady Mairi?"

"Keep silent," he hissed. "And I am not here. Ensure every soul who has seen me understands that he speaks of my presence under penalty of death."

"Aye, sir."

"Tell me true, have you received word from Robert Grant? Anything from the Earl of Cromartie?"

"Not a word."

"Ride immediately to Glenmoriston and tell Grant I need a response."

"Straightaway, sir."

"Thank you, and see to it my mother's chamber is prepared."

"Your mother's?" Ram's voice shot up.

"Are you deaf?"

"Nay, sir."

"Wait," said Dunn. "Where is my horse?"

"Beastie's growing fat in the lower paddock. God's bones, there's no chance I would have left him behind whilst you were on the run."

"My thanks. Now haste ye."

Cradling Lady Mairi's head to protect it from being bumped, Dunn proceeded up the wheeled stairwell. "And send up Mrs. Struan with a tincture for fever," he bellowed, the sound reverberating like he'd struck the church bell.

Not waiting for a response, he continued up until he stepped out onto the third landing. His clothing dripping across the floor, it was a relief to be home, regardless of the danger. Damnation, he'd taken every precaution possible to conceal his arrival. There was very little chance he'd been spotted by redcoats or the earl's men. Dunn opened the door to the chamber that adjoined his. Already a serving maid crouched by the hearth, striking a flint.

Startled, she quickly stood and gave a curtsy. "Sir."

"Good evening, Lilas. If you please, quickly turn down the bedclothes." Dunn moved to the bedside and gazed at Mairi's face. "Are you able to remove the lady's stays and kirtle?"

"I am." Lilas slipped in front of him and prepared the bed.

His jaw twitched. No matter how much he wanted to tend to Her Ladyship, it was proper for the maid to do it. "This woman needs a clean chemise as well. Are there any of my mother's remaining?"

"I believe so—in the cedar chest." While Lilas moved

to the trunk at the end of the bed, Dunn rested Lady Mairi on the mattress.

"Mm," she moaned, draping a hand over her forehead.

"Rest, m'lady. You're safe now."

Lilas moved beside him with a chemise in her hands. "Is that—?"

"Do not ask. And if anyone inquires, I have sworn you to secrecy. There is no one in this chamber. I am *not* here, and you have *not* seen me since I left for the gathering."

She curtsied. "Yes, sir."

"Have you seen Mrs. Struan?"

The door opened, and the head housemaid who also served as healer entered. "I'm here. I've brought the medicine basket." Concern etched the timeworn lines on her face as she held up a vial. "You needed a tincture for a fever?"

He gestured to Mairi, repeating the same orders to Mrs. Struan that he'd just relayed to Lilas.

The older woman gave him a deprecating once-over. "Have you been up all night, Duncan?" Good Lord, Mrs. Struan was the only person alive who still called him by his given name.

"Do not concern yourself with me, matron."

"Nay? If you have forgotten, *sir*, you were my care when you were a wee bairn. I believe that gives me the right to intercede when I see you behaving like an unmitigated mule. You are wet and, by the dark shadows beneath your eyes, I'll wager you've hardly slept in the past sennight."

Lilas sniggered and slapped a hand over her insolent mouth.

"I am fine," Dunn insisted. "Do not concern yourself with my welfare. Your patient is on the bed."

"I beg to differ." Mrs. Struan shook her finger. "You are soaked to the bone, and if you do not change into dry clothes, you will be as fevered as this wee lassie."

"Bless it, contrary to what you may believe, I do not aim to continue standing here dripping water across the floorboards." Throwing up his hands, he groaned. "Change Lady—*ah*—the lass into a clean chemise." He strode across the floor to the door that adjoined his chamber. "I will return anon."

"I implore you, Duncan. You need a good meal and a full day of rest."

He stopped with his hand on the latch. "Enough, woman. This lady is in my care, and tending to her is more important than *anything*. I trust you will address her ills with the same concern which you have for me."

Chapter Fifteen

*R*eluctantly, Dunn left the chamber that had once been occupied by his mother, allowing the women time to tend to Lady Mairi. One of the servants had ensured the fire in the laird's chamber was lit, which he welcomed. He stood in front of its warmth while he stripped off his wet clothes and hung them on the drying rack. Moving to the washstand, he poured water into the basin. Everything was ready and waiting as if he'd been there all along, but he knew Ram would have awakened the servants as soon as he'd been spotted. God bless them.

Naked, he lathered the soap between his palms, then made quick work of bathing where he stood, cleaning the loch weed from his hair and scrubbing away the mud between his toes. He stared at his reflection in the mirror while he used the silver-handled brush from his shaving kit to lather his face.

Aye, Mrs. Struan was right. The dark circles under

his eyes made him look like death. But he'd gone without sleep many times before. He'd neglected himself more often than he could remember, and this night would be no different. No one would protect Lady Mairi except him.

He'd taken a risk bringing her there. And now he was duty-bound to remain by her side and protect her at all costs. Her Ladyship would *not* succumb to the sweat, the ague, the plague, or to whatever illness ailed her.

He opened his razor and shaved a swath through the foam.

I am responsible for Her Ladyship's illness. I am solely at fault.

Though Mairi had ordered him to remain behind while she checked the trap, at the first sound of thunder, Dunn should have hastened to find her and take her back to the cave. Good God, the lass had stayed away far longer than needed, and he'd been bull-brained enough to allow it while he'd worried.

Dunn methodically shaved while he glared at his image in the mirror.

Aye, ye bastard. You just let her stay out in the squall, even though you had noticed her cough afore.

If anything happened to Mairi, he'd never forgive himself.

After splashing his face, he dressed in clean clothes and cracked open the door to the matron's chamber. "May I enter?"

"You should be abed," said Mrs. Struan from a chair beside the sleeping maid, tucked beneath the bedclothes. She pointed to the mantel clock. "'Tis nearly dawn."

He stepped inside. "I shall sleep when I am convinced of Her L—ah—the wee maid is feeling well."

"Surely, you can take your rest. The lass is sleeping comfortably."

"Very well." He crossed his arms. "That the maid is contented means you may take your leave and return to your bed."

"But you—"

"I am the laird of this castle and you are dismissed, madam."

Mrs. Struan stood. "And you are as hardheaded as your father...*sir*."

He gave her a steely-eyed glare—the one that always worked on the servants. "I consider that a compliment."

With a shake of her head, a grin spread across the matron's lips. "I see I cannot dissuade you."

"You are correct."

"I suppose I never have been. You've been obstinate since the day you were born." Sighing, she gestured to the bedside table. "There's willow bark tea in the cup and in the vial is a tincture of comfrey. Spoon what you can between her lips on the hour. The tea will help her fever, and the comfrey will help whether she has the corruption or the ague."

"Both on the hour?" he asked, studying the cup, the vial, and the wooden spoon.

"Aye." She gave his shoulder a pat. "You haven't eaten, have you?"

"Good-bye, Mrs. Struan."

"I'll send up a tray."

He nodded and, before the matron slipped out the door, he thanked her.

Once alone with Her Ladyship, Dunn took Mairi's hand in his palm and lightly brushed his fingers over her delicate skin. His heart twisted as he examined her slender fingers. Lily white, her skin was as supple as a rose petal.

A blessing from the Father.

He lifted her fingers to his nose and inhaled deeply. She smelled sweet as honey and magnolias—too sweet to be ill, too sweet to be caught in the middle of a mindless feud. A feud so baseless, he still wasn't sure how it came about.

I must write to Seaforth straightaway.

Dunn closed his eyes and clenched his teeth. Damnation, he was the cause of this. "Och, m'lady, I apologize from the bottom of my heart. It seems no matter how much I try, I always make a muddle of things. I never should have taken you to the Cavern of the Fairies. 'Tis a place for rugged Highland men to take refuge in times of battle." Holding her fingers ever so gently, he raised them to his lips and kissed her with reverence. "Though I ken my adoration is not returned, I cannot deny my love for you, bonny lass. Did ye ken I've loved you my whole life?"

Nodding, he smirked. "Aye, but in my heart I've always kent I could never win a lady as fine as you. I've always kent a woman of your stature would nay look twice at a hardened man like me." He sat and watched her for a long while, admiring her, praying she would open her eyes and smile at him.

But she did not.

Every man within miles, including Robert Grant, would call him a fool. Dunn could have his choice of all the lassies in the Highlands, even second- or third-born daughters of earls or dukes. But a firstborn daughter of an ambitious peer? A man who didn't care whom he destroyed on his quest for power and fortune?

Blast it all, his heart had to choose Mairi MacKenzie. For years, Dunn was unable to look twice at her because the maid had been betrothed to Seaforth. For years, he'd pined for her and had been able to do nothing about it. When the window finally opened and he approached her father for permission to court the lass himself, her refusal had cut him deeply.

After the mantel clock chimed the hour, he moved a hand to her shoulder and gently shook. "Lady Mairi? I must give you a tincture now."

Her eyes flickered open, then closed again. "My throat is burning."

His heart fluttered. She was still there, fighting the illness inside her. "I ken, *mo leannan*." He held a spoon of comfrey tincture to her lips. "This will help."

When her mouth opened, he poured a spoonful inside.

Her face soured, followed by a cacophony of coughing. "I feel awful," she wheezed.

"I am ever so sorry, but I aim to set you to rights." He gave her a teaspoon of willow bark tea, and when she didn't cough, he gave her another.

She shivered. "I'm so c-cold."

But her forehead was afire.

"I'll fetch another blanket." He found a tartan blanket draped across a chair by the hearth and tucked it around Mairi. "Is that better?"

But she was once again deep in slumber, the chattering of her teeth having subsided. Though a trickle of perspiration streamed down her temple.

Dunn had seen the fever before—many times. The lass might feel chilled, but she needed her flesh to cool. He took a cloth from the washstand, moistened and folded it, and placed the cool weave across her forehead.

She inhaled sharply with a pained expression. But still didn't wake.

All day and all night, Dunn held vigil, applying damp cloths and feeding Lady Mairi tincture and tea. Lilas had brought food and Mrs. Struan complained that he needed rest, but he would hear none of it. The burden of Her Ladyship's recuperation was his alone. And she would come through this sickness. He would see to it.

He neglected his fatigue, forcing his eyes to stay open, and every time his head nodded, he splashed water on his face. When the sun rose on the following morn, his chin dropped to his chest and he allowed himself to close his eyes—only for a moment. The poison of fatigue spread through his limbs and forbade him from raising his head. It was like being in his cups without the pleasure. Sleep threatened, and Dunn tried to fight her gripping talons while downward his head fell until it hit the feathery softness of the bed.

* * *

Mairi opened her eyes and stared at the canopy above. She was in a bed, a very cozy bed, but not her own. Pushing the damp cloth from her forehead, she thought back. *Where am I?*

She'd been fevered—still was a bit. Pain pounded at her temples.

Flashes of memories played through her mind—the clearest being wrapped in fur and riding through a dark forest. But she hadn't been afraid. Mr. MacRae had her cradled in his arms the whole way. There'd been a boat, a small boat. Somehow, she'd ended up in this chamber with the yellow canopy and bed-curtains embroidered with flowers, feminine décor for certain. Mairi swallowed and drew her hand to her neck. Aye, her illness had started with a sore throat and a cough. It still hurt, but not nearly as much as before.

She raised her head and peered downward. Good heavens, the laird was in a most awkward position. Though seated in a chair, his head rested on the bed, turned so he faced her. Motionless, eyes closed, breathing in a slow cadence, he clearly was sound asleep. "Mr. MacRae?" she asked, her voice barely audible as it grated drily in her throat.

She swept her fingers over his hair to see if he'd rouse. He didn't move. Heavens, his hair was unusually soft—like a seal pelt. Curious, Mairi threaded her fingers through those thick chestnut locks. "You are beautiful," she whispered.

The wee gesture sapped her strength. Leaving her fingers full of Dunn's locks, she closed her eyes against the pounding in her head. How long had she been abed? How long had the big Highlander been holding vigil? Where were they? Eilean Donan?

Most likely.

Opening her eyes once more, she shifted her gaze to Mr. MacRae—Dunn as he'd once asked her to call him. In slumber, his rugged features softened. It was difficult to believe the gentle soul resting on her bed was the champion of the Highlands and most trusted man to the Earl of Seaforth.

The pain eased some. Given how ill she'd been, Mairi should be feeling as if she'd been through the wars, but a smile turned up the corners of her mouth.

Had he spoken of love? Or was I dreaming?

"Mr. MacRae?" she tried again. When she was absolutely positive he hadn't heard a word she'd said, she took a deep breath and swirled her fingers again. "I love you as well. Even if you return my love only in my dreams."

Chapter Sixteen

Two days later, Mairi's fever broke for good. Though relieved beyond words, Dunn wouldn't allow her out of bed. She still had a cough and a sniffle, and until her ailment was completely gone, he refused to take any chances.

He turned the page of the book and started to read aloud, when a knock sounded on the door.

"Come," he said over his shoulder while Mairi leaned forward and looked to see who had arrived.

Ram strode in looking disheveled and in bad humor. "Forgive me for interrupting, sir. I've returned with a message from Robert Grant."

"At last." Dunn set the book aside and stood. "Well? Have out with it."

Thinning his lips, Ram's gaze shifted toward the bed. "Perhaps it would be best if we moved to the solar."

"Very well." Dunn stood and bowed to Her Ladyship. "Please excuse us." He should have uttered the courtesy *m'lady*, but he would not do so with anyone present no matter how much he trusted them. His orders stood. The entire staff of Eilean Donan knew to deny that he was in residence. Also, the woman recovering in his mother's chamber was not the only daughter of the Earl of Cromartie. In fact, the lass didn't exist. Neither Dunn nor Mairi had been seen since the gathering at Urquhart Castle.

He followed Ram into the solar and sat in his seat at the head of the table. "What news? Has Grant received a reply from my missive to Cromartie?"

"Aye." Ram shook his head, pulled a letter from inside his doublet, and slid it up the table. "The man is a tyrant."

Dunn snatched the parchment, unfolded it, and read the most ridiculous summation of drivel he'd ever seen in his life. The earl not only dismissed Dunn's plea to rescind the price on his head, he'd upped the bounty to one hundred guineas. The blasted fool demanded the immediate return of his daughter, at which time Dunn was expected to turn himself in and face grave discipline. The letter ranted about Dunn's sworn duty to Clan MacKenzie, which included not only the House of Seaforth, but the *equally important* House of Cromartie and, if anything untoward happened to Lady Mairi while in the MacRae chieftain's care, Dunn would be held accountable.

"Jesus Saint Christopher Christ." His blood boiled while he slapped the missive on the table. "Does anyone in all the Highlands actually believe I absconded with Cromartie's daughter? Did they not see the dead guards in the forest? Good God, a child of five might have pieced together the clues. And if it hadn't been for me, the lass would be ruined and quite possibly dead!"

"We all ken your innocence. As you said, the evidence

was clear." Ram sliced his hand through the air. "And when Seaforth vouched for you, Cromartie would have none of it."

Dunn slapped the missive, making a resounding bang. "One hundred paltry guineas for my head? He believes me worth so little? I'd like to show Cromartie the extent of my bloody worth."

"Given the drivel in that letter, I believe you have an unmitigated right to march the MacRae army against him."

"If only he weren't Seaforth's uncle, I'd not hesitate." Dunn drummed his fingers. "I am not admitting the woman in the matron's chamber is Lady Mairi, but it is my duty to see the lass safely home—without putting my neck in a noose."

"Jesu." Ram shoved his chair back and pushed the heels of his palms into his temples. "The bastard has his daggers at your flanks."

"Nay. *No one* stabs me in the back." Dunn fetched an inkwell, quill, and parchment from the cupboard. "I want you to take a missive to Seaforth."

"Aye? That might take some time." Ram cringed. "Word is His Lordship is off to Coxhoe House in the north of England."

Jesu, must everything be impossibly difficult? Dunn furiously scribed a letter explaining all that had transpired, excluding Lady Mairi's illness—besides, she was coming good. He made it perfectly clear that Lady Mairi was well protected with her virtue intact and he'd attempted to return her home only to be chased by a mob of dragoons intent on collecting the bounty placed on his head by Her Ladyship's father.

Once content he'd aptly described the absurdity of

Cromartie's demands, he implored Seaforth to reason with his great-uncle to enable Dunn to safely return his daughter home. He would not surrender to arrest, he would not be penalized, and he would not tolerate having his good name smeared throughout the Highlands.

"So, this is how I am repaid for performing my duty." He shook his head, and folded the missive. Holding a wax wafer to a candle, Dunn dripped a blob and applied his seal. "Take this to His Lordship. Show it to no one else. And if you must travel all the way to London to find him, do so forthwith."

"Aye, sir."

Dunn stood as he watched Ram leave. Damnation, he could not sit idle and bide his time, especially with Seaforth in England. Given favorable wind, it would take at least a fortnight for Ram to sail south and return, and most likely longer. Dunn must do everything in his power to strengthen his fortress. Furthermore, he sensed the lady in the matron's chamber mightn't be as averse to him as her father had made out.

Can I win Lady Mairi's heart? God bless it, I aim to show her I am not the boorish oaf she thinks me to be.

* * *

Mairi pushed the needle into the linen and pulled the thread through the other side. She'd tolerated about as much of being bedridden as a lass could stand. Mr. MacRae had treated her like a queen, too much so.

"'Tis a fine day outside," said Lilas, opening the window.

"Truly?" Mairi took in a deep breath of fresh air. "What I wouldn't do for a turn around the wall-walk."

"Aye, you haven't coughed since I came in. I reckon the laird will give you leave to rise from your bed soon."

"I am completely healed." She set her embroidery aside and pushed away the bedclothes. "And I will begin by dressing. Please help me don my stays and kirtle."

"But, miss—"

"I would thank you to help me now, Lilas, without the preamble." Mairi's hackles stood on end. On one hand, it was fun not to be referred to as "my lady," but on the other, she was accustomed to having her requests carried through without being questioned. At Castle Leod, if she asked Aela to help her dress, it would be done with efficiency.

Sighing, Lilas set her duster down and gathered Mairi's garments from the back of the chair where they'd been neatly folded. "Straightaway, miss."

That was better. Mairi smiled. At last someone listened to her without checking with the laird first. "Thank you," she said as Lilas tied her stays in place. "'Tis time for me to regain my strength, and I cannot do that whilst lying in bed."

"Agreed, m'l—um—miss."

It was hard not to laugh aloud. Lilas and Mrs. Struan had tried very hard to pretend Mairi was not the daughter of an earl.

Lilas held up the kirtle. "Over your head or step in?"

"Over my head." Mairi held up her arms and on went the gown. While the lady's maid smoothed the skirts, a clang resounded outside. Mairi hastened to the window and leaned out. "Oh my, it looks as if Mr. MacRae is sparring with a guardsman."

Lilas pushed in. "'Tis Curran, and have a look at that. No shirts." Patting her chest, the lass giggled.

"You did say the day was fine. I reckon the present view just improved on the weather." Mairi fanned her face, and not because she was overwarm. Good heavens, even from three stories up, Dunn looked magnificent, his muscles rippled beneath glistening skin—powerful shoulders, his sculpted back tapering to a sturdy waist.

"Mm..." And Lilas seemed to think so, too.

Mairi scraped her teeth over her bottom lip. "I can see why he's champion of the Highlands."

"Aye, but Curran is every bit as formidable."

"Curran?" Mairi glanced at the maid. She was completely rapt. "Do you fancy him?"

The lass blushed scarlet. "Me and all the lassies within twenty miles."

"Is that so? Why not the laird?"

"Och, Duncan MacRae is a man to be admired for certain, but a lass like me ought never dream of marrying him. Nay, the laird will marry a woman of great prominence."

"Hmm." Mairi didn't care much to continue a discussion about whom Dunn would marry. She much preferred to watch the battle down below. Inches taller, Mr. MacRae advanced, swinging his sword in his right hand and brandishing a targe in his left. Curran struggled to deflect Dunn's savage blows. Mairi's heartbeat raced when their cross guards met. As they bared their teeth, the opposing power between them was palpable as each man struggled to gain the upper hand. With a bellow, Dunn broke away, spinning outward. The two men circled, weapons held high, awaiting the next strike. Curran lunged. Dunn scooted aside, and the clanging swordplay resumed yet again.

"He's incredibly bonny," Lilas said.

Mairi blinked, as if snapping from a trance. "There are no words," she sighed.

"And faster than a fox."

"Like lightning."

A sword clattered to the cobblestones. Both women leaned through the window and watched Curran retrieve it, and then he waved—at Lilas, of course.

Dunn pointed his weapon at Mairi. "Why are you out of bed?"

"Because I am well, sir, and if you do not escort me for a stroll, I will have no recourse but to escape from this chamber and enjoy the day on my own."

His expression grew dark as he sheathed his sword and marched for the keep.

"Oh, dear," said Lilas. "I do believe he is cross."

"Mr. MacRae? Cross?" Mairi giggled. "When is he not?"

It all seemed amusing until the chamber door burst open.

"Miss Lilas, you are dismissed," Dunn barked, his stare boring through Mairi like an auger.

As the lass hastened out the door, Mairi stopped paying attention to the laird's eyes. Neither did she fret about being barefoot. At least she was respectably clad for the first time in days. Only one thing consumed her mind. *Good heavens.* She stared at the bare chest heaving from exertion—the enormous male chest, peppered with chestnut curls. A chest as powerful as a horse, and an abdomen ripped with delicious muscles. She splayed her fingers. What would it be like to touch him? His nipples were tight and erect, begging her to step forward and swirl her fingers over them. Did men have nipples sensitive to the touch? Mairi's certainly were tender.

He sauntered toward her, his gaze hard and unblinking. "So, you think you are well enough to leave your chamber?"

"I do." She raised her chin, determined not to allow him to frighten her into backing away. "I am no invalid."

"But it has only been a day since your cough subsided."

"And you told me that once it was gone, you would accompany me on a walk."

He pursed his lips and jammed his hands into his hips. "Och, ye ken we must exercise caution. And I intend to have you returned to pristine health when I accompany you to Castle Leod."

"But it might be ages afore Ram arrives with Seaforth. Did you not say the earl is in England?"

"The north of England, aye."

She licked her lips and stepped closer. Presently, her yen to take a stroll was trumped by a desire of a completely different nature, heaven help her. Mairi's mind clicked—what had he said when she was abed and fevered? Yes, she remembered clearly now. He *had* spoken of love. More than once he'd said how much she had hurt him and, every time, remorse crept up her spine. *Well, no more.*

"But I thought you didn't want people to ken you are here, either," she said, blinking her eyes and keeping her voice low.

"No one aside from the castle staff."

"See? We both must remain cautious." She stared at his chest, glistening and heaving with his breaths, while her knees turned wobbly.

"Do you mean to tell me what I can and cannot do?" Mairi took one more step. He smelled of freshly oiled leather and musk. Had Lilas tied her stays too tight? *No!*

"Forgive me, but when you venture out, m'lady, I must go as well."

"And you think that is fair?" she challenged.

"Of course 'tis not fair. I have a great deal of responsibility, and I shall not be cosseted within the walls of my own keep."

Unable to resist, she placed her palm on his chest and boldly eyed him. "Are your duties more important than me, Dunn?" Calling him by the familiar name made gooseflesh rise across her skin.

He drew in a sharp gasp as if he felt it, too. Staring at her face, his eyes smoldered with intensity and filled with the same yearning that churned through Mairi's breast. Not a word was said while his Adam's apple bobbed.

Kiss me.

His hand moved to her waist and rested there. Connected by the tension in the air between them, he uttered nothing, staring with a myriad of emotions swirling in those deep pools of midnight blue. But Mairi had come to know this man like no other. No, the smoldering look in his eyes was not anger. Dunn continuously battled with the storm raging within him. He was a good man, a great man with enormous responsibilities—obligations that prevented him from acting on impulse and forced him to withhold his opinions.

Do it. Kiss me with the same fervor and passion you showed me in the wood.

Sliding her hand to his shoulder, she did not avert her gaze while she moved closer. Dunn dipped his chin while his big hand tugged her closer. "God save me, Lady Mairi, I want to kiss you."

Her heart soared as she wrapped her hands around his neck and rose on her toes. Their lips met with more fervor than before. This was not a sweet kiss, but a savage joining that expressed more emotion than words could express in a lifetime of writing. She might not be a practiced kisser, but Mairi learned quickly. When he swirled his tongue, she matched him. When he gave a little suck, she did as well.

The deeper he probed, the greater her need. Something coiled deep inside grew insistent, heightening her desire. Every inch of her flesh was alive and craving more. He rubbed his hands up and down her back, coaxing her body flush to his. Her breasts molded against his powerful chest. His hands slid downward. Mairi's fingers sank into thick bands of sinew while Dunn's fingers cupped her bottom and pulled her even closer.

Something long and hard pressed into her abdomen, bringing a flood of hot moisture between her legs. Mairi's eyes flashed open as she gasped, suddenly realizing exactly the effect she had on him. Aye, she'd heard the talk among the servants at Castle Leod. She'd seen animals mate and knew how men were different beneath their kilts. And everyone knew men were made the way they were to mate with women.

She just wasn't quite sure how it was all accomplished. Right now, the doing of it didn't matter. All she knew was she wanted Dunn to hold her in his arms and press his body against her and kiss her until she could stand no more.

Still dizzy, Mairi dropped her head back and moaned while his kisses trailed down her neck like feathers. "My flesh is afire."

His lips stilled. "Has the fever returned?" he asked,

concern rolling in his voice as his warm breath made gooseflesh spread down her spine.

"Nay, nay." She moved a hand to his cheek and cupped it reverently while she studied his rugged features. "'Tis on account of you, Dunn. You have ignited a fire deep inside me."

He chuckled—a low, deep rumble that made her heart thrum. As if possessed by surreal forces, she arched her back, pressing herself closer to his hardness.

More, more, more!

Dunn's hot lips continued downward while his fingers worked loose the ties at the front of her garments. A hint of alarm registered in the back of her mind, but all she could do was hold on for dear life. "Wha-what are you doing?" she asked breathlessly, trying to regain a modicum of control.

"I'm kissing you, lass."

Good Lord, how did he raise her passion simply with the tone of his voice? Just when she thought she could endure no more, his tongue swept over the top of her breast while his finger flicked over her sensitive nipple.

Again, she gasped. When he covered her nipple with his mouth and suckled her, her defenses fell with a maelstrom of euphoria. Her knees went limp as she gave herself over to the power of his will.

Chapter Seventeen

Dunn thought he was in control, thought himself able to steal a single kiss and cool the raging passion that had lurked beneath his skin ever since he'd battled the dragoons and raced for the Highlands with Mairi between his arms. He wanted to woo the lass slowly. He wanted to be in complete command. But with his every stolen kiss, his control slipped further into oblivion. Good God, her wee sighs, her hips grinding into his cock—everything about this woman made him ravenous and totally, unequivocally, exceedingly unable to stop.

Could he take the chance and reveal the love he'd bottled up for years? He'd asked for a kiss, and she did not shy. The desire reflected in the lady's eyes showed him what she wanted, and when he'd finally lowered his chin and kissed her, in his arms she turned to potter's clay.

It took him less than three ticks of the mantel clock to slip her kirtle from her shoulders while he continued to ply her flesh with kisses. Arching her back and giving herself over to his seduction, she didn't seem to notice as he unlaced her stays. Ample breasts bounced free beneath her chemise, making him harder than forged steel. His hands and lips roved over supple flesh with only a thin bit of holland separating his fingertips from her. But it wasn't enough.

Hot and potent desire coursed through him. Unable to help himself, he worked loose the tie of her chemise and slipped his hand inside. His mouth continued across the silkiness of her skin, languidly tasting her. Every swirl of his tongue increased his desire. Seed leaked from the tip of his cock as at long last he cupped the fullness of her breast. Incredibly soft, pert, and perfectly round, her nipple drew tight, begging to be suckled. Demanding to be kissed. Dunn happily obliged. Gasping, Mairi dug her fingers into his back as her body arched into his cock. With his mouth full of divine and pure woman, he moaned and moved with the rocking of her hips.

The woman he'd loved for years swooned in his arms like one possessed, begging him not to stop. Holding her upright, he looked toward the bed. Hell, he looked at the floor as well. But a woman as fine as Lady Mairi must be treated with reverence and care. Gently, he lifted her into his arms, carried her across the floor, and rested her on the mattress.

When her head touched the pillow, she looked at him with seductive, half-cast eyes.

He grinned. "Do ye ken how desirable you look?"

She raised her arms. "I need more of your kisses."

"I want to kiss you forever." He climbed beside her and nuzzled into her neck. If only he could slide between those feminine thighs and claim her once and for all. Instead he rubbed his cock against her hip. "And I want to do so much more."

Mairi rolled on her side and thrust her mons forward, connecting with his erection. Her face took on not only passion but also a visage of challenge. "W-would you ravish me, sir?"

Her words came out breathlessly, but there was no mistaking her meaning. Dunn hadn't lost his sanity enough to take her like a harlot, though. Aye, he wanted Mairi, but he knew what taking her virginity meant, and the price of one hundred guineas on his head might possibly quadruple—unless he convinced her to reconsider, to vow to be his forever.

Nonetheless, it was the heat of passion making the innocent maid reckless. He knew it, but she did not. It was his responsibility to douse the fire under the steaming kettle. Now.

"I would never ravish you, m'lady." He kissed her, weighing his next words carefully, praying they would not be met with scorn. "If you consented to lie with me...ah...it must only be with the understanding that we marry." The last word hung in the air while neither he nor she took a breath.

"Marriage?" she asked at last, her voice shaky. Dunn held his tongue while she toyed with a lock of his hair, her eyes drifting away from his gaze as if a hundred thoughts swirled in her mind.

"I...um." She traced his finger along his jaw while her lips parted. "There is one thing I must know first."

Did he have a chance? "Anything," he replied all too eagerly.

"When you offered for my hand...was it out of pity?"

"Never." He reverently smoothed his palm over her

silken tresses. "Even when you were betrothed to Seaforth, I secretly wished you could be mine. I love you. You must believe I want you to be my wife. I did then, and I do more than ever now."

"Good gracious, you do." She placed her palm over his heart, her eyes welling. "And unknowingly I hurt you with my callous refusal. If only my father would have expressed the depth of your sincerity. He told me you were merely acting on your duty. I never dreamed you truly wanted to marry me."

"Believe it, lass." He traced his finger around her breasts. "Bonny doesn't begin to describe you. To me you are a goddess."

She stilled his hand, and then her gaze dipped downward and back up. "Please. I want you to make love to me."

Lord save him, he wanted her more than anything he'd ever wanted in all his days. "I want you to be my wife."

"I do, too. But my father..."

"What *you* desire is all that matters. What you, Lady Mairi MacKenzie, wish in the depths of your heart is the only thing that can influence my actions."

"*My* wishes?" She giggled. "Da has never considered my wishes."

"Though I respect your father, I covet neither his station nor his wealth. I do not fear him or what he thinks he can do to me. My only concern is for you and your happiness, m'lady."

"I want—"

Touching his finger to her lips, Dunn silenced her. "Afore you answer, think on it. If you want me, it will nay be easy. Your father and your kin could be lost to you forever. But I swear, even if I am forced to turn my back on Seaforth, I will never turn my back on you."

Her eyes shifted while her lips pursed. "You are more a man than my father, and I can no longer imagine myself without you."

With her words, Dunn's heart soared. "I love you, Lady Mairi." Before she answered, he captured her mouth, plunging his fingers into her hair, and showed her how much she meant to him. His lips wandered across her cheekbones to her tiny earlobes. She shivered and sighed as he kissed her neck and found his pleasure between the glorious valley of her breasts. As he worshipped her, his fingers inched her chemise up over her thighs, blessing him with the intoxicating fragrance of a woman aroused. When he stripped off the undergarment, he rocked back and feasted his eyes on her magnificence— long, slender legs, a flare of hip, a coppery nest of curls. A spike of desire hit Dunn so hard, his ballocks squeezed, making him come too close to losing his seed.

"No woman on earth is half as bonny as you, *mo leannan*."

She sat up and reached for his belt. "I must see ye bare." With a flick of her wrist, his kilt pooled around his knees. Mairi's lips parted as she took in a breath, staring at his erect cock. "You are so...so *large*."

He liked having her eyes on him, liked the admiration in her voice. "And I'm all for you. Only you, lass."

As she lay back down, her hair sprawled across the pillows. "Then show me."

Good God, with one stroke of her lithe fingers, his balls would explode. Needing to slow his fervor, he rolled beside her and gazed into her mesmerizing eyes. "Are you certain?"

She nodded, her gaze drifting to his manhood. "More certain than I've been in a long time."

He ran his finger around her nipple, aching to be inside her. "It can be painful for the first time. I-I do not want to hurt you."

"A wee bit of pain will be worthwhile if it binds me to you." She kissed him, her lithe fingers reaching down and brushing the tip of his cock.

Dunn sucked in a ragged breath.

"Sorry." Pulling her hand away, her eyes grew wide. "Did I hurt you?"

"Nay," he managed to utter, coaxing her hand back down. "Feel me. Feel my length. See how much I desire you."

"Do you like me to touch you…ah…there?"

"Aye, it drives me mad."

"Mad?"

Dear God, how could he think with Mairi milking his cock? With a feral growl, he moved atop her and kneeled between her legs. "Let me show you pleasure."

"Please."

Parting her curls, he brushed the pad of his thumb over her wee button.

Gasping, Mairi arched her back. "My stars. What— how—good Lord!"

He grinned, swirling his thumb in a languid rhythm. "Close your eyes and allow yourself to feel."

She did as he asked, and when her hips worked in concert with his thumb, he slid his finger inside her. "Think of me entering you."

"Mm," she moaned, her face enraptured.

He added a finger. "I will stretch you further than you think is possible."

The rocking of her hips sped. "Please. I want it. I want you."

Barely able to control himself, he held himself over her and slid his member up the channel of her parting. Back and forth he tempted her, his thighs shuddering while her hot moisture spilled over him.

As Mairi opened her eyes, she arched up and caught the tip of his cock at her entrance. Dunn's breath caught. Smoldering, completely aroused woman took ahold of him and looked him straight in the eye. "Take me," she whispered.

Jesus Saint Christopher Christ, he could come right now. He clenched his buttocks and tried to think of anything but plunging into her depths and burying himself to the root. Good God, he needed to make this the most memorable experience of her life. Show her the heights of pleasure. "I'll try to be gentle," he growled, trying not to sound too gruff.

She nodded, her hips continuing their seductive swirling rhythm. Christ, he was supposed to be the one seducing Mairi, but without a lick of schooling she'd proved an expert. Slowly, he pushed inside.

She sucked in a gasp.

Dunn froze. "Am I hurting you?" His hips rocked back. "If you want to stop…"

Mairi's fingers clamped into his bum. "I like it." With a firm tug, she urged him deeper while she made little gasps beneath him. By the saints, he adored this woman. He ground his back molars, his body shuddering, demanding release. But he denied himself while, ever so slowly, he slid into the length of her. When his tip reached a pillowy soft wall, he gazed into her sultry eyes.

"This is the nearest I've been to heaven." Aye, the torture of waiting, of going painfully slow, was all worthwhile as he held himself buried deep in her—joined as man and woman in the most intimate discovery known to humankind.

She rocked her hips beneath him. "We are one. It is a miracle."

"Aye, but you must come."

"Come?"

"As the pain ebbs, swirl around me. Find the spot that will drive you wild, and rub."

"Fast?"

"As fast as you want, lass."

While she rode him, her breath speeding, her face flushed with rapture, Dunn's ballocks clamped so tight, he forced himself to suck in deep breaths to keep from spilling. Until Mairi's eyes flew open, a cry catching in her throat. In an explosion of pure passion, frenzy claimed his mind. With Mairi's deft fingers kneading his backside, he lost all control. Her cries echoed in Dunn's ears, driving him over the top. Her wild scent ensnared him. Stars flashed across his vision.

Faster and faster he thrust. Mairi moved her hands up his back as she clung to him. And now that she'd reached her peak, he was free to drive with fury. Out of control, his breathing sped, his heart hammered. All at once the burst of euphoria flooded him. His body quivered with strain. His cock convulsed as he bellowed, "Mairi!" After one more deep thrust, he forced himself to pull out as he crashed into the wave of glorious release.

Dunn held himself over her, his head dropping forward as he fought to catch his breath. "Lord have mercy," he growled, while his heart began to steady.

Pushing up on his elbows, he raised himself high enough to regard the wildcat's face. Her lips swollen and slightly parted, her heavy-lidded gaze, red hair in a mass

of tangle. Mercy, she defined rapture. Her Ladyship be-
witched him mind and soul, and he would fight heaven
and hell to make her his. He would fight the Earl of
Cromartie. If it came down to it, he would face off with
Seaforth himself.

With a satiated moan, he trailed kisses down her neck.
"Was it good for you, *mo leannan*?"

She cupped his cheeks between her hands. "Never in
all my days did I imagine such pleasure."

"You are the world to me, Mairi." Breathing deeply
to catch his breath, he rolled to his back and pulled his
woman atop him. "Ye ken I adore you."

She rested her head on his chest, swirling her fingers
over his chest. "And I you."

He cradled her with love swelling in his breast. He
closed his eyes against the power of his emotions. Aye,
the woman in his arms made him swell with pride—made
him want to be a better man. A man of whom Her Ladyship would always be proud.

* * *

Brimming with joy, Mairi floated through the next several
days. Rarely did Dunn leave her side, though he still
wouldn't allow her to venture outdoors. They did explore
the keep, which had more rooms than Castle Leod. Fortunately, she no longer missed her freedom. Now she knew
why they sang ballads about love consuming a soul's
mind and body. Oh, how the laird knew how to fulfill a
woman's desires...in so many astonishing ways.

During an hour when Dunn had gone to tend to his affairs, Mairi sat in the window embrasure reading a book
about the uncomely Mooth-Toothed Meg and her improb-

able union with a borderland laird. She'd only managed to read the first chapter when the braw Highlander of her dreams burst through the door. "Mairi, I hope you are hungry for the evening meal." He wore a dress tartan, complete with velvet doublet, silk waistcoat, and lace cravat.

She set the book aside and studied him quizzically. "As a matter of fact, my stomach growled not but a minute past." Craning her neck, she looked around him. "I do not see a tray."

He made a sweeping gesture with his arms. "We shall take our meal in the banqueting hall."

"Aye? Will there be guests?" She clapped her hands together. On the tour she'd been impressed by the banqueting hall. The chamber consumed the entire first floor. The stone walls were adorned with life-size family portraits and tapestries. Nearly the entire room was filled by an enormous table.

"It will just be the two of us. I've asked the lads to rearrange things a bit."

"Tell me, will we need parchment and quill to communicate from opposite ends of the table?"

He chuckled. "I do not think I could bear to be so far away from you through an entire meal."

She liked that. Dunn always managed to say things that made her insides swirl as if filled with popping soap bubbles.

He took her hand. "If your stomach is growling, we mustn't tarry."

Mairi giggled all the way down the stairwell. As he pulled her into the banqueting hall, her eyes grew wide and her lips formed an O. The enormous dining table had been exchanged for a small round table in front of the grand hearth. It had been set with fine plates, utensils, and goblets all in engraved silver. "'Tis exquisite."

"The setting was my mother's." He held a chair for her. "M'lady."

"Thank you, sir." She glanced at him out of the corner of her eye. "My, you are ever so braw-looking this eve."

Smiling with a bit of color coming to his cheeks, he took a seat. "It is not often I am able to dust off the finery." He reached for a bottle of wine. "May I pour for you?"

"Please." Mairi watched the ruby liquid as it filled her goblet, the candlelight flickering through the stream.

The steward entered from the side door, carrying a tureen by its handles. "The first course is served."

Mairi inhaled. "It smells delicious."

"Thank you, m'la—"

Dunn cleared his throat.

"Thank you, miss." After placing the tureen on the table, the servant picked up a silver ladle. "Beef broth with leek."

Mairi shifted an amused gaze to the laird. She doubted a soul living at the castle thought she was anyone but the daughter of the Earl of Cromartie. "Mm, my favorite."

The meal consisted of four courses, complete with white bread of fine-milled flour, roast beef, and sugared plums with cream. Mairi used a dainty spoon and dipped it into the deliciously sweet concoction. "I am overfull, but this is far too good to pass by."

"I will give your compliments to the cook." Dunn took a bite. "The staff certainly have not disappointed this eve."

She closed her eyes while the tartness mixed with sweet spread across her tongue. "Heaven." Once she opened her eyes, Mairi watched as Dunn mimicked her expression. "What makes you happiest?" she asked.

He smacked his lips and swallowed.

She leaned toward him. "Aside from food."

His eyes dipped her way, fanned by dark lashes. "I must say, though we are still in a precarious situation, I have never been happier than in the last few days—ever since your illness passed." He took a sip of wine, his gaze shielded behind his goblet. "And you?"

"I agree." She looked to her hands and chuckled. "A month ago, I never would have guessed it to be true."

He took her chin in the crook of his finger and turned her face until she looked straight into his eyes. "I'm ever so content to ken you return my love."

Mairi's heart fluttered when he leaned forward ever so slowly and sealed his words with a kiss, his hand sliding back and kneading her neck.

"If you have eaten your fill, I have something else to show you."

"Aye? What is it?"

He took her hand and helped her stand. "Since 'tis dark out, I believe a turn on the wall-walk is in order."

"Out of doors?"

"Two souls silhouetted in the moonlight. I believe there isn't a spyglass in all of Christendom that would be able to make out who we are."

She followed him up the wheeled stairwell until they stepped out onto the walk of the highest part of the keep.

"From here Eilean Donan seems like a kingdom." Dunn led her around the perimeter. "On a fine day, to the north you can see all the way up Loch Long; to the south is Loch Duich, and to the west is Loch Alsh, which leads to the sea."

Mairi turned full circle. "And all around us are stately mountains. They're as rough and rugged as the men they breed."

When they approached the turreted tower on the northeast corner, lyrical music filled the air. Mairi drew a hand over her heart as a harpist came into view, his tune flowing like a gentle waterfall. "Och, Dunn, 'tis glorious."

The laird took her hand and twirled her under his arm before he bowed. "A feast would not be complete without dancing, m'lady."

Together they moved in harmony while the ballad from the Celtic harp swirled around them. Dunn hummed in a deep bass, complementing the dreamy notes. Light on his feet, he handled her with sure but gentle tenderness. "La dee da dee ya da da dee da."

The deep bass of his voice made her feel as if she was floating. "You sing so beautifully. Why have I never heard you before?"

"If you like it, then I shall only sing for you."

She laughed while not missing a step. "Aside from our brief dance at Urquhart, I don't recall seeing you dance afore—you always stood on the fringe, watching with one hand on the hilt of your sword."

"I suppose I haven't danced much, especially when Seaforth is near. After all, my duty is to watch his back."

"But still, you are an accomplished dancer."

"Bless my mother for seeing to that."

"Is Seaforth the reason you are always so serious?"

"Hmm." He locked his elbow with hers and promenaded in a circle. "I'd say much of life is serious."

"Except when you're with me," she whispered.

"Och, when I am with you, it is the most serious of all."

"But you laugh."

He stopped dancing and clutched both of her hands over his heart. "Lady Mairi, I allow myself to laugh when I am with you, because you make me happy. When I am with you, I feel as if there is music in my heart. I want to be yours. Your protector, your lover, your husband."

Speechless, she gasped as he kneeled, drawing her hands to his lips and kissing each finger. He slipped his fingers into the pocket of his doublet and met her gaze, while the moonlight's shadows made his face handsome beyond compare. "Lady Mairi MacKenzie, would you do me the honor of being my wife?"

Mairi wanted nothing more than to say yes, but how could she? Aye, they'd spoken of marriage, but there were so many problems yet to sort through. Her father had a price on the man's head, for heaven's sake. Making an irrevocable promise would be highly irresponsible at this juncture. And yet . . . A tear slid down Mairi's cheek. Taking in a deep breath, she nodded, unable to form the words.

"I ken this decision is fraught with challenges. I ken we need your father's blessing, but I am asking *you* as a woman fully grown with the ability to make decisions on her own. Once we set things to rights and have the House of Cromartie's blessing, I bid you, please, please, please accept me."

"Aye." Tears streamed down her cheeks. "I will marry none other than you, Duncan MacRae."

"Then wear my mother's ruby ring as a symbol of my everlasting promise to you."

Mairi's breath stuttered while he slid the ring onto her finger. It fit perfectly, and she held it up so the moonlight made the deep red of the stone flicker. "It is the bonniest ring I've ever seen."

Chapter Eighteen

*D*unn headed across the courtyard, returning from a sparring session with Curran, but he stopped short when pounding came from the main gate.

"Open these doors at once by order of Her Majesty the Queen!" a voice bellowed from the other side.

Dunn tightened his sword belt and changed direction, heading up the barbican stairwell and straight to the chamber housing the cogs for the portcullis. Placing his feet carefully, Dunn made no sound as he moved to the medieval arrow slit where he could observe unawares— not the first time he'd assumed such a position.

Curran met Mrs. Struan at the big wooden gate that was reinforced by an iron portcullis built to keep out clan enemies.

"What on earth do you want now?" asked the matron, opening the small wooden window allowing only her face to peek through. "You have already searched the entire castle."

A red-coated officer tightened his reins, making his horse snort and stutter-step. "We have heard rumors that the laird has returned."

Dunn's gut clenched. Aye, it was a risk to bring Mairi to his castle, but he trusted his kin to remain quiet. Did he have an informant in his ranks? Or had a redcoat with a spyglass seen him? He had been careful, but if the government troops had a soldier watching the castle, there might be a remote chance he was spotted when in the courtyard.

"Rumors?" asked Mrs. Struan. "So now the queen's dragoons have nothing better to do than roam across the Highlands, chasing rumors?"

"Hold your tongue, madam. We have probable cause and will search the premises. Mind you, if you try to stand in our way, I shall personally have you locked in the stocks."

Curran pulled on the portcullis chain and looked up—straight through the gap in the floor, good lad. Dunn circled his finger, indicating the "tour" should start at the kitchens, which would allow him time to spirit Mairi out of the matron's chamber and into the hidden crevice above the chapel.

While the noise of raising the gate rattled the barbican wall, Dunn hastened for the keep.

Mairi set aside her book as he entered, her expression immediately concerned. "What is it?"

He strode toward the bed to straighten the comforter and pillows. "Dragoons are searching the castle, acting on a rumor that I am in residence."

She dashed to the other side of the bed to help. "They ken you're here?"

"They're fishing. 'Tis likely some Sassenach outside the walls *thinks* he saw me."

After fluffing the pillows, he scanned his gaze across the room. "This chamber looks far too much as if it has been recently occupied."

"The fire." Mairi strode to the washstand and fetched the ewer. "We must douse it."

"Nay." Dunn grabbed the garments from the back of the chair and rolled them. "Wet coals will make them think we were here and received warning."

She replaced the ewer and smoothed her hands down her skirts. "What about the tray?"

"Come. Put everything in the trunk. Haste. We must head above stairs. I have a false ceiling in the chapel."

"Hiding in a house of God?"

He grinned. "See? Such a thing is unthinkable."

Working swiftly, they had the room looking as unoccupied as possible, aside from the fire. God save Mrs. Struan to come up with a good excuse for that.

Dunn led Mairi to the door and cracked it open. Footsteps echoed in the stairwell beyond. "Blast. They're coming." Damnation, starting the search in the kitchens should have allowed them at least twenty minutes. Shutting the door, he grasped Her Ladyship's hand and made a quick decision. "Behind the curtains."

"What about the dressing room?" she whispered.

"Nay, that's the first place they'll look." Heavy drapes hung from the ceiling and touched the floorboards. "We'll hide in plain sight." He held the curtain open as she slipped behind.

"But will they not see us here?"

The latch clicked.

Dunn slipped beside Mairi as the sound of footsteps clomped inside and slowly took a turn of the chamber. "There's a fire," said a man.

"And a vial and spoon beside the bed," said another.

Blast. How did I miss that?

The beat of his heart roaring in his ears, Dunn wrapped his fingers around the hilt of his dirk while footsteps marched across the room. The door to the dressing room creaked open. "Where are they?" the first man demanded.

"I have no idea to what you are referring, sir," said Mrs. Struan.

"Fool! It is as clear as the nose on my face someone is staying in this chamber."

"Stayed," Mrs. Struan corrected as if she were taking an oath with her hand on a Bible. "Please do not tell the laird, but my mother was deathly ill. It was her final wish to die in a fancy bed in Eilean Donan Castle." She sighed loudly. "Since I am the head maid and the laird is *not* in residence, I saw no harm in granting her wish."

"Your mother died here?"

"Last eve. Please, please, do not tell Mr. MacRae. He'll have my hide for certain."

One of the soldiers laughed. "Where MacRae is heading, I doubt he'll care."

"Ye ken," continued Mrs. Struan, "Eilean Donan is the last place the laird would go to seek refuge."

"Is that so?" asked the dragoon. "Tell me, where do you think he's gone?"

"Och, I've known Duncan MacRae since the day he was born. Whenever the lad is in trouble he *always* heads straight for the mountains."

"Where does he hide?"

"That, sir, is the quandary. If the laird does not want to be found, there is nary man in all of Scotland who can find him."

Aside from Reid MacKenzie or Ram MacRae. Dunn's fingers tightened on his hilt.

"So say you, madam." The officer didn't sound convinced in the slightest. "Let us continue on, and the next chamber had best not show any signs of being occupied or I will lock you in the stocks until you lead us to the bastard."

Dunn held his breath while they moved on. As soon as the door clicked shut, Mairi grasped his arm. "Your chamber is next. They'll find the fire."

"Nay, I prefer to keep things cool. The hearth is clean. Haven't used it since the first night when I brought you here."

"What about the bowl, the ewer, a drying cloth?"

"I threw the water down the latrine chute this morn," he whispered. The used drying cloth hanging on the washstand's rail might give them away, but with the hearth clear, Dunn hoped they wouldn't go so far as to test to see whether the cloth was still damp.

He moved to the door between the chambers and pressed his ear to the timbers. Footsteps and muffled voices came through, but it was impossible to make out the words. Mairi stared at him, pressing her fingertips to her lips.

When the footsteps faded and a door slammed closed, Dunn let out a deep breath only to be replaced by a sharp inhale. The dragoons should have proceeded down the passageway toward the west stairwell, but as sure as the sun rose in the morn, clicks from the soldier's boot heels headed east.

"They're coming back!" he shouted in a whisper, while he grasped Mairi by the arm and pulled her downward. "Roll under the bed."

Holding his sword to prevent it from clanking on the floorboards, Dunn followed her under just as the door opened.

Good God, his breathing sounded louder than a raging river while uncomfortable silence swelled throughout the chamber. Dunn glanced downward. Damn it all, the hem of Mairi's skirts was peeking out. Where were the soldiers now? Not a footstep sounded. *Christ, they're most likely staring at the damned bed skirt.*

Dunn clenched his teeth; the blasted green gown contrasted with the yellow décor. Where was Curran? Where were the MacRae guardsmen? How many soldiers must he fight while keeping Her Ladyship from harm?

He couldn't kill the bastards. If these men did not return to their regiment believing the rumors were false, everything would be ruined. Cromartie would most likely hang Dunn before Ram returned with Seaforth.

"Is there something I can assist you with?" asked Mrs. Struan, her voice strained.

"Where is your mother's body now?"

"Interred—*the sweat.*"

"What say you?" The soldier's voice shot up. "The crone died of the sweat? Why did you not say something before?"

"You did not ask, sir," Mrs. Struan replied sharply. "Now, if you will follow me, I can show you the rest of castle afore nightfall. 'Tis a very large fortress, sir."

Dunn almost snorted aloud. It wasn't yet noon. The tour had damned well better be over. *Now.*

"Lead on," the man clipped, clearly irritated.

The door slammed with a bang.

Mairi started to move, but Dunn gave her a tap. "Not yet."

He waited until the footsteps disappeared in the west stairwell before they climbed out from under the bed.

He pulled Mairi up by her hands while she gazed at him with wide eyes. "That was fantastically dangerous."

Dunn wasn't amused. "I cannot believe they had the nerve to return. And when they have no right to set foot on the premises in the first instance."

"They did not?"

"Well, they said they possessed an order of the queen, but I believe the order came from none other than your father."

Mairi grasped Dunn's hands. "This is ludicrous. Allow me to travel to Castle Leod with an escort. I will inform my father of your gallantry, how you saved my life, and how much I have come to adore you."

"I'm certain he will be overjoyed," Dunn said sarcastically.

Mairi groaned.

"Please, my love. We must be patient. Those soldiers were merely acting on a hunch. Seaforth will be here anon, and then together we will ride to Castle Leod and reason with your father. 'Tis the only way."

She stamped her foot. "Blast Seaforth. I loathe relying on him for anything."

"He's a good man, Mairi, despite his faults."

"He has never proved his gallantry to me."

Dunn drew her into an embrace and kissed her. Oh, how he'd been blessed with an entire fortnight of pure joy. "When we are wed, you will thank the stars that Reid MacKenzie fell in love with his ward, because you and I were meant to be together."

"Through thick and thin?"

"Through every hindrance imaginable."

A knock sounded.

Mairi jolted like a startled rabbit.

Dunn pressed his finger to his lips indicating silence, then gestured for her to slip behind the curtains. He'd had about enough of hiding in his own home. Drawing his dirk, he tiptoed to the door and stood aside it.

The knock came again, more insistent this time. "Duncan, may I come in?" asked Mrs. Struan.

He pulled down the latch. "Why didn't you announce yourself the first time you knocked?"

"Pardon me whilst I spout lies to government dragoons on your behalf." She looked at him with righteous indignation.

"Are they gone?"

"Of course they're gone. I never would have come back up here had I not seen the backsides of their horses for myself."

"You were supposed to take them through the kitchens first."

"I tried, but 'tis a bit difficult to tell a horse's arse he must start in the kitchens when he turns and marches for the keep's front door." She drew a hand to her forehead. "Dear Lord, I might have swooned. Do ye ken how exasperating it was to tell those men my mother had died in this chamber last eve?"

Mairi stepped out from behind the curtains. "And of the sweat. Goodness, we shall need to scrub the entire castle."

Dunn sheathed his weapon. "I reckon it was a stroke of genius. I'll wager they couldn't spirit away fast enough."

"Aye?" Mrs. Struan thrust her finger into his sternum. "But if they do any searching, they'll discover my mother met the Lord ten years past."

"Well, I think you performed splendidly," said Mairi.

"Perhaps we pulled the wool over their eyes this day, but sooner or later, someone will figure out you are hiding right under their noses. How much longer must we carry on with this charade?"

"Not long," said Dunn. "My Lord Seaforth will not fail me. Soon all will be set to rights; we just need to remain another sennight." Now that Mairi had agreed to his proposal, he could ride on the morrow and face her father. But having Seaforth's backing would only serve to strengthen his case. For Her Ladyship's sake, Dunn preferred to do what he must to avoid a bloody feud.

"At best," added Mairi.

Mrs. Struan looked between Dunn and Mairi, a frown stretching her careworn features. "I ken you are *both* high-ranking members of the gentry and I am but a lowly servant, but I have lived to see many great men fall to their ruin. I do not want to see either of you hurt. You may not want my opinion, but as your former nursemaid, I believe it is my duty to give it." She shook a bony finger. "Every soul in the Highlands kens the Earl of Cromartie is a shrewd and ruthless man. There had best not be anything untoward going on between you pair, lest there will be hell to pay. By my oath, I swear it."

Chapter Nineteen

As Mairi turned the page of her book, she glanced toward the noises coming from the laird's chamber and smiled. Dunn said he was preparing a surprise and had made her promise not to open the door until he came to fetch her.

Who knew the Chieftain of Clan MacRae could be so romantic? Who knew his brooding scowls and smoldering looks had been masking the love the braw man harbored in his heart all along?

Sighing, she hugged the book to her breast. The past fortnight had been marvelous. Though she desperately wanted to be able to venture outside or explore the castle alone, Dunn had done so much to make the isolation bearable. Since her fever broke, her days had been filled with new love, filled with the exploration of the flesh, of passion between a man and a woman she'd never dreamed possible.

The only thing she lacked was freedom. But soon

Dunn would have everything set to rights. She would explain the depth of their love to her father, and they would marry in the Cathedral of the Church of Saint Andrew. Mairi had always dreamed of an enormous wedding with all the Highland lords and chieftains in attendance. There would be a feast after, and she would dance and dance into the wee hours of the night.

"M'lady." Dunn peeked his handsome head through the door and smiled broadly. Och, how she loved his smile. "The evening meal is served."

"In your chamber?"

He pushed the door wider and bowed. "An outdoor meal with a bonfire, brought inside."

She took his offered hand and stepped through the threshold. The furniture had been pushed aside, and in its place were pillows of all shapes and sizes set in a half circle around the hearth. She drew a hand over her mouth. "How gloriously diverting! But..."

"What?"

"You have lit the fire in your hearth. Any dragoons who come snooping will be doubly suspicious."

"I doubt they'll set upon us this night." He led her to the cushions. "The fare this eve is finely milled white bread, roast lamb, cheese, and strawberries. I hope that meets with your approval."

"I am impressed, thank you. It all looks delicious." He helped her slide down and recline against a pile of pillows. Mairi licked her lips at the banquet spread in front of the hearth, illuminated by two tapers burning in the center. Her gaze rested on the squat wine bottle in the center. "And to drink, sir?"

"A full-bodied Bordeaux." He uncorked the bottle and poured two glasses.

Mairi sipped. "Mm. I do believe this is the most flavorful vintage we have tasted yet."

Dunn slid down beside her and tapped his glass to hers. "May we share many more bottles of wine, each one better than the last."

"Agreed," said Mairi, craning her neck for a kiss. "I am looking forward to so many hours of enjoyment."

"And I am looking forward to telling all of Scotland that you are mine."

Warmed by the fire, together they feasted as if they were still in the cave. The fire flickered in Dunn's eyes and gave him a mysterious look. Who but he would have thought to dine inside as if they were sitting before a campfire? All her life Mairi had sat at the dining table with her father in Castle Leod with her back ramrod straight, her shoulders tense, her stays laced so tight that she scarcely ate more than a few bites. Heavens, at Eilean Donan, Dunn removed her stays nearly as fast as she put them on.

"What were your parents like?" she asked.

Dunn drew in a long breath and looked to the relief on the ceiling. "They have been gone for so long, I fear I have forgotten times gone past."

"What do you remember most about your father?"

He smiled reflectively. "No tougher man than my da held this fortress."

"Was he as tall as you?"

"Aye, and I reckon he was broader in the shoulders."

"Truly?"

"He was a man to be reckoned with, but a good father as well, mind you. He may have been a bit harsh with a switch in his hand, but his discipline was fast and finished. There were no grudges held by my da, unless you were a MacLeod, of course."

"Of course," Mairi agreed. The clans who feuded with the MacRaes also feuded with the MacKenzies. "And your mother?"

"A bonny highborn lady who was gracious to everyone. Did ye ken she was the youngest daughter of the Marquis of Montrose?"

"I did not."

"Aye, and as such she was referred to as Lady Harriet, just as you will always be Lady Mairi." He grasped her hand. "No one can take your birthright away from you."

"It concerns me not at all to be given a courtesy. Truth be told, it hasn't bothered me in the slightest to have it omitted by the servants since I've been in hiding."

He swirled one of her curls around his finger. "I find that ironic."

"Oh?"

"According to your father, you will marry no less than a baron."

"Da said that?"

"You're surprised?"

Mairi sighed. "Nay, I should not be. I ken my father. He has grand plans to expand Cromartie lands, and 'tis very difficult for him to bow to Seaforth, his grand-nephew."

"It must be a bitter tonic for him to swallow, indeed. Your father must be thirty-five years Reid's senior." Dunn traced his finger along the length of her neck. "But the Earl of Cromartie does not hold my interest, lass."

Shivers coursed all the way down her arms. "I do believe you are attempting to seduce me, sir."

"I beg to differ, m'lady," he growled into her ear. "I am a slave to your seductive wiles, Mairi. For, simply by being, you inflame the ravenous beast within me."

Heat pooled in her loins with a craving that had proved insatiable. She pushed her fingers into his thick, shoulder-length hair as he dipped his chin and captured her mouth in a kiss—not a sweet, slow kiss, but one filled with greedy desire that carried the promise of steamy passion to come.

"I want to play a game with you, *mo leannan*."

"What kind of game?" She wiggled her shoulders with eagerness.

"One of anticipation. One that I promise will make you soar to the stars."

"I like the sound of that, sir. What must I do?"

"Lie still. But you mustn't touch me."

She frowned. "That doesn't seem fun at all."

"It will be, because after I'm finished with you, it will be your turn to torture me."

She grinned, liking his idea better. "Torture?"

"Delightful torture." He grasped the front lace of her kirtle and slowly pulled open the bow. "Now lie back."

"Is this why there are so many pillows strewn across the floor?"

"Mm-hmm." Once her kirtle was unlaced, he tugged open the ties of her stays. As he pulled the garments away, Mairi took a deep breath, smiling, no longer nervous to disrobe in his presence. He made her lift her hips as he tugged off her petticoats.

When his fingers slipped to the bow on her chemise, she grasped his hand. "More kissing."

Gradually, those thick eyelashes raised and he met her gaze. "You mustn't touch me, m'lady."

Gooseflesh pebbled her skin, even as she began to smolder within. "I am your servant."

"That's what I like to hear." With just a few flicks of his fingers, Mairi was completely naked, excepting her hose and slippers. Dunn stood, stepped around her, and allowed his gaze to linger. "You are exquisite."

She smiled, unashamed to pose nude for his eyes alone. "When will I have a turn?"

"Only after you have been unequivocally satisfied."

A thrill made her heart flutter. "I am yours. Do what you will with me."

Dunn dropped to one knee and removed her slippers. His fingers tickled as he untied her ribbons and languidly slid her hose down each leg. By the time he pulled the last one from her toes, Mairi's inner thighs were already quavering. Her gaze dipped to his kilt, catching the outline of his thick manhood. Tapping her tongue to her lip, she yearned to sit up, unbuckle his belt, and draw him atop her.

Exposed and completely naked, she held very still, planning her attack.

He moved to her side and kissed her forehead. Though he did not touch her with his hands, his lips caressed her cheeks and found her mouth. Mairi opened for him, and when he swirled his tongue with hers, she arched up and met his fervor. Still, only their mouths joined. Nothing else.

Dunn continued to tantalize her with feathery kisses moving down her neck and each arm, licking each finger as his dark, sultry eyes watched her. The need simmering in Mairi ratcheted up with the warmth of his mouth, the tiny little sucks, and his warm breath as it tantalized her skin—her breasts aching for his touch, her desire growing hotter as he slowly issued his torture. She inhaled sharply when he finally arrived at her breasts. His swirling mouth lingered, teasing her nipples, suckling them until she cried out.

He issued a low rumble of laughter as he kissed down

to her navel and swirled inside it with his tongue, giving her an erotic preview of his cock entering her core. Mairi prayed he would part her legs and lick her there, but he slid his kisses down and up each leg. When he kissed her arches, she slid her fingers between her legs and pressed to ease the longing.

"I cannot take much more."

His eyes grew even darker with his wicked smile. Sliding down to his stomach, he shouldered open her legs. Panting, Mairi lay completely prone, on the edge of soaring into oblivion, while he gaped at her womanhood and inhaled. "Good God, you are divine."

He moaned as he licked her.

"Again!" she demanded, so close to release she bucked.

Dunn lapped her again. "Like this?"

"Please!"

"Or like this?" He sealed his mouth over her and suckled.

Blinded by the intensity of the flame coiled at her apex, Mairi cried out, thrusting her hips, circling them around his merciless mouth.

Stars darted through her vision as her body exploded with shuddering ecstasy. When, finally, her breathing returned to normal, she rose to her elbows and grinned. "May I touch you now?"

"Are you satisfied, or do you want more?"

"I believe it is my turn to be the executioner." She pulled him into her arms. "Where did you learn such wicked wiles?"

"Hmm. I believe it is a prerequisite for a Highland chieftain to ken how to pleasure his woman." He rested his head on the pillow beside her. "I love you."

She looked deep into those pools of midnight blue and saw honesty, trust, sincerity, and most of all, love. And by her oath, Mairi returned Dunn's love with every fiber of her being. "And I you," she said from the depths of her soul.

And the best part? It was his turn.

* * *

Never in all her days would Mairi grow tired of gazing upon the man's magnificence. Removing his clothing was like unwrapping a precious jewel or opening a treasure chest. Except the experience was more thrilling.

She took her time drinking him in with her eyes before she touched him. Even in repose, his chiseled muscles made him look like an Adonis. A quite hard and virile Adonis. "You are fine to me, MacRae."

Grinning, he waggled his eyebrows. "How fine, m'lady?"

"Would you like me to show ye?"

"Aye." He shifted his shoulders against the cushions while he raised his arms.

Mairi shook her finger. "No, sir. I am in charge of this seduction."

"So, you aim to seduce me now?"

"I do."

He spread his arms to his sides. "Then let us see if you can turn me into sweet cream butter."

"Hmm." She kneeled beside him and kissed his lips. "Cream?"

He stretched his neck as she kissed him there, inching up until she nibbled his earlobe. "I rather think you become a *wild man*."

His chuckle aroused another bout of stirring in her center. But she would ignore her pleasure. Seeing Dunn squirm was far too much fun. He moaned and shifted as she tasted him. She dared to take his nipples into her mouth and suckle them as he had done to her. She swirled her lips down the ripples in his abdomen until she neared his manhood. So tempting, the base of the shaft rested on his belly, but the tip arced up as if he was ready to burst.

Careful to draw out the torture, Mairi kissed his arms and legs, paying particular attention to his hands and feet. Dunn jolted when she kissed him between his toes. "Now you're not playing fair."

"No?" Grinning, she kissed him again, only to make him squirm all the more. She laughed aloud. "Have I found a wee ticklish spot?"

"I am not ticklish."

"Oh, but I think ye are." She kissed him again and again.

He yanked his foot away. "Stop."

She pulled it back. "Not until you admit you might have one solitary weak spot on your body."

"All right. I admit it." He grasped her shoulders and pulled her up. "You are far better at this game than I imagined."

"But I'm not finished." She rolled off him and looked downward. "There is one spot yet to be tortured."

A low growl rumbled from his chest, reverberating all the way to Mairi's toes.

Smiling with wickedness, she scooted lower. Dunn gasped and arched his back with her first lick. She used her fingers to grip and massage him while she tasted and gradually grew bolder. A quick glance up showed his pure desire. Then suddenly, as if possessed, he slammed his fists into the floor, and released a feral bellow.

"My word," Mairi marveled. "I never kent I could wield such power with mouth and hand."

Taking in a calming breath, he coaxed her atop him and kissed her. "Only you can control me mind, body, and soul."

She rested her head on his chest and swirled her fingers through his downy soft curls. "I feel as if we are living in a dream. One I never want to end."

Chapter Twenty

Shaken awake, Dunn snatched his dirk from beneath his pillow and sprang to his feet. Crouching, he readied his body to fight.

Eyes wide, Ram took a step back, holding up his hands. "'Tis just me, ye boarheaded bull."

Releasing a deep breath, Dunn rubbed his neck and glanced to the bed. Thank God he'd insisted Lady Mairi return to her chamber lest Mrs. Struan string him up by his cods—not that he'd allow it, but the matron had been right. By allowing his heart to take over his judgment, he was playing with fire. It was best to be discreet until things settled. "It is about time you returned. What the blazes took you so long?"

"I beg your pardon, sir, but I believe nary a soul would make it all the way to Coxhoe and back as fast. I even took a ship from Newcastle to Inverness, mind you."

Coming awake, Dunn looked past his lieutenant and knit his brows. "Where's Seaforth?"

"On his way to London, I'd reckon."

"What say you?" Dunn's fingers twitched, ready to strangle the numbskull. "I gave you explicit orders to return with His Lordship and—"

"He was summoned by the bloody queen." Ram reached inside his doublet. "But he was very troubled about your news, *very*. Seaforth told me that after Cromartie announced the purse of fifty guineas, he pulled his uncle aside and reasoned with him until Cromartie admitted you acted heroically. He was aghast to hear Cromartie had gone back on his word and taken things so far as to up the bounty."

Dunn tossed his dirk onto the bed. "Och, that helps like a blow to the head with an iron hammer."

"To aid in clearing your name, His Lordship penned two missives." The lieutenant pulled out a pair of sealed letters and gave Dunn the first. "This one's for you and the other is for Cromartie—Seaforth advised you should deliver it yourself, sir."

Dunn snatched the first. "Before or after the lying bastard puts my head in a noose?"

"The MacRae would never allow that to happen."

Growling, he opened the missive and read. It was written in Seaforth's hand, all right. The contents explained what Ram had just relayed, and expressed the earl's sincerest apologies. It profusely held forth that had anyone aside from Her Majesty the Queen summoned him, Reid would have hastened to Eilean Donan forthwith. Since he was unable to ride beside Dunn and confront his great-uncle, he was providing a missive for Cromartie, *ordering* him to drop the bounty on MacRae's head and explaining that MacRae had acted with heroism, protecting Lady Mairi from assured ruination by three uncouth dragoons.

This was not what Dunn wanted. He'd ridden roughshod for Seaforth more times than he could count. Did Reid honestly believe Cromartie would come to his senses after reading a missive? Even if Mairi professed her love, the chances of Cromartie behaving with reason were slim. Seaforth's letter to Dunn spelled it out: Gilroy MacKenzie hadn't listened to him at Urquhart. Why in God's name did the earl think Cromartie would pay heed to a slip of parchment? The situation needed an army, not a quill. Dropping his shoulders, Dunn reread the letter, then looked to Ram. "Are the roads still being patrolled?"

"Aye, sir." The lieutenant handed over the missive addressed to Gilroy MacKenzie, Earl of Cromartie. Dunn turned it over, his fingers itching to break the seal and read the contents.

No matter, 'tis just more of the same drivel.

"Well then, we shall ride at once, but we'll not take the road to Strathpeffer. We shall ride north to Loch Fannich, cut due east at Garve, then wind our way through the Heights of Brae. Just before Dingwall, we turn west. They'll never expect such an approach. Chances are the patrols are doubling their efforts at Tarvie to the north and Marybank to the south."

"Aye, Tarvie and Marybank make the most sense." Ram scratched his head. "But you want to leave now, sir? 'Tis the middle of the night."

"Yes, now. Summon Curran. I want to ride with a small party that will not attract attention. And if we wait until daylight, government troops are sure to make chase." Dunn headed for the door between chambers. "I shall wake Lady Mairi. Be ready to ride within the hour."

But he didn't walk through the door. Not yet. As much as he abhorred writing letters, there were three he needed to scribe before setting out. This time Dunn would leave nothing to chance.

* * *

Being back in the saddle did nothing for Dunn's ire. Blast Seaforth. Why didn't the earl send his regrets to the queen—or at least inform her that he was on his way and would be there as soon as a small matter with his great-uncle was resolved?

Dunn wouldn't have thought twice before he'd done the same for His Lordship.

Now he was leading two of his men and his betrothed on a roundabout journey, taking days longer than it should. He rode Beastie into the ruins of an old kirk near Loch Fannich in the shadows of the mountain peak Sgurr Mor. He'd used the remote location before, and though he didn't expect to see a soul, he gave Curran and Ram instructions not to light a fire while he scouted in a mile-wide perimeter. When that was done, he used what was left of daylight to ride up the mountain and scan the landscape for encroaching redcoats. He returned to the roofless kirk only after he saw for himself they hadn't been followed.

He hobbled Beastie near a burn with the other horses, pulled off his bedroll, and headed inside the ruins.

"Did you see anyone?" asked Mairi, rising to her feet.

"Nay, but that doesn't mean they're not out there." Dunn dropped his roll and nodded to his men. "I'll take the first watch."

Mairi stepped to the crumbling doorway and peered through the gap. "I can take a turn."

"No, you will not, m'lady." Since they were en route

to Castle Leod with his two most trusted men, Dunn had dropped the pretense that Her Ladyship was anyone other than herself.

She eyed him, crossing her arms. "But you men need your sleep as well."

"A few hours of sleep is all we need. Besides, you are under my protection and I cannot allow it. What if you were confronted by a mob of musket-wielding redcoats?" He sliced his hand through the air indicating he'd entertain no more discussion on the matter.

Ram handed him a parcel with a piece of dried meat and two oatcakes. "We've already eaten. This is for you."

"My thanks." Dunn plopped against a large stone that must have been part of the kirk's masonry.

Mairi moved beside him while the two men spread out their blankets and settled down to sleep. "When we arrive at Castle Leod, I will talk some sense into my father."

Dunn shoved the meat into his mouth and shook his head. She might be the love of his life, but she knew bugger all about the dealings of men. "When we arrive, I will do the talking. In fact, I do not want you with me until we've reached a truce. After all that has transpired, I don't care if Cromartie is your father, I do not trust the man any more than I trust an asp."

Releasing an exasperated breath, Mairi crossed her arms. "But if anyone can reason with him, it is I."

"Och, m'lady. You speak as if your da will be amenable to reason. But I cannot be so sure." He pulled two of the letters he'd written from his doublet. "These are insurance, an alternative plan in case something goes awry."

Mairi took them and read the addresses. "I understand the one to me, but another for Seaforth?"

"Aye. If anything happens to me, you are to ready your missive and immediately dispatch the earl's. Understood?"

She knit her brows. "You're worried?"

"I'm cautious."

"I believe everything will be fine. I feel it in my bones." Shaking her head, she passed the letters back, but Dunn refused to take them.

"Hide them in your cloak."

"Very well."

He tossed the leather parcel aside and stood. "You haven't made up your pallet."

"I was waiting for you."

"You need sleep. We'll be riding afore dawn." He grabbed the bundle, hating that Her Ladyship must bed down in a rocky old ruin without a fire. Finding a patch of grass that looked reasonably comfortable, he unrolled the pelt of fur and the blanket. "Here, Mairi. This ought to be the last night you must endure such crude accommodations."

"Have I complained?" With a shake of her head, she marched over and crawled under the blanket. "Heaven's stars, you're acting as if you're heading into battle."

Dunn's gut clamped into a hard ball. "Mayhap I am."

* * *

They awoke before dawn. After breaking their fast with two oatcakes each, they headed down the mountain—whatever mountain it was. Unaccustomed to sitting on a horse for hours on end, Mairi's backside ached. Yesterday they'd ridden from the wee hours, climbing up and down endless Highland routes that were no better than game trails covered with thorns, burns, and bogs. With Dunn trying to avoid running into all of humanity, they seemed to be riding in circles.

It didn't matter. It was best they were under way early. The old kirk in the mountains was cold, damp, and miserable. No wonder it was left to ruin. Moreover, Dunn hardly looked her way, as the old, brooding glint returned to his eyes. Worse, he acted cross with her. It didn't matter what she'd say, he'd grouse back like a curmudgeon.

Aye, it was a setback that Seaforth had been unable to join them, but he'd sent missives. Her father might be shrewd, but he wasn't daft. Besides, Mairi never expected Reid to come to their aid. The Earl of Seaforth had done nothing but let her down. Why should this be any different?

On top of everything, the Earl of Cromartie was her *father*, as she had tried to point out last eve. She'd been annoyed when Dunn discounted her influence on her own sire. But now his behavior was nothing short of infuriating. Mairi positively believed she could win her father's favor. In fact, her certainty buoyed her sprits regardless of Dunn's bad temper.

She would have her grand wedding within a month— and only because it would take that long to dispatch all the invitations.

After riding half the morning, Dunn led them out of the forest and straight to the shore of Loch Ussie—only two miles from home. Goodness, they hadn't seen a single town, not even Dingwall or Strathpeffer. They'd crossed roads, seen crofts and the wooden posts denoting miles to the next village, but they had not ridden through a town. Nor had she even glimpsed Inverness. They had circumvented all of civilization. Heaven's stars, when it came to navigating the Highlands, Dunn's skill was pure genius. In no way did Mairi realize they had come so close to Castle Leod.

Once they arrived in a clearing, Dunn dismounted and helped Mairi down from her horse, though he didn't smile or give her a lingering look—the type of fiery meeting of the eyes she'd come to adore.

"We'll wait here until dusk." He took a stick and drew a big circle. "This is the eastern shore of Loch Ussie." He drew an *X* where the loch should be, then another *X* above it. "Castle Leod is on the mound here."

Mairi pursed her lips. Of course, everyone knew it was on a mound.

"Do you intend to ride straight up the drive?" asked Ram.

Dunn scratched the dark two-day stubble along his jaw. "Nay, we'd be seen for certain. We shall ride in through the Peffery Burn. It cuts across the northeast quadrant of the estate."

It did. Mairi looked on, surprised that Dunn knew so much detail about her home. He couldn't have visited more than once or twice. "And then what?" she asked. "How do you intend to gain entry? Storm the keep? Smash through the front gate with a battering ram?"

Dunn cut her a stern look. "If need be. But I thought to knock first."

"And ask for an audience with my father?"

"Aye."

"With me beside you, or will Ram keep me tied up at the edge of the forest?"

"Bloody hell, m'lady, what is needling you? Ram and Curran will remain in the forest with you whilst I present Seaforth's missive to your da. Then I will be the one to tell him you have accepted my proposal of marriage."

"And you think he will allow you into his chamber for a wee chat?"

"Why would he not?"

"Because I ken my father. If I am not there, he will not see you until he reads the missive, and once he does, he's more likely to seize you and send out scouts to find me."

"We can plan for such a reaction."

"Or I can go with you."

Dunn chopped his hand through the air. "Absolutely not."

Mairi wasn't about to back down. "But I can spirit you inside the castle without the need to go through the front door."

That made him stop and look. "How?"

"Only if I can go with you."

"No, m'lady." He shook his head. "I refuse to put you in harm's way."

"Have you forgotten that the Earl of Cromartie is my father? I can reason with him far more effectively than *your* Lord Seaforth, especially since he is absent."

"She does have a point," said Ram.

Dunn turned to the lieutenant and thrust his finger toward the man's sternum. "Wheesht. I will decide how we proceed." He returned his gaze to Mairi. "Where is the entry to which you referred?"

Pursing her lips, Mairi crossed her arms. "Will you take me with you?"

Groaning, the laird rolled his eyes skyward. "Bless it, what if he draws a sword? You might be hurt simply by being present. Your father has thrown the gauntlet, and until I set things to rights, I am very concerned for your safety."

Gracious, she loved Dunn to his core, but she'd had

enough of his overbearing bullheadedness. Did he not realize how much she could help? They were on her lands now and she would not be ignored. "My father may have a quarrel with you, but he would never lift a finger to hurt me." Pointing at MacRae's chest, she stepped nearer. "Besides, you taught me how to fend off an attack."

"Aye, and as I recall, I said the best thing for a lass to do is run."

She raised her chin and stood a bit taller. "'Tis *my* home. Either I go in with you, or you will have no recourse but to enter through the main door and take your chances."

* * *

Dunn didn't like it one bit, but in the end, the lass's argument was too persuasive. Mairi did have clout with her da—he'd observed it on a number of occasions. Still, it was risk, but in this day and age, with war on either side of Britain and the kingdom itself on the brink of conflict regarding the succession, merely breathing bore a risk.

Against his better judgment, he left orders with Ram and Curran to wait for his return. After dusk, Mairi led Dunn though Castle Leod's gardens to the family crypt while he carried an unlit torch fashioned from hickory bark. At the rear of the building, stairs covered with moss led downward at a steep angle. Once they reached a dirt floor where they were completely out of sight, he gave Mairi the torch and struck the flint, igniting the sap-soaked tinder.

She led him through the crypt bearing medieval stone

effigies of knights in armor and newer tombs of granite. At the rear of the chamber, Mairi ran her hands along the wall. "I need to find the loose stone."

"I thought you had used this passage many times afore."

"Aye, but not for years." Stopping, she grasped one of the masonry blocks and shifted it. She glanced over her shoulder and grinned. "See? 'Tis a bit lower than I'd remembered." She pushed in on the stone, and a hidden crawlspace opened. "Through here."

Dunn watched as she went down on hands and knees. "Wait. You hold the torch. I'll go first—who kens what lies beyond this wall."

After he pushed through a myriad of cobwebs, Mairi passed the torch through, then followed him.

Beyond, a tunnel led into darkness—a tunnel filled with more cobwebs and Lord knew what else—definitely no place for a lady. "How far does this go?" he asked.

"We follow until we find the iron gate."

He swiped the torch back and forth while he peered deeper inside. "It looks as if no one has used this passageway in years."

"Three years, most likely. I oft used it when I needed solace from my governess."

"Not your father?"

"Nay. He's too busy to badger me overmuch. But my governess could be a dragon."

"Were you not afraid to pass through alone?"

"Not when it meant freedom."

True to her word, after a bend, they came to a gate. Dunn tugged on the latch, but it wouldn't budge. He swept the torch downward and found the reason for its obstinacy. "Padlock."

"Let me past," said Mairi, squeezing in front of him. "I ken where to find the key."

Dunn gave her room while holding the torch aloft. Her Ladyship reached between the bars and pulled away another loose stone. Sure enough, from inside she pulled out a key and used it to unlock the gate. After they passed through, she refastened the padlock.

He took the key and slipped it into his sporran. "I'll keep the key as insurance."

"Very well." Mairi pointed. "This way."

The passageway twisted and climbed until it opened into the cellars with vaulted ceilings. Unable to stand straight except in the center, Dunn ducked while leading Mairi out of the maze.

Footsteps echoed from the stairwell.

Mairi tapped Dunn's arm. "Hide in here." She pulled him into a room lined with beer casks. Dunn snuffed the torch in a barrel of water before he ducked behind it.

The footsteps stopped outside the brew cellar, and the light from the person's torch flickered across the entryway. "Bloody rats," said a man's voice before he continued.

Dunn peered around the wall and watched until the man disappeared into a room. "We must make haste." He grasped Mairi's hand and together they slipped to the stairwell. "Where would your father likely be?"

"The study or the billiards room," she whispered. "If he's alone, then 'tis the study."

"Let us hope he's not entertaining this eve." Dunn gestured. "Lead on."

"The southeast stairwell opens right to it—three floors up."

"Are we likely to see anyone?"

"Only Da. The servants use the north staircase."

Quietly, they proceeded upward through the dim light while Dunn ducked his head. Mairi exited into a passageway lit by a lamp burning in a sconce—a good sign. She stopped at the first door and nodded.

Dunn grasped the latch. "Stay close to me," he whispered, then pushed the door open.

Gilroy MacKenzie sat in a high-backed chair, smoking a pipe and reading a gazette. He looked up from his paper and hopped to his feet. "Mairi!" Casting the gazette aside, he rushed forward with a smile on his face.

"Da!" She opened her arms.

Dunn moved between them. "Halt! I have brought your daughter home, but there is the matter of a hundred guineas on my head that must first be resolved."

"Guard!" Cromartie shouted. "You, sir, should be tried and hanged for kidnapping."

"No, Da. You misunderstand." Mairi stepped around Dunn and approached her father. "Mr. MacRae saved me from attack by three dragoons. He tried to take me home the very next day, but before we reached Castle Leod, we were chased by redcoats."

"And you placed a bounty on my head," Dunn continued, sauntering forward. "How was I to return Her Ladyship when every man with a musket in all of Ross Shire is out for my head?"

"I will have your head and it will not cost me a farthing." Cromartie turned to Mairi. "Did he ravish you?"

"N-nay." Dropping her gaze, she shook her head. "I love him. I want to marry him."

"MacRae?" Cromartie blurted the name as if it were a curse. "Preposterous."

Dunn drew Seaforth's letter from inside his doublet before the situation spiraled out of control. "M'lord, I am carrying a missive from the Earl of Seaforth addressed to you. He would have been here himself had he not been summoned to court."

"What is my meddling grandnephew up to now?" Cromartie took the letter, ran his finger under the seal and opened it, taking a moment to read.

"Does it matter?" asked Mairi impatiently.

"No, it does not." Cromartie waved the parchment in Dunn's face. "A pardon granted from Seaforth in no way excuses your irresponsible behavior."

The chieftain's jaw twitched. "I see, so it is permissible for a man to place a bounty on an innocent man's head?"

"Innocent? You absconded with my daughter." Looking toward the open door, Cromartie craned his neck. "Guards! Guards!"

"Stop this madness. You cannot blame Mr. MacRae for saving my life!" Mairi shouted, bless her for trying.

From the passageway, the stairwell echoed with approaching footsteps.

Dunn slammed the blasted door and locked it. "Do not be so hasty, Your Lordship." He tugged Mairi under his arm and held her protectively. "I have asked your daughter to marry me and she has accepted. I love her with all my heart. Furthermore, I can provide her with a home where she will live in the style and comfort befitting her station."

"Please, Da."

"Have you lost your mind, Mairi?" Cromartie's voice was sharp. "I forbid it! I cannot allow you to throw your future away on a henchman." He took another step closer to the door. "Guards!"

Keeping Mairi at his side, Dunn backed up until he

blocked the earl's path. "I beg your pardon, m'lord, but I am not leaving until you bless our betrothal."

"Are you deaf? I cannot and shall not." The earl threw out his hands. "I'm only relieved to have my daughter returned in time to travel to London for the Royal Autumnal Ball." He shifted a pointed stare to Her Ladyship. "We've discussed this, Mairi. I have an alliance to make with your hand, and it will not be with a mere Highland chieftain, mark me. When Seaforth rescinded his duty, it opened the door for mé to make an alliance that will bolster our line."

"You would put your quest for wealth before my happiness?" Mairi asked.

Fists pounded on the door. "It's locked!" shouted a guard.

"Lay an ax through the timbers!" bellowed Cromartie, eyeing his daughter. "Nearly a month hiding with this swine and you've already forgotten the roots of your kin?"

Rage boiling in his chest, Dunn shifted Mairi behind him. "I will not leave without her. She will be my wife with your blessing or not."

"So now you're threatening me?"

Dunn drew his sword. "'Tis no threat. You read the letter from the Earl of Seaforth, *your* clan chief—*your* superior, and yet you refuse to acknowledge it. You have not removed the price on my head—"

"And I shall not."

Dunn seethed. "Believe me, m'lord. You do not want to start a feud with Clan MacRae."

"Please, Da." Mairi stepped between the men, holding out her palms.

Cromartie ignored her. "And I'll tell you, young pup, I will have the queen's dragoons put Eilean Donan to fire and sword if you do not stand down."

"Mairi, come." Dunn lowered his sword and beckoned with his fingers.

"Nay. I have forbidden it, and my word is final. Do you not see, daughter? He is merely using you to clear his name." Cromartie grabbed her arm.

"I have proclaimed my love. I have offered my hand." Again, Dunn raised his sword. "Release her."

"I choose MacRae." Gnashing her teeth, Mairi twisted her arm from her father's grasp and dashed toward Dunn.

Protecting her with his body, he leveled his weapon at the earl's sternum. "I wish things could have been different, but Mairi is mine now. Call off your guard."

The earl's gaze grew dark and deadly. "If you dare leave with my daughter, you will never be safe. I will hunt you to the ends of the earth."

Dunn backed the lass to the door. "I have Seaforth's protection. It is you who are wrong, and all of Ross Shire will testify to it before a magistrate. I ask you once more," he hissed through bared teeth. "Tell your guards to stand down."

"Let them pass." Cromartie raised his voice, his hand disappearing into his sleeve.

Dunn opened the door to a half-dozen guards looking stunned. "Stand back," he growled.

Mairi turned, stretching her fingers toward her father. "Please, Da. Don't do this!"

"I shan't!" In one motion, Cromartie grabbed Mairi's wrist, pulled her into his body, and pressed a dagger to her neck. "Seize him, you fools!"

"Not this night." Dunn's sword hissed through the air as he kept the guards at bay. "You would rather murder your own daughter than allow her to marry me? *You* are mad, Your Lordship."

"She will do my bidding. And that is final." Cromartie scowled and backed away. "Surrender your sword."

"You are making a grave mistake," Dunn seethed.

Mairi whimpered. "Stop this lunacy! I love him."

But Cromartie's hard stare reflected no compassion. "Guards!"

The earl might have been bluffing, but Dunn couldn't take the risk and call Cromartie out. His heart twisted. Seeing the love of his life with fear filling her eyes while her own father held a dagger to her neck ripped Dunn's heart into a thousand shreds. He gulped against the thickening in his throat, lowered his arm, and dropped his weapon to the floorboards. The guards rushed in and seized him. "You have not heard the last of this," he growled.

"Oh? I believe I have." Cromartie nodded to his men. "Take MacRae to the prison and let him feast with the rats."

"You will be my wife, Lady Mairi!" he shouted as he allowed them to haul him away. Aye, Dunn may have lost this battle, but if his surrender meant saving Her Ladyship's life, then so be it. Cromartie had no grounds on which to accuse him, and God save His Lordship once this was over.

Chapter Twenty-One

*W*hen Da finally released his grasp, Mairi clutched her neck and stumbled away.

My very own father threatened me with a knife! Never in all her days would she believe he was capable of such madness.

She coughed and sputtered, trying to regain control while blood trickled through her fingers. On top of it all, Dunn had taught her how to defend herself and, at the first attack, her efforts had been totally inept. Could things grow worse? She glared at her father in disbelief. "You would murder your own daughter?"

"I did not act upon my threat, did I?" the man grunted with a snort. "I bluffed and fooled him. Have you seen that Highlander fight? If I hadn't done something rash, he might have cut down the lot of my guardsmen—perhaps killed me in the process."

Mairi jammed her fists into her hips. "But there was no

need for any of it. I love him. I intend to marry him with or without your consent."

"Good God." Da threw out his hands. "Clearly the man has taken advantage of your naïveté. You couldn't possibly love him. In my opinion, he's nothing but your cousin's hired muscle."

"He is a hero. A chieftain who owns land and cattle. A man who is loved by his clan and kin. How dare you treat him like a common felon?"

"Och, you are a fool, your head filled with fanciful ideals." Da shook his dagger and eyed her. "I cannot believe you allowed him to convince you that he is in love with you."

"He did *not* need to convince me. How many times must I tell you, if it weren't for Mr. MacRae, I would have been violated?"

A rueful laugh rumbled through Cromartie's throat. "You mean to say that rogue didn't lay a single finger on you?"

Mairi's cheeks burned. It was none of her father's concern if she had accepted Dunn's love and returned it in kind. After all, he never would have made love to her if she had not given him her permission. "He acted honorably."

"Well, something happened. I'd wager Seaforth's stallion colt on it."

"That colt is mine."

"Oh please, Mairi, nothing is *yours*. Seaforth gave me that horse in payment for *my* burden upon his withdrawal of your betrothal."

Seaforth had also given Da coin that ought to be part of her dowry. *I suppose he has forgotten that as well.* "What say you? I am merely a woman—nothing but a burden."

"Och, stop feeling sorry for yourself. 'Tis time you realized you are a mere lass clearly incapable of choosing your own husband." He smoothed a hand over her hair. "I will ensure you are well positioned. You might even be appointed as one of Her Majesty's ladies."

Mairi's spine shot up straighter than a bedpost. "I believe I am a far better judge of character than you, Father."

"Is that so? I will make an alliance that will ensure your children become powerful peers of Britain. I am thinking only of you and the posterity of my progeny." He stuffed the dagger into his sleeve. "Besides, I have already received correspondence from the Earl of Buchan, the Viscount Lymington, and the Marquis of Beverly."

Mairi rolled her eyes to the ornate ceiling relief. "Not a duke in the offing?"

"I've yet to hear from the Duke of Kent, and many more will be in London, where you *will* make me proud. Never forget your place, or I shall ensure you face dire consequences."

Mairi lowered her hand from her neck and looked at her bloody palm. Who was this man who purported to be her father? Had she ever truly known him? "What will you do with Mr. MacRae?"

"If he weren't fast allies with the Earl of Seaforth, I'd have already ordered his hanging. Though satisfying, such an act would bring dissention to this house, which I can ill afford." Da paced. "But Seaforth will be required at the Autumnal Ball as well. I reckon he will not be able to help MacRae for at least two months, possibly more. Perhaps given time to ponder his misdeeds whilst wallowing behind bars, the man will reconsider his suit."

"But he won't."

"Then I will have you married afore we return from England."

"I will refuse your choice!"

"If you dare defy me, I will not hesitate to execute the bastard—Seaforth or nay. Do you understand? If you try to run, he dies. If you deny a legitimate offer for your hand from a titled gentleman, he dies. Have I made myself clear?"

Mairi clutched her hands against her roiling stomach while tears burned her eyes. "Exceedingly clear." The words tasted bitter in her mouth.

A guard appeared in the doorway. "MacRae is behind bars, m'lord."

"Well done." Da flicked his wrist at Mairi. "Now take my wayward daughter and lock her in her chamber. Post a guard at her door. The only person permitted within is Aela. She'll need new gowns for London."

Mairi gulped as the guard appraised her like vermin. "When are we departing?" she asked.

Da returned to his chair and picked up his gazette. "As soon as I can arrange transport."

* * *

Locked in her chamber, Mairi threw herself facedown on the bed and shrieked into her pillow. For the love of God, if she'd only realized what an unfeeling cur her father could be. Never had he treated her with such disdain. In fact, until now, she had been cossetted. Aye, she'd heard rumors about his ruthlessness, but never saw this side of him until now.

He has played me like a marionette for my entire life.

Her body shook as tears streamed in her eyes and wet the pillow.

I've been so blind.

And all the while Dunn was right. He knew she should have stayed in the wood with Ram. He knew Da would behave cruelly.

And I did not believe him.

She sat up and drew a fist to her mouth. Ram and Curran had orders to wait. What would they do if Dunn did not return? If the lads were to approach the castle bearing arms, Da might make good on his threat and hang MacRae.

Mairi hopped to her feet and dashed to the door, pulled on the latch, and shook it with all her might. "Let me out. Please!" She pounded her fist against the timbers. "I am being held against my will and I have done nothing wrong."

"Apologies, m'lady," said the guard. "Orders are you must remain within. Shall I send for Miss Aela?"

"Yes, do so. I need her at once."

Footsteps approached in the corridor. "I am here, m'lady."

"Thank heavens."

The lock clicked and Aela slipped inside. "Och, m'lady, I've been ever so worried. I feared you might never return."

"Well, your worry has been unfounded." In a blink an idea came to mind. She pulled the lady's maid into the dressing room so as not to be overheard. "I need your help forthwith."

"Of course, but I've been sent to pack your trunks."

"There'll be time for that later. Quickly, I need to change into your costume." Mairi pulled open her kirtle laces. Aela was near enough in size, and she wore her brown hair tucked under a coif. If Mairi passed the guard quickly, he'd never notice.

"But I cannot possibly—"

"I *order* you to disrobe immediately. 'Tis a matter of life and death."

"But what if the earl discovers us?"

"I can count on the fingers of one hand the number of times the earl has visited my bedchamber in the past one and twenty years. Am I not wrong?"

"You are correct. I don't recall ever seeing him in this wing."

"Still, we must act with caution. Once I've donned your costume, you will climb under my bedclothes, pull them over your head, and pretend you are fast asleep."

"Are you certain about this? 'Tis risky. What if you are caught?" Aela removed her apron.

"Then I'll be no worse off than I am now, will I be? Now haste." As soon as Aela stepped out of her kirtle, Mairi slipped it on. "Climb into bed and do as I say. I shall return with an armload of wood and say you—I mean *I* have a chill."

Aela removed her coif and handed it to Mairi. "What do I do if someone comes in?"

"Ignore them." She pulled a frilly white dormeuse cap from the peg. "Put this on. It will hide your hair." Mairi grasped Aela's hand. "Now, quickly, pin up my tresses so no one can see the color beneath my coif."

Within minutes, Mairi stood at the door and knocked, giving the maid a nod.

"I'm ready to come out now," Aela called from the bed before hiding beneath the comforter.

"Straightaway, miss," said the guard, unlocking the door.

"My thanks," Mairi replied, impersonating Aela's voice to the best of her ability and curtsying with her head down. But she didn't wait for the guard's reaction. Walking briskly, she headed straight for the servants' stairs, dashed down three flights, then raced outside and across the courtyard to the guardhouse. Catching her breath, she stood against the wall and gradually inclined her head until she was able to peer inside the archway. A light flickered from within, but she saw no one.

Movement above caught her eye as two guards met on the wall-walk, looking outward toward the forest. "Have you seen anything?" one asked.

Mairi froze in place, her back flush against the wall. If either of those men turned around, they'd spy her for certain.

"Not a thing."

"Do you think MacRae's men will attack?"

"I doubt it. The bastard might have been able to slip into the castle with Lady Mairi, but all the shire would ken if he'd ridden here with an army."

"Mayhap you're right."

"But I might be wrong…"

Unable to hold her breath any longer, Mairi slipped into the archway and crept toward the tower's passageway leading to Castle Leod's single gaol cell. She'd seen it once when she went exploring as a young lass—in the days when she was insolent and incorrigible and her governess drove her mad. As she tiptoed forward, she listened for voices, but only heard a snore. The man guarding the passageway was sound asleep, sitting on a stool with a musket across his lap. Mairi searched for keys, praying they were hanging from a peg on the wall, but saw none. The guard didn't have them hanging from his belt, either. Her gaze slipped to his sporran.

Her fingers twitched. *Oh no, he'll wake for certain.*

Quiet as a mouse, she slipped past the man and hastened down to Dunn's cell.

"Dunn," she whispered, only able to make out his outline in the dim light.

"Mairi?" The big chieftain stood and grasped the iron bars.

"'Tis I."

He reached through and flicked the coif with his finger. "What are you wearing?"

"My maid's costume." She drew a hand over her mouth, blinking back tears. It was no time to simper like a weak-minded waif. "Da has ordered me locked in my chamber until we leave for London. He said he will kill you if I defy him."

"Christ, he's worse than even I imagined."

She wrapped her fingers around the bars and gave them a fruitless shake. "I must find a way to free you."

"Nay. You must not take any further risks."

"I beg your pardon?"

"Your father must believe everything is running according to plan—*his* plan. Now tell me, when will he set out for London?"

"H-he said soon—ah—when he can arrange transport."

Dunn pulled the key to the hidden gate from his sporran and held it up. "Take this and go back through the tunnel. Find Ram. Tell him I have been captured."

Her heart raced. "And to plan your escape, raise an army, and march on Castle Leod."

"Wheesht. He kens what to do."

"He does—then we shall plot your escape for certain."

"Leave that to my men. I mean it, Mairi. Remember when I said I would leave nothing to chance? Believe me when I say I'm finished biding my time, but the earl must think otherwise until Ram and Curran have raised the alarm."

"But—"

"Make no bones about it, your role is the most important. You must convince your father that you know nothing of any contingencies. I am keeping you in the dark for your protection."

"I want to do more." She hid her face in her palms. "King's crosses, I cannot bear to see you caged like a criminal!"

Dunn cupped her cheek, his hand cool, but ever so gentle. "You must go along with your da until I can set things to rights. And I swear on my life, I will."

"But—"

"Go—find Ram, and do not take such chances by coming again."

Mairi refused to budge. "I cannot. Not without knowing you will be all right."

"Och, lass, I've been taking care of myself for thirty years. You needn't worry about me."

"I hate this."

"Just do as I say. Promise me you will not try to do anything rash. Please."

She cringed. Her own foolishness had created this mess. "I will. I promise." Her mind raced. "W-what if Da takes me to London? What should I do?"

"Do you still have the missives I gave you?"

"Yes."

"Keep them hidden. Take them with you. Gain an audience with Seaforth. Tell him everything. I swear, that man owes both of us a great deal."

"The pox on Seaforth. What if he doesn't listen?"

"Then I will no longer pay him fealty." Dunn took her hand and kissed it. "Trust me on this, Mairi. You will be mine whether Seaforth helps or not. But having his backing will only help matters."

He pushed the key into her palm. "Haste."

She closed her fingers around his hand and squeezed while her heart bled. "I don't want to go—I can't leave you here like this."

"You must. I need you to be stronger than you have ever been in all your days." He again pulled her hand through the bars and kissed it, the expression in his gesture filled with passion so overwhelming, words could never explain. He straightened and smiled while he cupped her cheek in his palm. "You have the bonniest eyes of any lass in the Highlands. I see incredible goodness in them and stalwart strength. Know you have the courage to weather this tempest, *mo leannan*."

"I do. Because of you, I do."

"There's a good lass." He kissed her again and released her hand. "You must be careful not to let anyone see you, lest your father punish you more."

She swiped away a tear. "I don't want to go."

"Remember I love you. Now more than ever."

"I love you, too." She rose on her toes and kissed him, then slipped through the shadows of her home, not making a sound.

* * *

Mairi waited to light a torch until she had entered the blackness of the tunnel. She made her way through the dark cavern quickly, constantly checking over her shoulder and peering into nothing but blackness. The long walk through the passageway had always been eerie, but she'd never traversed it at night and never with the stakes being so high. At each bend in the tunnel, her heart jolted, ready for a ghost or wicked fairy to leap in front of her.

No matter how unnerving the passage, Mairi tightened her grip on the torch and continued onward until she met Ram and Curran exactly where she and Dunn had left them.

"Where's MacRae?" asked Ram.

"My father has taken him prisoner."

"God's blood." Curran threw up his hands. "I kent walking in there for a wee chat was folly. Cromartie is a snake. I beg your pardon, m'lady, but everyone kens your father is a viper."

"And now I do as well."

Ram bowed respectfully. "I'm sorry it has come to this. MacRae gave us orders we must carry out at once. He feared this would happen." He turned to Curran. "We ride."

"Ride?" Mairi stamped her foot. "Where?"

Ram headed for his horse. "Forgive me, but I'm not at liberty to say."

"Not at liberty?" Her heart raced. "You do not understand. My father is taking me to London…soon… mayhap on the morrow."

Ram stopped. "What say you? Cromartie is leaving?"

"Aye. To attend the queen's Autumnal Ball, where he expects to find a pompous old duke who will agree to marry me."

Curran thwacked Ram on the shoulder. "If Cromartie is heading for London, the army remaining at the castle ought to be reduced by half."

Ram mounted his horse. "You're right."

Mairi glanced between the two Highlanders. "Tell me what you're thinking. Are you riding for more men?"

"We're no' exactly heading for home."

"Aye," Curran agreed. "But the laird swore us to secrecy."

Things were spiraling out of control so fast, Mairi's chest tightened as if she were drowning. "Please. Whatever you are up to, I expect you to act with haste. I *do not* want things to go so far as to leave me with no alternative but to venture to London. Understood?" She pulled the key from the pocket of her apron. Giving it to Ram, she explained how to go through the crypt and find the entrance to the passageway. "There's a padlock on the gate, which I will secure upon my return. Use this key. The passageway opens in the cellars. After you climb up the stairwell to the kitchens, head through the courtyard to the guardhouse at the main gate. Dunn is imprisoned there."

"Thank you, m'lady," said Ram, taking up his reins. "Now return home afore you're caught."

Chapter Twenty-Two

*T*he footman helped Mairi into the coach, followed by Aela. Da walked around the team, inspecting the harnesses as he always did before a journey, then told the driver all was well and climbed in the coach and sat opposite the two ladies. He smiled with a great deal of smug satisfaction. Clenching her fists at her sides, Mairi returned his gaze with a stony leer.

Nothing was settled. As she feared, she'd been awakened at dawn and told the coach was waiting. Escorted by armed guards, she hadn't even been allowed a chance to see Dunn. The guards had marched her to the courtyard as if she were heading for her own execution.

My life is shattering.

As the coach rolled through the gate, she glanced out the window toward the gaol. Dunn sat alone cooped up in his miserable cell for naught. His crime? Saving a maid in distress. And there Mairi ambled along, riding in a stately coach as if she had not a care, on her way to board a galleon that would transport her to a royal ball. It tore her insides to shreds to leave Dunn alone. What would happen to him? What did Ram and Curran have planned? Was a feud imminent?

Mairi loathed sitting across the coach from her father while the horses took them farther away from Dunn. Her heart twisted, tormenting her as if she were a wretched traitor guilty of sedition, leaving her man behind bars and in chains.

"Mairi, you are like an open book," said Da. "You're not even trying to disguise the anguish you think you're feeling."

She sifted her gaze to her father's recreant face. "How would you know what I'm feeling?"

He smirked. "You will enjoy this venture to London. I have gone to great lengths to secure superior marriage prospects for you, and I will not abide your indifference. Your infatuation with MacRae is merely that—an infatuation brought about by your rescue and then close proximity. A few days away will give you time to clear your head, and you'll see the folly of your ways."

Beside her, Aela cleared her throat. "I believe attending a royal ball would be astonishingly romantic."

Da opened his snuffbox and took a pinch. "You are quite right, miss. I have no doubt Mairi will forget the Highlander as soon as we arrive in London and she mingles with many other fine gentlemen much more fitting to her position."

I will never forget Dunn. Clasping the hands in her lap as tight as her fingers could grip, Mairi shot her lady's maid a glare. Was everyone intent on rallying against her throughout this voyage? As soon as she got the lass alone, she would set her to rights. For the love of everything holy, Aela knew the depths of Mairi's desolation.

It took three hours to travel ten miles to the confluence of the Cromarty Firth with the River Conon, but it seemed more like an eternity. Any other day, Mairi would be thrilled to board a ship and sail for London. She would be thrilled at the opportunity to attend a royal ball and see the opulent ladies' gowns and dapper gentlemen in their finery. She would relish the chance to shop for the latest fashions on High Street. But doom and sadness were better descriptors for this day.

A skiff waited on the shore to ferry them to the three-masted brig moored in the Firth. Mairi obediently climbed in, allowing the sailors to help her to a bench. She sat, patting the seat beside her to beckon Aela. "What would you like to do in London?"

The maid looked astonished and drew a hand to her chest. "Me, m'lady?"

"Aye. After all it is your first voyage, I would think there would be a great many things you would like to see." Honestly, Mairi would relish any excuse to avoid outings with her father. Perhaps she would slip away with Aela for some shopping or take a coach along the Thames.

If only dreams were real.

Once the skiff was tied alongside the ship to hoist the guests aboard, the sailors used a winch with a seat that looked like a tree swing. Da made Mairi go first. When she swung out over the sea, she glanced down, her stomach lurching. Should she leap into the gray swells? If she did, she would swim back to Castle Leod and set Dunn free. That is, if she weren't wearing volumes of woolen skirts that would fill with water and drag her beneath the surf. No, such a folly simply wouldn't do. She must stay alive to help Dunn. She would deliver his missive to the Earl of Seaforth, and when the time came, she would take a stand against her father.

Once the Cromartie reached the deck and all were aboard, the captain introduced himself and shook hands with Da. He turned to Mairi and bowed. "I do hope you and your father will join me in my cabin for the evening meal."

Mairi curtsied and smiled pleasantly, though she nearly asked for a tray to be delivered to her stateroom. "It is very kind of you to invite us."

"I shall have the boatswain show you to your quarters, where you can rest. I'm sure the journey from Castle Leod was tiring." He gestured to the sailor on his right—obviously the boatswain.

"My thanks."

The captain returned his attention to the earl. "Your Lordship, I trust that you will find my ship comfortable and accommodating during this voyage. With a good wind and calm seas we should arrive in London by Thursday eve, Friday morning at the latest."

A lump swelled in Mairi's throat. *Three days of sailing farther away from Dunn.*

"Very good," said Da. "You'll sail right up the Thames then?"

"Aye. We shall navigate her all the way to the Pool of London."

"Excellent."

The boatswain gestured to the luggage that had been hoisted aboard. "Which portmanteau is yours, m'lady?"

"The two nearest." *And the one with the red ribbon contains the most precious cargo of all, Dunn's letter.*

Mairi looked over the rail to see her trunk being winched upward. "Where will my chests be stowed?"

"The trunks will go in the hold." He picked up the portmanteaus. "Have you packed what you need for the voyage in these?"

"I have. My trunks will be secure in the hold, I assume?"

"Yes, of course, m'lady, locked away. Only I and my boatswain have keys."

"That will be fine." Mairi gestured for Aela to follow the man as he headed aft.

Once they were alone, she sat on the bed. "I believe I just heard someone shout to weigh the anchor."

"I heard the call as well, m'lady." Aela set one of the portmanteaus on the table and opened it. "Shall I unpack for you?"

"Not yet." Mairi pulled Dunn's missive from her cloak, unfolded it, and patted the bed beside her. She'd read it last night, but intended to read it over and over again. "Would you like to know why I will marry Dunn MacRae and none other?"

Aela took a seat. "Is that missive from him?"

"It is, and I want to share it with you. If it were proper, I'd climb to the main deck and shout it for all the crew to hear." She cleared her throat and read aloud:

My dearest Mairi,

I only have a few moments to write this as my men prepare for our ride to Castle Leod. If I am not beside you when you open it, then my worst fears have been realized.

I want to tell you how much you have enriched my life, how happy you have made me during our

*adventures together. When I approached your father
and offered for your hand, I did so believing in my
love for you. I was enamored of your high spirits,
your lovely laugh, the way your eyes sparkle in the
candlelight. But at the time, my love was only half
of what it is now. I tell you true, my admiration has
grown tenfold. Aye, I still admire all the things I
stated above, but now there is so much more.*

*You, Mairi MacKenzie, are a remarkable woman.
I am honored to have found your favor, and know
that I love you with every fiber of my being. Ever
since we met, I have pondered your poem. It is high
time I share it with you:*

The first time I saw ye bonny lass, ye caught my e'e,
Though I could do naught but pass ye by.
I watched from afar whilst many a year passed,
Watched as ye grew,
Into a bonny lass,
An' a fine woman ye are, 'tis true,
I watched ye from afar wi' my heart tied,
I offered fer yer hand and was denied,
Then fate brought us together at last,
And we discovered our love was vast,
Now ye are mine and so, so nigh,
My love fer ye shall ne'er die…

*…Know you are in my heart always, my lady.
Know whilst I still breathe you will have my love
and my sword.*

*Your devoted servant,
Duncan MacRae*

"Och," Mairi cried, pulling a kerchief from her sleeve. "I cannot bear to leave him in that horrible cell."

Aela clasped her hands over her heart. "What are you to do, m'lady? Surely you cannot marry one of your da's suitors."

"I will refuse them all—string them along. I vow on my mother's grave I will not agree to a hasty marriage. Da owes me at least that." Mairi buried her face in the kerchief. "Mr. MacRae is so wonderful, and my father is being such a bull-brained mule."

"Mr. MacRae is a true gentleman." Aela sighed loudly. "And ever so romantic."

"He *is* romantic." Mairi set the missive aside and blew her nose. "I once thought he was frightening with his dark features and brooding eyes. But he's nothing like that. It was only because of Seaforth that he kept his feelings hidden. Thinking back, at every gathering I ever attended, he always looked my way. I looked at him as well, I suppose, though I didn't realize how much I liked him. His watchful gaze always made me feel unnerved, but..." Mairi slapped her hand through the air. "Forgive me. Mine are the silly musings of a daft maid."

"Not at all, m'lady. I think 'tis wonderful. Tell me, for I've never been in love. How did his attentions make you feel?"

"Beautiful," Mairi sighed. "And Seaforth never so much as made me feel anything aside from unsuitable."

Aela returned to the portmanteau and fished out a brush. "Thank heavens he married someone else then. Because you are an astonishing lady, and anyone who doesn't realize it does not deserve you." She gestured to the chair before a looking glass bolted to the wall as the ship began to sway. "Come. You must dry your eyes and dress for the evening meal."

Groaning, Mairi plopped into the chair, nearly teetering off for the sway of the ship. "We are under way."

"And on an adventure."

"I only wish my heart was filled with eagerness rather than foreboding."

Aela shook the brush. "Och, if his letter is any indication, Mr. MacRae will find a way to win you; I am positive he will. You've naught but to try to play along with the earl's antics and enjoy the voyage as best you can. With all your fine gowns, simply stepping out amidst London society ought to be amusing."

Using a tactic Dunn had taught her, Mairi snatched the brush from Aela's hand, stood, and wielded it like a sword. "I doubt anything will amuse me on this journey."

Aela's mouth dropped open. "M'lady, you wrested the brush from my hand with no effort. How on earth did you manage to do it?"

Mairi slashed the makeshift weapon through the air in an *X*. "Mr. MacRae is good for more than poetry. If anyone dares attack my person, I shall not simper and wilt." *I swear it—even if he is my father.* She resumed her seat, presenting Aela with the brush's handle. She might be captive on this ship for three days, but she vowed to use the time to practice disarming her lady's maid.

I shall never be helpless again.

Chapter Twenty-Three

A sudden screech awoke Dunn from a deep sleep. Groggy, he reached for his dirk but only grasped a handful of straw. Grunts echoed through the passageway. He pushed up from his pallet and peered through the iron bars. Shadows flickered in the torchlight beyond.

"Tie him up," a man hissed.

Damnation, Dunn couldn't see a thing.

Moments later, Ram and Curran hastened toward the cell, holding the keys to his freedom.

"Where are the others?" Dunn asked while the tension in his shoulders eased tenfold. Good God, he was relieved to see his men.

"Beyond the walls—ready to attack if need be." Ram used a key to unlock the door. "Once Lady Mairi told us the earl was sailing for London, Curran and I realized the MacKenzie guard would be reduced by half at least."

"I like it—a quiet escape." Dunn pushed the creaking door open. "Were you seen?"

"Nay, we slipped through the tunnel in the crypt. Her Ladyship gave us instructions," said Ram.

Curran chuckled and pointed his thumb over his shoulder. "We had a wee skirmish with the guard, but he's dreaming with the fairies at the moment."

"Did you kill him?" The last thing Dunn needed was a murder on his hands.

"He's still breathing, but he'll have a sore head when he comes to."

"What is the hour?"

Ram dropped the ring of keys to the dirt floor. "Three, near enough."

Dunn rubbed his wrists. "Where are the horses?"

"Out the back—tied in the wood where we left you days ago."

"Very well, we shall head through the cellars then." Dunn led the way through the corridor and stopped at the guard, lying on the floor with his wrists and ankles bound.

Blood ran from his nose as he opened his eyes. "Cromartie will hang you for this."

"I doubt that." Dunn pushed into the armory and found his sword, dirk, and sporran. "Where's my coin?"

The man smirked. "A wee payment for your stay."

Gnashing his teeth, Dunn slammed his fist across the braggart's jaw. "I'll be taking back what's mine." He fished in the man's purse and pulled out a handful of coins. "Witness this, men. Cromartie's guards have robbed me and I am recovering only a pittance of my property."

"Duly noted, sir," said Ram, presenting a leather purse. "This is for you. From your coffers."

"He thinks of everything," said Curran with a snort.

"You are a good man." Dunn took the coin and belted

on his weapons. "Let us haste afore anyone else decides to pay us a visit."

"This way." Curran beckoned, taking the lead.

"How many guards?" Dunn whispered, drawing his sword.

"Four posted on the wall-walk," said Ram.

Curran stopped at the edge of the courtyard and popped his head through the archway, searching back and forth. "'Tis clear."

Dunn pointed ahead. "Skirt to the kitchen entrance."

"Aye, that's where we're heading," whispered Ram, taking up the rear.

Slinking around the perimeter took longer but enabled them to keep to the shadows...until someone's blade scraped the stone wall.

"What's that?" shouted a guard from above.

"Run!" Dunn hissed.

Curran stepped up the pace.

Crack! A musket blasted behind them.

"Faster!" yelled Ram.

Dunn stole a glance over his shoulder as they made a sharp turn and headed for the kitchen entry. Above, three men dashed toward another who stood lining up the sights of his musket.

Two steps to the door.

Crack! The guard's musket fired.

Dunn grunted as something smacked his heel. Keeping up with the pace, he lunged forward. Searing pain burned his foot and shot up his leg. His knee gave out.

"Jesus Christ," Ram swore as he shoved his hand beneath Dunn's armpit.

Steeling his mind against the pain, he ran, favoring his left foot, only tapping the ball of his right. Agony punished him with his every step. But he was committed. He either fled or faced the noose come dawn.

As they charged through the kitchen, Dunn grabbed a cloth.

"Thieves!" the cook shouted, snatching a poker from the hearth.

Ram swung the door shut in the man's face.

"This way," growled Curran, turning into the stairwell.

Clenching his teeth, Dunn hobbled down the steps, leaving a trail of blood.

"Will you make it?" asked Ram.

"Bloody oath, I will."

Without stopping to light a torch, they dashed into the passageway. It wasn't long before the shouts of the guards echoed behind them.

Ahead, Curran pushed through the gate. "You're limping like a lame nag."

"I'll be right as soon as I mount Beastie." Dunn ground his molars as he sprinted through the gate and up the stairs, the pain lessening.

"They're gaining," hissed Ram, catching up and taking the lead.

A volley of musket fire blasted from the wood. "We have you covered, MacRae! Run!" bellowed Robert Grant. Cromartie might have been alerted to MacRae Highlanders in the area, but not Grant.

Aye, Dunn loved it when a plan came together. Only paces to freedom, he bore down and kept running. Cromartie's guard did not stand a chance. As he reached the edge of the wood, Robert stepped from the brush. "Are you hurt?"

"Not bad."

"Then go. If our muskets haven't convinced them to

turn tail and go back behind Castle Leod's curtain walls, we will keep them busy as you make your escape."

Dunn shook his friend's hand. "I am in your debt."

"That's right, and I'll be looking for payment one day."

Dunn beckoned Ram and Curran. "Let us ride, lads."

As he neared his horse, Beastie snorted. The big horse could smell his master from fifty paces. Dunn released the stallion's reins and shoved his left foot into the stirrup. "Are you ready to run?"

The horse nodded. Aye, Beastie sensed the danger and flared his nostrils. Once he was mounted, the big fellow reared. "Follow me," Dunn bellowed.

He took the northern route, circling toward Contin. There was no chance Cromartie's men would think he'd waste that kind of time, but that's why Dunn couldn't be tracked. He never traveled the expected route.

When they arrived at the Y in the road outside the village, he pulled Beastie to a halt. Ram and Curran rode in beside him. "We must split up. You men ride on to Eilean Donan. Ensure she's protected from attack. Double the guard."

"But you're bleeding, sir." Ram pointed at the swath of slick blood glowing in the moonlight on Beastie's barrel. "You need a healer."

Dunn snarled. "'Tis but a scratch."

"When will we see you next?" asked Curran.

"I can't say. There's a wee lassie on her way to London who needs rescuing."

"You're heading for London?" Ram's voice cracked. "After that bastard locked you in the bowels of hell?"

"Aye." Dunn reined his mount southward. "What better way to clear my name when I have both Cromartie and Seaforth in the same city?"

"What?" The lieutenant's voice shot up. "Are you mad?"

"Perhaps, but I'll not stand idle while Mairi's father attempts to marry her off to the loftiest bidder."

* * *

With the coming of dawn, the skies opened into a deluge. A tempestuous wind drove the droplets sideways, piercing Dunn's clothes. He hunched over Beastie's withers as the rain turned to sleet. His heel throbbed with the stallion's every step. Riding into Inverness, he reined his horse to a stop outside the harbormaster's rooms. A lamp shone from within.

Dunn stepped inside, grinding his teeth against the pain.

"We're closed. Don't open for an hour yet," said a man seated at a writing table with a quill in his hand. He didn't bother to look up.

Undaunted, Dunn stepped forward. "I need to purchase fare to London forthwith."

"The next ship sails on Friday. You'd best return then."

"No. I must leave today."

The man looked up. "You are brash coming in here smelling like a bog and demanding passage. Run along and do not return until Friday morn at ten o'clock."

Dunn grabbed his dirk and slammed the point into the center of the man's parchment. "I beg your pardon, but I am Dunn MacRae, chieftain of my clan. I've been wronged by the Earl of Cromartie, and I *will* sail for London this day. If ye do not want your throat cut, I reckon you'd best tell me where I can find a boat leaving within the hour."

"Th-there's none."

"None?" Dunn pulled up the dirk and leveled it at the man's neck.

Sweat beaded the coward's brow. "Ah...you might try Mr. Murdoch. He's taking a load of livestock south—I reckon he'll h-help you."

"Is that Murdoch with a barque?"

"Aye, a single-masted barque. He's the one."

"That's better." Dunn sheathed his weapon and strode out the door, doing his best not to limp, the top of his right boot flapping without the sole.

The activity in the dockyard had grown busier with the hour. The rain turned to a heavy mist. Fishermen with sea galleys were unfurling their sails. At the end of the pier a flock of sheep was being herded onto a barque—the same boat Dunn had hired two years past to deliver his livestock to market in Glasgow.

He led his horse to the gangway. "Mr. Murdoch, please."

The master stepped to the ship's rail. "MacRae?"

"In the flesh. Do you have room for a paying passenger?"

"I do. But why would you be heading to Hull?"

Jesus Saint Christopher Christ, Hull was a good three-day ride from London. The blasted harbormaster probably knew it as well. "I need fare to London. 'Tis urgent."

"I have no qualms taking you down the eastern seaboard. Perhaps you can find a transport to London at the port in Hull."

"I suppose it will take me a mite closer than we are now." Determined to change the master's priorities, Dunn limped up the wooden gangway, pulling Beastie behind.

"Are you injured?" asked Murdoch.

"Nothing a dram of whisky won't set to rights, my friend." He smiled as if the throbbing pain were a trifle. Once aboard, he planned to slowly wheedle the master until he agreed to ferry him all the way to London.

"Well, I reckon you should go below decks and pay a wee visit to the galley. Cook's salve is the best I've seen." Murdoch beckoned a sailor. "You there, lower this horse into the hold."

"My thanks—and have a care with the big fella. He's a rare find." Dunn handed over the reins and proceeded down the narrow steps toward the galley.

A large man scooped a pan of oats from a barrel.

"Are you the cook?"

"I am."

Dunn took a seat on the stool. "Master Murdoch said you might have a remedy for my foot."

"Perhaps. What happened to it?"

"Caught by a musket ball."

"Shot, aye?" The cook wiped his dirty hands down the front of his apron. "Let's have a wee peek."

Crossing his leg over his knee, Dunn took his first good look at the damages. With the heel missing, there wasn't much leather remaining on the sole, either. Gingerly, he pulled off the boot, then hissed as he peeled away his hose.

"God's bones, that is one mangled pound o' flesh," said the cook, pulling up a stool. Grasping Dunn's ankle, the man examined the wound. "'Tis a godsend ye had heels on those brogues, else your foot might have been shot clean off."

Dunn hissed. It hurt more now that he'd seen it. The bottom of his foot looked like mincemeat. "Can you fix me up?"

"I reckon it'll need a good soak in a pot o' briny water afore we apply a dressing."

Dunn nodded. "Is there a spare boot about? It seems mine is damaged beyond repair."

The cook stood and grabbed a cast-iron pan. "It might cost you some coin."

"Fair enough." He watched as the man prepared the water and salt, then clenched his teeth until they throbbed as he submerged his foot in the tincture while the salt attacked him like a hundred angry hornets.

Chapter Twenty-Four

Due to inclement weather, the Earl of Cromartie and his retinue did not arrive in London until Saturday. During nearly the entire journey down the coast, the brig had creaked and groaned, tossing about in the midst of a tempest. Mairi spent most of the journey in her berth overcome by seasickness. The weather didn't sour Da's mood, however. By the time they arrived at the London town house, he had an entire sennight of activities planned, including private parties, symphonies, operas, and luncheons.

He allowed her the first night to rest, but this morn she was expected to attend services at Westminster with the queen. Though it wasn't proper for Mairi to venture out alone, especially on a Sunday morning, she slipped through the gardens and out the alley. Reid MacKenzie kept his rooms only blocks away. It was difficult to believe, but she had never been invited inside Seaforth's town house, a fact she still resented. Twenty years of being betrothed to the man, and he'd never shown her any affection. Aye, he was always pleasant, but the more Mairi thought about it, the more she realized the earl had forever tried to evade her. He was polite, yet distant. How had she never once considered he might not want to marry her? *I was so naïve.*

As a matter of fact, she'd never questioned her duty to marry him. Their forthcoming nuptials had always been a part of her future. She had a task to perform for kin and clan, and she would have obediently allowed her father to lead her down the aisle of wedded bliss.

Wedded misery is more likely.

Now that Mairi knew love, she realized how miserable her life with Reid MacKenzie would have been. Though he was an attractive man, she didn't love him. Heavens, he hardly noticed her. *Who would want to go through life being treated like an inconvenient consort? Especially when Mr. MacRae has so much love to give.*

Arriving at the earl's town house, she took in a deep breath, climbed the stairs, and rang the bell.

After a great deal of time, an old butler answered the door. A puzzled expression furrowed his weathered face. "May I help you, madam?"

"Lady Mairi MacKenzie here to meet with His Lordship, please."

"I am afraid the earl has not yet risen." He moved to shut the door. "Perhaps you should return at a more appropriate hour, my lady... and with a proper escort."

With a jolt of ire, Mairi slid her foot forward to keep the door from closing. "No." She pushed inside, throwing her shoulders back. "I will speak to His Lordship, *my cousin*, forthwith. It is a matter of life and death!" Reid wasn't a first cousin, but that didn't matter. They were kin, and that's all this pompous butler needed to know.

The man's jowls shook. "This is highly improper. And before the worship service with the queen."

"I do not care whether my presence here is proper or not," Mairi shouted, thrusting her finger toward the staircase. "Either you fetch His Lordship this instant, or I will open every door in this house until I find him."

The butler bowed. "Of course, my lady. I shall wake him straightaway." He gestured with an upturned palm. "If you would take a seat in the parlor."

Mairi heaved a sigh and retreated to a settee. Thank the stars the man hadn't drawn a dagger and waved it under her nose, though she would have been ready for such an assault.

It seemed like an eternity before the steps creaked and the earl entered, barefoot, wearing no more than a shirt and kilt. "'Tis rather early, is it not, Cousin?" he asked, dipping his head in a semblance of a bow.

Clutching Dunn's missive, Mairi hopped to her feet. "Seaforth. Things have grown dire since Mr. MacRae's last correspondence with you."

"MacRae? I thought you and he were planning to marry."

"That is exactly what we want, but my father has other plans." She shoved the missive into his hands while filling him in on all that had transpired, right up to riding out of Castle Leod's gates while the poor chieftain suffered in the bowls of Da's prison.

"Good God, will your father stop at nothing to further his estates?"

"You have no idea. I'll tell you now, Dunn does not give a fig about my dowry—he would marry me this very day if he weren't imprisoned. Dunn only surrendered his weapons because my father held a knife to my neck and threatened to kill me."

"Thought you said Cromartie was bluffing."

"Aye." She rubbed her throat where she now had a small scab. "But it seemed real enough at the time."

Seaforth opened the letter and gestured to the settee while he took a seat near the hearth.

But Mairi refused to sit. Not at a time like this. "Da told me he would release him, but only after my hand had been spoken for."

Looking up from the letter, Reid arched an eyebrow. "Only after you've said *I do*, I'd surmise."

"I will never utter those words unless they are when I am standing beside Duncan MacRae."

Seaforth held up his hand as he read. Then he folded the parchment thoughtfully. "Do you truly love him?"

"With my whole heart. With my entire being."

"Then why did you refuse him when he offered for your hand before?"

"Because Da said he was merely taking pity upon me."

"Hardly."

"Hardly?"

Seaforth crossed his ankles. "I reckon Dunn has carried a torch for you since your fifteenth birthday."

Mairi thought back. There had been a clan gathering at Castle Leod. A young man of four and twenty, Dunn had attended with his father—and Seaforth. Heaven's stars, that was about the time when she first noticed his brooding looks from across the hall.

"Is that why you rescinded...?" Her voice trailed off. *No use opening wounds that have only begun to heal.*

"Nay, lass. But hear me true, you are a fine, bonny

young woman. My heart strayed, is all. I have no further explanation, aside from offering my sincerest apologies for any suffering I may have caused you." He shook the missive. "I will confront your father directly. After all, he owes me fealty, not the other way around. I will demand that he dispatch a missive to the constable at Castle Leod for MacRae's release forthwith."

"Thank you, m'lord." Mairi drew her hands over her heart. "And what of Dunn's proposal of marriage? Can you *please* convince my father to relent?"

"Unfortunately, you will need to have a reckoning with your da on that account. I may be the chieftain of Clan MacKenzie, but your father has every right to arrange your marriage, though you have a right to refuse his choice as well." Seaforth tapped his lips with his pointer finger. "I'll do what I can to intervene whilst we are in London, and ensure Cromartie does not act too hastily in negotiating your betrothal."

"You would do that for me?"

"Let us say I will try. Dunn MacRae is the best ally a man can have, and he deserves a chance to pursue happiness. If you love him as you have declared to me, you will have my blessing and my support." Seaforth stood. "Now if you will excuse me, I must dress to attend the queen's service."

Both happy and miserable at the same time, Mairi slowly curtsied. "Thank you, m'lord." Seaforth might be able to force her father to release Dunn, but his hands were tied when it came to whom she married. She suppressed a groan, fully aware that was the way of it.

How am I to keep Da at bay until we return to the Highlands?

* * *

Thrown from his narrow cot, Dunn startled awake as his backside collided with the deck. His stomach roiled with the violent lurching of the ship—port to starboard like an overzealous cradle. Above decks, thunder boomed and rumbled. His weapons and effects slid, clanking from wall to wall in the tiny berth used by paying passengers.

With the ship's next roll, Dunn grappled to grab onto the legs of the bed as he hurled toward the wall.

"She's on her beam ends!" a voice shouted from the main deck.

"Tack west," bellowed another.

In the dim light, Dunn fumbled for his new hose and boots, which had cost him thrice what he'd pay a cobbler. The ship jerked and jolted as she changed course until the rocking shifted from side to side and then bow to stern.

Dunn gritted his teeth as he forced his foot into the boot. "Jesus Saint Christopher Christ, that bloody hurt!" Grumbling under his breath, he bumbled to his feet while the ship continued to lurch. Good God, he was no virgin to the sea, but even the most hardened of sailors might lose their guts in this storm.

Biting back the pain, he staggered out the door and to the steps. He pulled himself upward using the rope rail, taking in a deep breath when his face met pelting rain. The deck awash with seawater, his feet slipped, causing a shot of pain from his heel all the way up to the small of his back.

Clouds hung so low, there was little visibility as the ship broke through one enormous white-capped wave after another.

"She'll not weather this storm much longer," shouted a sailor.

A man wound a sail rope around a belaying pin. "We'll run aground, for certain."

"Not on my bloody watch," hollered Murdoch from the helm.

Dunn barreled aft toward the ship's wheel. "Where are we?"

"Should be rounding Spurn Head—hold on to the timbers. Once we enter the Humber Estuary, the seas will calm. Mark me."

"I bloody will," Dunn said, looping his arm through the ship's rail and planting his feet squarely. "What were you thinking, sailing into this squall? 'Tis rough enough to roll her over."

"It hit us fast—no time to outrun the wind."

"Land ho!" shouted the navigator, lowering his spyglass just as a lightning bolt struck the mast. Sailors scattered as the great pole crashed to the deck, splintering the timbers.

"Jib boom to port!" the master bellowed. "The mast is no' done in. She has a good fifteen feet. Cut the rigging and bid the wind fill the main course sail!"

Dunn watched as the men worked to regain control while a wave hit broadside, making the boat heel all the way to the top rail. Volumes of salt water gushed across the deck, knocking two sailors from their feet, the wave carrying them to the portside wall.

He could do nothing but hold fast. If they made it to Hull, no ship in Britain would take a chance on sailing in the open sea until this storm passed.

Chapter Twenty-Five

*M*airi sat before the looking glass while Aela removed the rags from her hair, revealing fresh and bouncy new curls. "I do not ken how you do it. I can barely pull a comb through my locks, they're so thick." Though she tried to sound cheerful, inside a wretched tempest brewed. Her father refused to tell her anything about his meeting with Seaforth. She only assumed Da had done the honorable thing and dispatched word requesting Dunn's release.

The maid smiled. "Practice, I suppose." She twirled the length of hair in the back into a chignon and pinned it in place.

Mairi glanced to the tray on the table in front of the hearth. "Thank you for bringing my breakfast so I could avoid eating with my father." If she had to face his pinched expression one more time while he told her to tend to women's affairs and practice her charm, she would scream.

"I kent you'd prefer a tray. Besides, I'm most likely more eager to ride along the Thames than you are, m'lady."

"Oh yes." Mairi clapped her hands together. "It will irritate Da to no end. We must slip out the servants' entrance so as not to be seen. Then we can hail a coach on Church Street."

"Hailing a coach." Aela sighed and set the brush on the dressing table. "It sounds ever so daring."

"As long as we are together, no one will pay us much mind."

"Lady Mairi?" called the butler while a knock sounded at the door. "Your father has requested your presence in the parlor straightaway."

"A moment," she said loudly, then turned to Aela. "Curses, they're starting early this morn. We were not fast enough."

The poor lass's face fell. "Perhaps there will be time later."

"I truly hope so."

Resolutely, Mairi followed the butler to what she knew would be another introduction to a pompous nobleman. 'Twas only Wednesday and no more than five complete and utter aristocratic bores had graced the parlor thus far.

"Lady Mairi MacKenzie, may I introduce the Earl of Buchan."

She affected an air of indifference as she stepped inside. Surprisingly, the earl wore Highland dress. Graying at his temples, the man looked to be at least forty, and was reasonably tall and slender, if not too thin. He bowed deeply. "M'lady, it is a pleasure to meet you at last."

She curtsied, all too aware of her father's watchful eye. "You are a Scot, m'lord?"

"Aye, from the shire of Buchan, near Aberdeen."

Ah, that's why she couldn't place him. Aberdeen was quite a distance from Castle Leod.

Da gestured to the settee. "I've ordered a pot of coffee and biscuits."

"Splendid," said Buchan, waiting for Mairi to sit first, then taking the seat beside her.

With a sigh, she took the seat on the settee. Doing so would be a great deal easier than listening to her father complain later. Buchan's gaze slipped down and up as he smiled and pulled on the cuffs of his velvet doublet. "Your father tells me you have a fondness for dancing."

Her mouth popped open as she searched for words. True, she enjoyed dancing, but the only person she cared to dance with was Mr. Duncan MacRae. "Ah...my dance master once told me I am light on my feet."

"I should like to see you at the ball...dance, that is."

"She is as graceful as a swan," said Da, as if he were a traveling tinker selling his wares.

Her cheeks flooding with heat, Mairi gave her father a pointed look. "You are biased." Hoping the time would pass more quickly if she were to ask the questions, she folded her hands and faced the earl. "Tell me, m'lord, are you here for the ball, or have you come to London on other matters?"

"Alas, a bit of both, I'm afraid." Buchan was polite and well-spoken, and by far the most affable courtier she'd met. However, Mairi doubted the man would last two minutes in a sparring session with Dunn.

"Alas?" she asked. "Have things been unfavorable for you?"

"They have." The earl looked to Da.

Cromartie nodded. "Go on, you may as well tell her. She'll draw it out of you soon enough."

"Very well." Buchan looked at her directly with a pair of soulful brown eyes. "My wife died giving birth to my son. It was a tragedy that cut me to the quick."

"Oh, I am sorry. You must be bereft with melancholy."

"I am—er—was. It has been a year, and the time is nigh for me to find a mother for Henry."

"And a wife," said Da.

"Aye, and a wife," Buchan echoed, not as convincingly.

"Do you feel you are ready to marry?" Mairi asked, curious. If her intuition was correct, he was no readier to wed her than she was willing to wed him.

"I wouldn't be here, otherwise." He shifted in his seat.

The butler stepped into the parlor carrying a silver tray. "Coffee and biscuits, my lord."

Cromartie certainly beamed with good spirits this day. "Thank you, Maximillian. Please set the tray on the table. Will you please pour, Mairi?"

Trying to look pleasant, she did as her father asked, though she hadn't acquired a taste for the Turkish drink that had taken London by storm. Even with milk, it was bitter and made her on edge. "How are your crops, m'lord?" she asked, opting for small talk.

"Good so far, we're expecting a bountiful harvest."

"And your son, Henry, is it? Is he a happy bairn?" She took a bit of biscuit, savoring the sweetness and wishing she had a nip of Dunn's whisky on hand to take away the stupefying boredom.

"He is, as are my other children." Looking away, the earl picked up a porcelain cup and sipped. "It is a fine day for a coach ride. They're saying it will be clear by

noon." Light rain pattered on the window, though that
hadn't stopped Mairi from planning an outing with Aela.

But Mairi had stiffened at the words *other children*.
Nonetheless, she chose not to query him on the subject.
After all, Buchan's offspring were no concern of hers.
"Fancy that, I was just speaking to my lady's maid about
the very same thing." She beamed at her father. "Wouldn't
it be lovely for my lady's maid to chaperone us on a ride
along the Thames?"

"Aela?" asked Da, stretching his collar.

"How charming of you to think of your maid," Buchan
interjected with a warm smile. "Are the pair of you
close?"

"Quite close." Mairi sat back, and twiddled her
thumbs. She'd be able to keep her promise to Aela and
a ride with the earl ... without her father. Who knew how
interesting the conversation might be without Da there to
hang on every word?

* * *

It was only by the grace of God the barque managed to
sail, damaged and broken into the port at Hull. Even if
Master Murdoch had agreed to take Dunn to London, it
wouldn't have happened. And with the weather still blow-
ing a gale, he had no choice but to disembark with Beastie
and ride the remaining distance. As he left the village, he
passed a signpost that read "London 178 miles."

At a fast trot with requisite rest, the journey would take
him two and a half days, if not three. If nothing went
wrong.

He crouched over the horse's mane and rode through
the drizzling rain, shielded by not much more than a

leather doublet and a woolen plaid draped over his head. Still swollen, his heel burned and stung, though the pain trumped the ache from the bruises he'd sustained from falling off his bunk on the ship. At least the ride would give his foot an opportunity to heal. Dunn had endured many injuries before. The foot was a bugger of a place to be injured, though he couldn't think of anywhere on his body he'd like to be shot. In fact, a musket ball to the foot ought to bear a lower mortality rate than anywhere else. With no lead ball lodged in his flesh, the wound was clean.

Neither rain nor wind nor sleet nor his agony would stop him. Three days until he again held Mairi in his arms. Squaring his jaw, he set his sights on the long road before him and cued his horse for a posting trot.

He clenched his fist around his reins. *Something always goes awry.*

And Mairi had no idea he was so close. There wasn't even a way to send her a message—at least not one with a chance of arriving before he did. Had she gained an audience with Seaforth? Had Cromartie come to his senses? What was she doing now? Being fitted for gowns, most likely. He hoped.

* * *

The lady's maid sat with her head craned out the coach window. Aela's exuberance was amusing. "Look at London Bridge, m'lady. Do people actually live there?"

"They do," said the Earl of Buchan from his seat across the coach. "'Tis a treasure trove of shops, though very congested at this time of day."

Mairi sat back, enjoying herself for the first time since

she arrived. "I kent she would fancy a ride along the Thames."

"She's dear, her excitement infectious."

"Thank you for humoring me. I'm afraid my father has been a wee bit overbearing as of late." Mairi dug her fingers into the velvet seat while the coach jolted and bumped along the cobblestones.

Buchan didn't seem to notice as he swayed with the motion, not paying much attention to the passing scenery. "He's eager to see you happy and matched with a suitor who he feels is worthy."

"Aye." Her gaze trailed away along with her voice. Surely, her father still cared about her happiness, though he had an odd way of showing it of late. "I think he's nervous."

"I suppose I will be when it comes time for my first daughter to wed. She'll be of age soon."

"First daughter? How old is she?"

"Fifteen."

Aela popped her head inside and pointed. "Look, m'lady. 'Tis the Tower of London!"

Too busy pondering Buchan's revelation, Mairi ignored the lass. "If I am guessing correctly, you have more than one daughter and a newborn son."

"I do."

"Pray tell, how many children have you sired?"

He stroked his fingers down his cleanly shaven chin while deep creases formed between his brows. "Nine. The eldest is a lad, aged eighteen."

"Nine children?" She didn't bother hiding her astonishment. "My heavens, you have quite the ready-made family."

"I do." He grinned. "Phillis and I always wanted a big family."

"Always? How long were you married?"

"Twenty glorious years." He closed his eyes and patted his chest as if bereft.

"Nine children in twenty years?" Mairi asked, still flabbergasted and placing the earl's age somewhere between thirty-five and forty. "She must have been with child a great deal of that time."

"Indeed, she was." He proudly beamed.

"How did you meet?"

He shrugged. "She was a Forbes. Her family and mine have always been fast allies. I knew her most of my life."

"Did you love her all that time?" Mairi was prying, but she didn't care. Besides, the earl seemed willing to openly discuss his affairs.

"I suppose I did. As children, we oft played together. It was natural that we would marry."

"And you miss her."

He nodded, looking to his hands. "Very much."

"At least your marriage was happy while it lasted." Mairi flipped open her fan and cooled her face. "Growing up, I always thought I'd become the Countess of Seaforth, but it wasn't meant to be."

Buchan met her gaze. "I'd heard the news and I must express my regrets."

"There is no need. I would not have wanted to endure a loveless marriage."

"I think the best marriages begin with a solid friendship."

Mairi pulled off her glove and twisted Dunn's ring on her finger, admiring it. "I agree. And . . . I would be remiss if I did not inform you that I am in love with another."

"Oh?" The earl frowned, though his eyes didn't reflect surprise. "Is your father aware of this?"

"Alas, yes. Though he does not believe a mere Highland chieftain to be worthy."

"I see. His decision must have been very difficult for him."

"I'm not certain if he is being difficult or obstinate but, nonetheless, he has refused his consent."

"I am sorry." Pulling a pipe from his waistcoat pocket, Buchan dipped it into a pouch of tobacco. "Hmm. *If* we were to marry, at the least we would be able to support each other in our sorrows."

Chapter Twenty-Six

*T*he eve of the ball arrived with overtones of doom. During the coach ride from the town house to the Banqueting House at Whitehall, Da announced they would be staying in London for another fortnight at the request of the Earl of Buchan. Regardless of Mairi's efforts to convince the earl of her affection for Dunn, dear old Papa had eased Buchan's concerns by telling him Mairi had merely been infatuated at a gathering of Highlanders, an understandable diversion to take her mind off Seaforth's untimely retraction.

"Have you sent word for Mr. MacRae's release?" she asked, avoiding mentioning her visit with Reid MacKenzie. If her father discovered she'd gone behind his back, he'd be livid.

Da opened his snuffbox and nipped a pinch. "I did," he said, as if the decision had been his alone. "There was no sense in keeping him incarcerated now that you are in London, though it will take a fortnight for my orders to reach the castle. 'Tis best to ensure a clean separation once and for all. And if you marry Buchan, you mightn't ever see the MacRae rascal again."

"So, you would hope." Mairi sighed, dressed like a queen in a gold gown with gossamer lace while a wretched chasm stretched in her heart.

The coach rolled to a halt.

"Come, Mairi, would you give up the chance to marry an earl for a Highland chieftain? Think of your children, my dearest. If you married MacRae, they would be born commoners."

"Yet still members of the gentry. Is that so awful?" she asked as the footman helped her alight. "I would prefer my children to be sturdy Highland folk, well loved by a father who would dote on them, not by a man whose only care was to make alliances. Be careful, Father, your lust for riches and power is eating away at your sensibilities. I'm afraid if you do not stop, you will have no heart left."

After following her down the steps, Da grabbed her elbow and squeezed. "You will cease spewing this derisive drivel at once. Hold your head high and act like the proud daughter of a peer, or I might go off and choose the oldest, most hideous nobleman I can find to marry you."

With a subtle jerk, she yanked her elbow away. "I would never agree."

"I'll see to it that your approval is not required."

"You wouldn't!"

"I suggest you do not put it to the test." He presented her with a gloved hand. "Enough of this. You will make me proud this eve. I miss our amiability, dear. Let us put this business about MacRae behind us."

Never.

Mairi glanced over her shoulder. The coach had moved

on and was replaced by another. All around them people clad in opulent finery converged into the courtyard, processing through the enormous double doors. Only one year ago, excitement had flitted about her insides while she passed through the same entry into the Banqueting House with its ornately painted ceiling. But at that time her hand had been promised. Unfortunately, this visit made her throat swell closed while each couple was led inside and announced by the master of ceremonies in a booming voice.

Mairi pictured herself as a prized heifer being led by her sire as they approached the throne. Queen Anne sat holding a scepter, her back so straight, she looked to be laced to an iron rod. Her Highness wore a crown atop swirls of brown locks, looking on with a frown that receded into her double chin. Indeed, the woman had aged in the past year.

"The Right Honourable the Earl of Cromartie and the Lady Mairi MacKenzie," the master of ceremonies announced.

On cue, Mairi curtsied, bowing her head. If only she could drop to her knees and grovel at Her Majesty's feet and bemoan how poorly her father had behaved toward the man she loved.

The queen leaned forward with a pinch to her brow. "I say, Lady Mairi, you were formerly engaged to wed Lord Seaforth, were you not?"

"She was, indeed," Da said before Mairi uttered a word.

"I bid you hold your tongue, Cromartie. My question was not addressed to you." Her Majesty returned her attention to Mairi. "I do hope you will find this royal ball *rewarding*."

Mairi cringed, the weight of her misery sinking to her

toes. *A quick exit would be my greatest reward.* "One can never be certain, Your Highness."

"You are a lovely young woman. Many a maid would give their dowries for tresses such as yours."

"Indeed, she is bonny, thank you, Your Highness," Mairi's father said, a beaming smile stretched across his lips.

With a flick of the queen's wrist, they were dismissed. Mairi groaned under her breath. She could hear it now, her father spending the evening boasting about how the queen complimented his daughter on her *coiffure*.

The hall was a bustle of lords and ladies standing in circles gossiping, no doubt. Above on the gallery musicians were playing, though the dancing had not yet begun. Mairi searched the faces for someone familiar. She hadn't attended court often, and friends like Janet Cameron rarely visited London, if ever.

A familiar face came from the crowd—unfortunately not a welcome face. "My lady, it is ever so good to see you," said the Countess of Seaforth, grasping Mairi's hands as if she and Mairi were best of friends, which most certainly was not the case. The last time the two had been in the same room, Audrey Kennet, now the Countess of Seaforth, was kissing Mairi's intended.

Completely at a loss for words, Mairi's jaw dropped as she searched for the woman's husband. The earl's formidable size usually made him easy to spot in a crowd, but Seaforth was nowhere to be seen.

To make things worse, Her Ladyship kept ahold of Mairi's hands and looked to Cromartie. "I hope you do not mind my absconding with your daughter before the dancing commences." She raised a fan to her cheek and leaned in. "Ladies' chat, if you will."

Nodding, Da flicked his wrist. "Very well, but stay nearby. I have many introductions to make."

Mairi allowed the woman, who by all rights should be her archenemy, to pull her through the crowd to a window seat. Lady Seaforth sighed as if relieved to be on the outer fringe of the throng. "Yours is the only familiar face I've seen at this entire gathering."

Mairi took a seat beside the countess, still craning her neck and searching the swarm of finely dressed courtiers. "Where is His Lordship?"

"Alas, Seaforth sailed this very morn with the Earl of Dartmouth." Huffing, Audrey fanned herself—it was quite a lovely fan, painted with a pastoral scene. "The queen asked him to be part of an envoy to initiate peace discussions with the members of the Grand Alliance."

Why must Mairi's luck continue to grow worse? She needed Seaforth's influence with her father. Just because he'd intervened to see to Dunn's release, things hadn't been set to rights by far. "'Tis a great honor for him," Mairi said, unable to keep the disappointment from her voice. "I truly hope he is successful in bringing peace to the Continent."

"I hope this venture is successful, indeed. It is ever so lonely to be without him, and he hasn't even been away a whole day as of yet."

Mairi flexed her fingers. A good strangling simply wouldn't do. Did this woman not realize how dreadful she had made Mairi's life? Worse, her words were like rubbing salt into a wound. *Without Seaforth for a day? Try visiting him in your father's gaol, no less, and then traveling to London and enduring the attentions of inquisitive courtiers while being prodded by one's own father.* "I'm certain you must be out of sorts," she mumbled drily.

The countess gave Mairi a long look, then patted her chest. "Forgive me. I didn't lead you over here to talk about my woes. I wanted to say that I have thought about you a great deal since..."

"Since?" Mairi asked.

"Since I married Reid." The woman blushed. "I want you to know I was unaware of Reid's promise until the day I arrived at Brahan Castle and met you."

"Truly?" Mairi held in a snort. That was the very day Seaforth rescinded their betrothal.

"I feel somewhat responsible for your current state of affairs and want to offer my help. I found love and ever so much want to see you happy as well." Lady Audrey patted Mairi's arm. "Were you aware that Seaforth spoke to your father about releasing Mr. MacRae?"

"Da mentioned he sent a missive to Castle Leod, though poor Mr. MacRae will have to endure another fortnight behind bars at least."

"Such a travesty. MacRae is a good man. Never in any way would he deserve to be incarcerated."

"No. His only crime is giving his heart."

"I feel badly for you."

"For me?"

Lady Audrey nodded. "Though I do not regret what transpired between my husband and you, I am not without guilt. And I most certainly sympathize with your plight." She tapped her lips. "Oh dear, I'm afraid I'm not very good at apologizing... Know this: If you should ever require my help, it will be given. All you need to do is ask."

Tingles fanned out across the backs of Mairi's arms. Oddly, she felt little resentment toward this woman. In fact, Audrey seemed quite human and endearing. "If I can manage to survive the next fortnight without my father promising my hand to anyone aside from Duncan MacRae, I will consider myself fortunate."

"What are your plans after?"

Mairi shrugged, though she had thought of little else. "We will return to Castle Leod. And with luck, somehow news of our arrival will reach Eilean Donan."

"Hmm." The countess arched an eyebrow. "It does sound like you have something brewing."

"Brewing, but not yet ready for enactment."

"Once again, if I can assist…"

"You shall be the first to know. In fact, I believe you are the only person in all of Britain who has taken my side."

"Seaforth has your side."

Groaning, Mairi looked to the opulent ceiling. "And he is on the Continent."

Audrey's shoulders dropped. "He is. But not forever. My husband and I would love to see you and MacRae happy."

A contredanse began. The countess raised her fan to her lips and leaned closer. "The only good thing about the earl's departure is that no one will expect me to dance."

"Do you not care for dancing?"

"I'm hopelessly clumsy. I'd much rather be in the orchestra."

Mairi stifled a nervous laugh. "But that would be scandalous."

Audrey gave a knowing roll of her eyes. "Women are only allowed to perform at private recitals. I've heard the same drivel my entire life."

"You must be very accomplished. What, pray tell, do you play?"

"Harpsichord." The countess giggled ever so endearingly. Of all the noblewomen Mairi had met, Audrey Kennet MacKenzie surely had a way of brightening things. "The dance master at my finishing school said I would be better suited for the orchestra to save gentlemen's toes."

"He didn't."

"He most certainly did. Until I met Seaforth, I believed myself to be the stalwart wallflower for any ball."

"I have been at a great many gatherings, and I'll certainly put forth that you are no wallflower, m'lady, and I doubt you ever were."

"There you are," said Da as he pushed through the crowd with the Earl of Buchan on his heels. "I thought I told you to stay nearby."

Mairi sighed. "Goodness, Father, at least we didn't take a stroll in the courtyard."

"Forgive me, my lord," said the countess. "I'm afraid I am not overly fond of crowds. And since Seaforth—"

"Is home ill," Mairi hastily interrupted. Goodness gracious, who knew what cunning father would resort to if he discovered Seaforth was on the Continent. And though Da said he'd dispatched a missive to Castle Leod, she wouldn't be surprised if the letter was still sitting on his writing table awaiting the courier. No, no. It was too easy for something else to go awry.

The orchestra stopped, followed by a round of polite applause.

Buchan stepped forward and bowed. Dressed like an Englishman this eve, he wore ivory silk knee-length breeches with his hose secured in place with ribbon of the same color. Brass buttons shone on his stylish navy doublet tailored to fit perfectly over a gold silk waistcoat topped by an exquisite cravat. Atop his head, a dark brown periwig had not a hair out of place, as if it had been fashioned for this very occasion.

Mairi gulped. She didn't want to be attracted to this man, but of all the courtiers she had met since their arrival in London, Buchan was the most agreeable.

"M'lady, it is invigorating to see you again. I must say you are absolutely radiant this eve."

Mairi bowed her head. "Thank you, m'lord."

He shifted his gaze to Audrey. "I hope we are not interrupting, m'lady."

"Not at all."

Da grasped his lapels and puffed out his chest. "Of course not."

It was impossible not to gape at her father with a frown.

"May I have this dance, Lady Mairi?" asked Buchan.

Watching her father, she placed her palm in the earl's hand and allowed him to help her rise. "I would be delighted," she replied flatly.

"I'll be here should you need a confidant," the countess said as Buchan led her away.

They joined two lines of dancers right before the orchestra commenced a minuet. The earl smiled. Mairi's muscles clenched as she forced a polite smile in return. Curses, the situation was a mess. If she outright spurned every potential suitor, Da would choose someone for her. If she encouraged Buchan, the earl from Aberdeen would think she was actually interested—in a man of forty with *nine* children, the eldest of whom was only three years younger than herself.

It didn't matter that Buchan looked handsome in his finery and danced with flawless precision. He needed a woman who already had experience raising children. He needed a seasoned matron who'd be overjoyed to take on a ready-made family.

As the dance ended, the royal trumpets sounded. All eyes shifted to the throne, where Queen Anne stood with her cabinet members in attendance. "I bid you all a happy celebration. I am afraid my dancing days have passed. I expect the young among us to draw pleasure from the music and dancing as much as I have enjoyed watching you. *Adieu.*"

While everyone in the hall reverently bowed and curtsied as Anne gracefully swept out the door, Buchan leaned toward Mairi's ear. "Poor dear. Since the death of Prince George, she has grown goutier and more listless every time I see her. I fear Her Majesty's days are numbered."

A stone sank to the pit of Mairi's stomach. The country had been at relative peace during Anne's reign because she was a descendant of the Stuart line. Her father spoke of the succession endlessly—out of both sides of his mouth. At times he would side with Seaforth and assert that James, Anne's exiled brother and rightful king, should ascend the throne. But when in the company of Protestants, he spoke like a Campbell, supporting the queen's fear of popery. When the time came, the only thing Mairi knew was that her father would be on whichever side he thought would win. And his decision might very well split Clan MacKenzie down the middle. Moreover, now that there would be no alliance with the House of Seaforth, Cromartie was not as honor-bound to side with his grandnephew.

The evening proceeded in a whirlwind. Mairi was not allowed a moment of respite while Da introduced seemingly half the men in attendance. The Earl of Buchan stood along the wall like a hawk, watching intently. The poor man obviously was desperate to find a wife, and his eagerness did nothing to endear him.

Mairi's new shoes made her feet ache, and by the time the tower clock struck the tenth hour, she wished the orchestra would pack up and head for home. Nonetheless, aside from a few brief intermissions, they tirelessly played on. Dancing with a crusty old viscount whose name she couldn't recall, Mairi was forced to tap a kerchief to her nose as often as possible to prevent herself from being overcome by the exorbitant amount of cologne water the man wore.

As the music ended, she halfheartedly curtsied. "Thank you, m'lord."

"Lady Mairi," a masculine voice uttered behind her, a voice that made gooseflesh rise across her skin. A voice so deep, it resonated throughout the hollow cavity in her chest.

Hands perspiring, Mairi gulped. Unable to allow herself to hope, she slowly turned.

In the blink of an eye, her heart beat like the gossamer wings of a hummingbird.

Handsome as a gallant knight, Dunn drew a finger to his lips, bidding her to remain silent.

Covering her mouth, she nodded as a muffled, high-pitched squeal escaped her lips. "What? How?" Her fingers trembled, her breathing unsteady. If she were not seeing him with her own eyes, she never would have believed he was there.

"I'll tell you all later." He bowed and offered his hand. "May I have the pleasure of this dance?" His luminous eyes bored through her like beams of light. Gracious, they were even more intense than she'd remembered.

"You may." As she placed her fingers in his palm, she wished she could run them around his waist and pull him into a fierce embrace. Indeed, he looked braw in a finely pleated kilt, velvet doublet, and crisp neckerchief. "Father's missive requesting your release cannot have reached Castle Leod. In fact, I'd wager he hasn't yet dispatched it."

"If I ken your da, he would do everything in his power to ensure I wasn't released until the festivities ended." He assumed a position for an allemande, tottering a bit. Good Lord, he looked powerful and commanding, his tartan and doublet every bit as stylish as any man's in the hall. "I had a bit of help from Robert Grant. In fact, it wouldn't surprise me if your father received word of my escape within the week."

"Escape? Was anyone injured?"

"Only me." He glanced downward. "Shot in the heel."

"Shot?" Mairi looked down, her stomach churning as he stepped with a pronounced limp. "And you risked traveling? You should be abed."

"Och, a wee graze isn't about to turn me into an invalid. Especially not when my woman is being paraded through London whilst her father searches for her husband."

"You amaze me."

"Is that so, lass?" With a wicked grin, Dunn waggled his eyebrows and grasped Mairi's elbow, leading her away from the dancers and toward the courtyard. "Come. I've much to say and we're not safe here."

Chapter Twenty-Seven

*B*efore Dunn stepped into the courtyard, he caught a glimpse of Cromartie and another overdressed peacock he recognized as the Earl of Buchan. The two men flailed their arms and gestured toward them. Clearly, the earl was smitten with Mairi. It had been written on the man's face as they were dancing. Doubtless, Cromartie was concocting gossip to incite the crowd. And right now, the last thing Dunn needed was to run from a mob of misinformed courtiers or, worse, armed dragoons. He might be able to outrun anyone when he had two healthy feet, but with his injury, he doubted he'd be able to beat an old woman across the street.

Grasping Her Ladyship's elbow, he hastened to take her outside. A blast of cool wind hit his face as he quickly searched for a place for a modicum of privacy. "Over here."

Mairi giggled. "In the egress? 'Tis scandalous."

He stopped. "Forgive me, m'lady. I wouldn't want to tarnish your reputation."

Shaking her head, she pulled him along. "I think it would be thrilling—have all of London talking about the earl's daughter caught kissing a Highland chieftain in the shadows of Whitehall's courtyard." She pulled him into the egress and grasped both of his hands. "I'm so happy to see you, my entire body is tingling."

Unable to restrain himself, he tugged her into him and wrapped her in an embrace. With one deep breath all his tension shed from his shoulders. She smelled of sweet wildflowers and salvation, and he could do naught but cradle her in his arms and drink her in. "Och, *mo leannan*. I cannot tell you how happy I am to finally hold you in my arms. Ye feel like heaven."

As she raised her chin, he plied her lips with a kiss.

"Ah, Dunn, you have made me the happiest lass in all of London."

He grinned with a chuckle. "Seeing your bonny face makes all the trials worthwhile."

"Tell me what happened at Castle Leod."

"Before we left Eilean Donan, I sent a missive to Robert Grant and requested his army remain on alert— that way, no one suspected me of marching the MacRae men and posing a threat. But do not worry, lass, I escaped without killing any MacKenzies. Ram and Curran slipped into the guardhouse. Gave the sentry a good ache in the head, took his keys, and opened the door to my cell."

"And how were you injured?"

"Fleeing. A musket ball clipped my heel—shot the bottom of my boot clean off. But I don't want to talk about that. Not when there's so little time." He tightened his embrace and buried his face in her tresses. "Dear God, I've missed you every moment of every day." Heaven help him, he never wanted to let her go.

Mairi tilted her face up to him, her delicate lips glistening in the moonlight, her eyes wide and incandescent. Dunn's heart swelled. Holding this woman in his arms made everything worth the effort. He might be insane, but he would endure Cromartie's gaol, he would withstand musket balls and tempests while riding in the driving rain. Whatever she needed, whatever *they* needed to convince all of Christendom they should spend the rest of their lives together, he would do.

Closing his eyes, he dipped his chin and covered her mouth with a claiming, devouring kiss. Joined with her in a sensual dance only the pair of them shared and savored. His entire soul ached as he kissed her, craving to possess her. His heart bursting with the enormity of his love for the bonny woman in his arms. He swirled his tongue with Mairi's as her low sigh curled like a melody around them.

But his euphoria did not last long.

The hair on the back of Dunn's neck pricked as his mind registered shouting. People swiftly moved toward them, a light growing nearer.

"Mairi?" he whispered.

"Mm?"

"I'm unable to stand and fight this eve, but I will not be rebuffed by your father ever again. He has no grounds on which to accuse me and no grounds on which to refuse me. I am a man of property and I can provide you anything you desire. Anything."

"I only want you."

"Be ready."

"Release my daughter at once!" shouted Cromartie, gesturing to the crowd. "You all are witnesses to this debauchery."

Pushing Mairi behind him, Dunn wrapped his fingers

around his dirk. He would have justice and let the truth speak for itself. "I am Dunn MacRae, chieftain of Clan MacRae, defenders of Clan MacKenzie, which includes this ungrateful clodpoll. I witnessed him, the Earl of Cromartie, hold a dagger to his own daughter's throat and draw blood. He is a disgrace to our great kingdom. I have asked for Lady Mairi's hand in marriage and she has accepted my suit. But this pompous flapdragon does not deem me worthy."

The crowd gasped while all eyes shifted to the earl.

"Blast you for your impertinence. I will never allow a mere laird to wed my daughter."

"But I love him!" Mairi slipped to Dunn's side and squared her shoulders. "I want to marry him."

Cromartie lunged for her arm. Before the earl reached her, Dunn darted in and grasped the bastard by the throat. "You will never wrongfully imprison me again. Men like you are parasites. You harbor not a care for your daughter's well-being. You are a fortune seeker of the worst sort. You would sell her to the highest bidder without remorse. I would like to crush you here and now, but I will not. Do you ken why?"

Gasping for air and shaking, the earl garbled indecipherably.

"Because you are Lady Mairi's father and I have sworn to protect you. You are alive because you are under Seaforth's shield." He leaned in so his face was a hair's breadth from the sniveling maggot. "Remember that when you're in your bed at night. Seaforth is the only reason you have not been reckoned with, for I do not take lightly to someone who incarcerates me for naught."

"S-stop!" the earl croaked.

Dunn shoved the earl away and drew his sword. "I want no bloodshed this night."

Behind him Mairi shrieked. "Release me!"

Dunn spun, dirk and sword ready for a strike. The Earl of Buchan had pulled her into an armlock. Not about to back down, Dunn sauntered forward. "I warn you, m'lord. Release Her Ladyship now and I will not run you through."

The man shuffled back, taking Mairi with him.

Dragoons charged into the courtyard at a run.

Coughing, Cromartie thrust his finger toward Dunn. "Seize him. An uninvited guest has disrupted the eve's activities!"

"I have done nothing of the sort," Dunn shouted, swinging his sword in an arc as twenty soldiers closed in, muskets at their shoulders.

"Is that right, mate?" asked a sergeant. "Lower your blade now afore I lodge a musket ball in your skull."

"Take him to the Tower!" shouted Cromartie.

"No!" Mairi shrieked, struggling to free herself. "He has committed no crime."

The barrels of two muskets pushed into Dunn's temples as the sergeant closed in. "You're walking out of here nice and slow, mate." He inclined his head to one of his men. "Seize his weapons, Ensign, and bind his wrists."

Dunn's gaze locked with Mairi's as they marched him away. "Remember the words from my letter."

She again struggled, but Buchan still had a firm hold on her.

Forced into the back of a barred wagon, Dunn seethed. Cromartie had struck him again, and with no grounds.

After the wagon was under way, a coach stopped them. Dunn craned his neck, but it was too dark to see anything.

Words were exchanged with the sergeant—muffled, indiscernible words.

God's bones, there he was again, behind bars, but now he had no contingency plan. Blast it all, he should have taken Mairi away from the ball before he wrapped her in his arms. He was smarter than that. *Jesus Saint Christopher Christ.*

At a snail's pace, the wagon ambled along. When the brooding outline of the Tower of London came into sight, he thought for certain they'd stop, but the wagon continued over the Thames. After another few miles passed, Dunn shook the bars. "Where are you taking me?"

No one replied while the cart creaked and ambled along the cobbled road for another hour, possibly more.

"This is far enough," said the sergeant, and the wagon stopped in the middle of nowhere. No lights aside from the single lantern swinging from the driver's seat. And a grove of trees prevented Dunn from any chance of gaining his bearings.

One of the soldiers hopped down and opened the cage door. "This is where you get off, mate."

"Here?"

"Aye."

Dunn squinted, trusting no one. "You've taken my side?"

"Not at all. I believe you caused a stir at the ball, but the Countess of Seaforth paid us not to incarcerate you." The sergeant tossed down Dunn's sword and dirk. "Just ensure you stay away from the Earl of Cromartie, else I'll have no choice but to lock you away and let the magistrate decide your fate."

Dunn picked up his weapons and secured them while the wagon rolled away.

*Audrey must have been in the coach that stopped us.
God bless that woman.*

* * *

Mairi paced the chamber floor, her mind racing. Yet again
her father saw fit to lock her within. Moreover, it was
midmorning and Aela still hadn't brought up breakfast.

Does my father intend to starve me into submission?

She had been in Dunn's arms last eve, and she'd lost
him again. Where had the dragoons taken him? The
Tower? She bit her knuckle and looked toward the window. If only there were a trellis leading up to her third-
floor window, she would climb down.

If ever she needed Reid MacKenzie, it was now. *Blast
Seaforth for leaving. Again.* Must the earl continually
disappear when he was most needed? Obviously Mairi
meant nothing to him and never had.

There must be something more I can do. Mairi clasped
her hands and paced until something popped into her
head. All this time she had been cursing the man, but she
might still be able to seek help from Seaforth's house.
How can Lady Audrey help? Surely Her Ladyship had influence at court—though she hadn't been a countess for
long. Her father had been a well-respected businessman,
however. Perhaps she knew a number of influential people in London.

With a loud knock, Da burst through the door, leaving
it ajar behind him. "Now you've gone and ruined everything!" he shouted, waving a piece of parchment in the air.

Mairi spread her palms to her sides. "How could I
have done anything locked in this chamber without even
a crust of bread?"

He thrust the document into her hands. "Before MacRae showed his face, I was convinced Buchan would make an offer of marriage. But he took one look at MacRae and the spineless weasel is heading for home. Says he's not ready to wed." Da shook his fist. "Nine bloody children! The man needs a wife in the most extreme way."

Mairi glanced at the missive. "What he needs is a governess, perhaps two." Not that she would ever be civil to Buchan again after he held her against her will last eve.

"What would you know about the Earl of Buchan's needs?"

Who gives a fig about the earl's needs at a time like this? Buchan is perfectly capable of solving his own affairs.

About to jump out of her skin, Mairi changed tack. "Please, Father. Must you continue to behave like a villain? Do you want me to hate you for the rest of my days?"

"Oh, so it is I who is the evil one? I, your sire, the man responsible for your enduring happiness and the longevity of our clan's line? I say you are being *childish*."

"I vehemently disagree. I know what is in my heart. It is full of love for Mr. MacRae and none other."

"I have made my decision, and you will *not* marry that man."

Mairi thrust her fists to her sides. "Why?"

"Because he's the hired muscle for that louse my cousin called his son. I do not want you aligned with MacRae *or* Seaforth."

"Though Seaforth was good enough for me for all but a few months in the past one and twenty years. My word, you are a hypocrite. Do you aim to stand against them when it comes time to decide the succession?"

With a twitch of his head, Da's eyes narrowed. "What drivel is this? Has MacRae put such thoughts into your head?"

"No, Father. If you haven't noticed, I am quite capable of thinking for myself." She pushed past him. "I am leaving."

"I forbid it!" He caught her arm and yanked her back, putting himself between her and the open door.

"Unhand me!" Jerking her arm toward the weak point of his grip, Mairi freed herself and lunged to the side.

"I have had enough of your impertinence." Da drew his dirk, pointing it at her heart. "Until you are wed, I am your lord and master and you will obey me."

Trembling with ire, Mairi focused on the knife. "Or you'll run me through?"

"Perhaps. Or I will petition the queen to lock MacRae in the Tower and toss the key in the Thames."

"For falling in love?" Mairi dared to take a step to the side, planning her next move. "Tell me, where in all of Christendom is that a crime?"

Da's eyes shifted. Mairi lunged, grabbed the hilt, and twisted it against his thumb. The weapon popped from his hand. Shifting her gaze to the door, she grasped the dirk with the point downward and sprinted out the door.

"Mairi MacKenzie! You come back this instant!" Her father's voice boomed from behind with the clatter of his footsteps.

But she didn't stop.

As she hit the stairs, he yelled again, "You will be left without a dowry!"

His threat only served to spur her on faster.

Chapter Twenty-Eight

*E*xhausted, Dunn let himself in through the kitchen door at the rear of Seaforth's town house. A loaf of bread sat on the counter. He broke it, shoving a bite into his mouth, devouring it like he'd been starved for a sennight. It had taken him all night to hike back to London, but he'd made it. As soon as he splashed a bit of water on his face, he aimed to organize Seaforth's men and break down Cromartie's door. Christ, if Mairi weren't within, he would put the earl's town house to fire and sword and face the consequences.

While he planned his attack, yearning to face the earl man-to-man, brawn against brawn, a ferocious pounding came at the front door.

Dunn wiped his mouth, his ears homing in on the butler's footsteps hastening through the entry. "Lady—"

"I must see the countess at once!" Good God, he knew that voice. He loved that voice.

"Mairi!" Dunn bellowed, dropping the bread and bounding toward the entrance hall.

"Dunn!" Her face brightened with surprise. "You're here."

"Just arrived."

She ran into his arms. "My father locked me in my chamber." Out of breath, she stepped back and waved a dirk through the air. "H-he threatened me with this!"

"Again?"

"My stars," said Lady Seaforth as she hastened down the stairs.

"Blast it all. I should not have tarried last eve. If I'd hastened to take you away from Whitehall, we would be boarding a transport home." Dunn gently removed the knife from Mairi's hand and pulled her into his arms. "I'll not let him touch you. Ye are safe now, lass."

"Not for long," said the butler from the door. "Cromartie is marching half a dozen men up the road.

"Quickly, out the back." Lady Seaforth ushered them through the corridor. "Saddle my gelding for Lady Mairi. I'll do what I can to stall."

Dunn clasped the countess's hands and hastily kissed them. "I owe you a debt of gratitude, m'lady."

She shook her head, smiling warmly. "Oh no, not after everything you've done for Reid. Now go!"

Grasping Mairi's hand, Dunn raced through the kitchen, gritting his teeth against the needling pain in his heel. He had his woman by his side, and there was no chance he'd let her go. Not this time. Not ever. They dashed out the rear door, across the gardens, and into the stable. "Laddie!" Dunn called to the stable hand. "Rig up Lady Seaforth's mount. Haste. 'Tis urgent."

Dunn found Beastie in his stall chomping at a

trough filled with hay. "Sorry to interrupt your meal, big fella, but we must ride." By the time he tightened the girth on his saddle, the stable hand was helping Mairi to mount.

"I ken she's here!" Cromartie's voice roared from the house.

"You will not come into my home and make baseless accusations. I do not care if you are the king of creation; I will tolerate no more of your beastliness!" Her Ladyship shouted so loud, the timbers in the stable shook.

"She has a backbone, Seaforth's wee lass." Dunn grinned and looked to Mairi. "Are you ready to ride?"

"I've been ready for days and days."

He gave a nod to the lad, who then opened the door to the alley.

At a canter, Dunn led them over London's cobblestones toward the Thames, away from Cromartie and his men. Since the earl was on foot, they had a good head start—one Dunn intended to put to his advantage.

Forced to slow to a walk as they approached the congestion on London Bridge, Mairi rode in beside him. "Where are we going? The bridge will take us south."

"That's the last thing your father will expect, am I right?"

"True, but Scotland is north."

"Aye, but the Chatham dockyard is southeast. I reckon we'll find a transport to Glasgow there and then another to Loch Alsh."

"We're sailing to Eilean Donan?"

"Taking a roundabout route, but aye, I reckon we'll be sitting before home's hearth in a fortnight, perhaps a wee bit more." Together, they rode down the tunnel of shops and houses built along the bridge while merchants bid them to stop and sample their wares. London Bridge was like a city within the city, and it stank of piss and rot.

Halfway, Dunn glanced behind at the swarm of activity. Thank God there wasn't a redcoat in sight. Cromartie was thrown off the scent. For now. If, in all his years serving Seaforth, Dunn had learned nothing else, it was to never underestimate the cunning of his enemy. Heaven help him, he wanted to stop in the middle of the bridge, pull Mairi into his arms, and declare his undying love. He wanted to find the nearest priest and make her his wife. But stopping now was too great a risk.

* * *

Dunn figured they'd been riding for nearly five hours when Mairi teetered and wiped her hand across her eyes.

"Are you unwell?" he asked.

"I'm hungry. Da did not allow me to break my fast."

The lout. "Unforgivable." His jaw twitched as he clamped his fingers tighter around his reins. Bloody hell, Cromartie would never cease to be an arse? "The signpost said Dartford is a mile on. We ought to be able to find an inn or an alehouse there."

"Are you upset?" Mairi asked.

"Angry with myself. I'd hoped your father would see reason, but now I realize that will never happen. I once asked for your hand like a gentleman, and he convinced you to refuse me. He has made his position clear. Forgive me, Mairi, but there is no longer a chance for me to settle things with your Da amicably. There's no chance of gaining his blessing."

"There is nothing to forgive. My father has also lost a daughter. I never want to see him again."

"Such a travesty for any man to place wealth ahead of clan and kin."

"I do not understand it. I remember when Da received his earldom. I was but thirteen years of age. Before, he was the Viscount of Tarbat, clearly below and beholden to Seaforth. Now that he is on equal footing and the marriage agreement has been rescinded, it is as if he has adopted a maniacal desire to further his lot. Is it not enough to be an earl? Is it not enough to be the lord of estates so vast, one cannot ride across them in one day's time?"

"I cannot say. Though I have never envied Seaforth for his exalted rank. It seems as a clan chief, I have everything he has without the pomp. The queen hardly kens I exist, and I prefer it that way."

"I think I do as well. Did you see the courtiers last eve, strutting in their finery, each one trying to outdo the other?"

"Unfortunately, court has always been about impressing, posturing, and outdoing."

"Funny, but I think my father was happier in those early days afore he ascended to his earldom."

"Now that, I believe." Dunn pointed to a stone building with a shingle out front. "There's an alehouse ahead and a stable beside it. The horses can enjoy a bit of hay while we eat."

"Do you think Da will come this way?"

"I doesn't matter what I think. I learned ages ago, it is best not to guess what any man will do. When you're running, there are but two rules: Do nothing to draw attention to yourself, and suspect everyone."

"Have you been on the run a great deal?"

"In these perilous times, if a man stands up for something he feels strongly about, sooner or later he'll end up on the wrong side of right. And then he'll have no choice but to head for the Highlands and wait."

"Or take up arms."

"Aye, if there's no other way."

After they dismounted and arranged for the horses to be fed, Dunn escorted Mairi to the alehouse. "Have you ever been in such an establishment?"

"Once. I was with Da, and the only ladies were unsavory types."

"He took you into an alehouse filled with wenches?"

"I suppose he didn't have much choice at the time, much like we do not now."

"All right then, stay near me. Look no one in the eye. We'll eat, have a pint of ale, and be on our way." He pulled open the heavy medieval door with blackened iron nails and ushered Mairi inside.

An unkempt candelabra hung from the ceiling, encased in wax. Midafternoon, there weren't many patrons. Three men stood at the bar who looked to be fishermen and, as Dunn neared, the stench confirmed it. On the other side of the room, a table of men carried on loudly. A pair of serving wenches were seated on laps, but nary a one looked their way.

"Where do you hail from, friend?" asked the barman. Though the question was a simple one, the man's dark stare filled with distrust.

"Glasgow," Dunn said. "Traveling home."

"What brings you to these parts?" The man leaned over the bar, giving Dunn's kilt a deprecating look. "We don't see many costumes like yours in Dartford."

"I'd reckon not."

"What's your business here?"

"Just passing through." Dunn tightened his grip on Mairi's arm. "Have you a bowl of pottage and a pint of ale for each of us?"

"That can be arranged." The barman pointed to a few empty tables near the door. "Sit over there and don't cause no trouble."

"We?" Mairi asked, drawing her hand to her chest. "Cause trouble?"

The man behind the bar the man poured the ale. "Beg your pardon, madam, but any woman walks in that door looking tastier than a honeyed crisp had best stay close to her man and keep her mouth shut."

Dunn's hackles stood on end as he took the glasses and ushered the lass away, trying not to limp. "We do not want any trouble. Just a meal and we'll be on our way."

After holding a rickety chair for Mairi, Dunn moved around the table and sat with his back to the wall, where he was able to keep an eye on the activity. In an establishment like this, a man might end up with a knife in his back if he wasn't careful. He reached under the table and grasped her delicate hand. "If we didn't need to eat, I'd teach that barman a lesson about speaking to ladies."

"'Tis best if he doesn't ken I'm a lady," she whispered.

"Aye, but you should be given your due respect, highborn or nay." Dunn's gaze swept across the scene. Two more burly tinkers entered, looking around as if they were prowling for wenches. Dunn knew the look. All men did.

"Don't turn around," he whispered, sliding his fingers over the hilt of his dirk as one shifted his gaze to Mairi. Then the rogue leaned to the side for a better look.

Dunn slid his chair back far enough to display his weapons—and his brawn. It didn't hurt to have a chest as wide as a horse's arse when rubbing elbows with folks who lived in the gutter.

The man's gaze slowly shifted from the back of Mairi's head to Dunn. MacRae gave a thin-lipped nod, telling the bastard to move along.

"You there, Harry. 'Tis your turn to buy us a round," a man hollered from the table of ruffians.

Sniffing, Harry smirked and arched an eyebrow before he sauntered off to join his colleagues.

Mairi leaned forward and cupped a hand to her mouth. "Tell me why my hackles are standing on end."

"I reckon the barman's comments about honeyed crisps were founded."

She shuddered, clutching her arms across her chest. "How vulgar."

A woman pushed through a door behind the bar carrying a tray with two bowls. "Lamb pottage for the pair of you. You'll never taste better this side of London," she said as she walked toward them.

Clasping her hands, Mairi sat a bit straighter. "Sounds delicious."

The woman placed the bowls and spoons on the table. "More ale?"

Mairi nodded. "Yes—"

"No thank you." Dunn picked up his spoon. "We mustn't tarry."

"Where are you pair headed?"

"Glasgow. We're catching a transport from Chatham," Mairi said, seemingly impressed with herself. The lass clearly didn't understand how not to draw attention to her person.

"Where is that?" asked the woman.

"Up north," Dunn said, flicking his wrist at Mairi. "Eat up, wife. Else we'll be riding until past dark."

Mairi's eyes grew round while she took a bite. "Mm. This is very good."

"See? I wouldn't lie to the likes of you." With a contented smile, the woman headed back to the kitchen. Dunn figured with a remark like that, the wench was accustomed to telling tall tales.

"Eat fast," he growled, watching the men across the room. During the entire interchange with the serving wench, they'd been looked on with undue interest.

"Shall I wipe my mouth on my sleeve?" Mairi whispered. "It might make me look uncouth."

"Just eat."

The crowd grew while they finished their meal. Dunn stood and held the chair for Her Ladyship. "Do you think they might have a privy out back?"

"No."

"But I have to go," she hissed through her teeth.

"We'll find a shrub on the way to Chatham." He tugged her arm. They had made use of Mother Nature's shrubbery many times before.

Mairi followed without another word, thank heaven for small mercies. Dunn always trusted his intuition whenever he visited a strange place, and right now his senses were charged and telling him to ride. In all honesty, he was probably being overly cautious. The men across the alehouse had mostly kept to themselves aside from stealing glances. Good God, if he'd been among the party, he would have been looking for a chance to espy Mairi's face.

He grumbled under his breath.

Do not start doubting yourself. If Cromartie convinced the queen's dragoons to search high and low for Her Ladyship, men may be riding in their direction at this very moment. And if not, word could spread via the waterways as it always did. And they were heading to Chatham. Aye, the town was east of London, but it was still on the Thames.

The alehouse door screeched behind them.

"If it isn't the blackguard wearing a kilt and showing off his weapons."

Dunn cringed at the menacing voice—that of a braying ignoramus looking for a fight. Aye, drink had a way of making foolish men bold. He stopped, turned, and pulled Mairi to his rear. Damnation, he'd forgotten to hide his limp. "Hello, friend. I'm afraid my wife and I are about to collect our horses and ride." He was careful not to tell anyone where they were headed, though Mairi had made a slip earlier on.

"Scots aren't welcome here." The unflappable codfish moseyed forward.

"Aye? Then 'tis fortunate we're leaving," Dunn countered.

"What say you?" the man persisted.

Dunn crossed his arms. "I said if my wife and I are not welcome, we'll make haste to be on our way." He watched the man move closer while his accomplices stood on the footpath outside the alehouse looking on with smirks on their faces. They'd called the scrapper Harry. He was obviously the leader—beefy arms, but he had a gut like a pregnant cow.

Dunn was all too familiar with men the likes of Harry. Bigger than most, they bolstered their pride by picking fights. And the reward for this one was too much for the bastard to pass by. No doubt the man had noticed Dunn's limp and saw him as an easy mark.

Harry raised his fists. "Sorry, *Scottie*, but you cannot leave Dartford without paying the toll."

"Ballocks, ye have me over a barrel. How much?" It galled Dunn to no end to fork over coin, but a fight would draw more attention than they needed—especially any nearby dragoons.

"A pound."

Jesus Saint Christopher Christ, a farthing or two would be ample, but a pound? "That's robbery."

"I meant a pound of flesh," Harry continued, raising his fists. "Cast your weapons aside, and face me man-to-man."

"Can you not see, he is injured," Mairi piped up from behind.

Dunn sliced his hand through the air. "Silence." He pushed up his sleeves. "You don't want to do this."

"I do. And I will."

One of the buggers by the door sniggered.

Dunn looked toward the coward and pointed. "When I'm finished with this varlet, you'll be next."

Harry removed his knife belt.

Ah, hell. Now if Dunn tried to run, there would be anarchy for certain.

Might as well have it over with.

Dunn removed his dirk and sword and handed them to Mairi. "Hold these."

"You cannot be serious," she whispered, taking the weapons.

"What choice do I have?"

She gulped and glanced to the stables. That's right, it was even riskier to try to run. The horses were in the

stalls with their bridles removed and their girth straps
loosened. Pursing her lips, she gave him a look that said,
Do not fail me.

A drop of rain splashed on his face as Dunn turned and
raised his fists.

Harry rushed him. In less time than it took to blink,
Dunn analyzed the man's attack. Going for brute strength,
the bull aimed to restrain Dunn by the arms as he tackled
him to the ground—an aggressive starting move, and if
unsuccessful, it was stupid as well.

One step before impact, Dunn dropped into a deep
squat. Harry's arms hissed through the air, connecting
with nothing while MacRae used the man's momentum
to flip him onto his back. The movement stretched his
heel, tearing at the newly formed scab, but Dunn was
all in now. Steeling his mind against the pain, rage shot
through his blood as he pounced, jabbing fists into the
man's pasty face. The dastard wheezed, trying to catch
his breath, his body flailing beneath Dunn's crushing
legs.

Harry took an uppercut to the jaw, his eyes rolling
back. Then his head cocked to the side and fell limp.

One varlet down.

Dunn hopped to his feet, looking to the alehouse door
for another challenger. No one moved, but their gazes
shifted, and Dunn knew to where.

Ice shot through his blood with Mairi's scream.

Harry's partner in crime grabbed her by the wrist and
started for the alley.

"Stop!" In a bold move, the lass dug in her heels,
jerked back, and twisted her arm free while Dunn barreled toward them.

The coward's face filled with terror before Dunn's

fist met his temple. In one blow, the man dropped, out cold.

The buggers crowding the alehouse door stood motionless.

Dunn reached for Mairi's hand. "Haste afore someone else tries to be a hero."

Chapter Twenty-Nine

*M*airi stood with her hands clasped, trying to play the part of a good matron while the harbormaster at the Chatham dockyard shook his head and frowned. "'Tis after six. There's not another merchant ship sailing afore the morrow."

"What about a naval transport?" Dunn asked.

Mairi glanced out to the ships moored in the Thames. The enormous, heavily gunned galleon was one of Her Majesty's fleet for certain.

The harbormaster pointed to the same ship. "The *Royal Sovereign* will be sailing across the channel one day hence. She's headed for battle, that one."

Dunn pursed his lips. "Very well, then which ships *are* sailing come morn?"

"There's a whaling boat headed for Newcastle at dawn and a transport scheduled to leave for Portsmouth at half past nine. And there's a handful of fishing boats, but they all will return to Chatham."

"We'll book two passages on the transport to Portsmouth, if you please."

Once Dunn reserved a berth, he led Mairi to the King's Arms Inn near the waterfront. Inside, the alehouse bustled with activity and boisterous laughter. A matron with a jolly face stopped. "You pair look like you could each use a tankard of ale."

"Aye, madam, a room for me and my wife, and a meal as well."

"You are in luck. We have only one room available. It will be a shilling for the meals and ale, and one shilling sixpence for the room."

Dunn pulled the coin from his sporran. "Done. Can you have a lad bring the meal up to our room?"

A shiver coursed across Mairi's skin. *Our room.* If only they were truly husband and wife. If only they could live the rest of their days at Eilean Donan without fear of reprisal from her father.

"Weary travelers, are you?" the matron asked as she started up the stairs, pulling a ring of keys from her apron pocket. "I think you'll find the bed to your liking, though it is a bit narrow. Where do you hail from?"

"Scotland," said Dunn.

"My, you are a long way from home."

"We are."

"What brings you to Chatham?"

"Business—cattle."

"Drovers, are you?"

"Aye." Dunn gave no more information than necessary.

On the second floor, the woman stopped and looked to Mairi. "How long have you pair been married?"

"It has only been a month." She looked at Dunn with a smile, though inside she felt as if she'd just lied to Moses.

The matron opened a door with a knowing smile. "Ah, newly wed. I understand why you need your privacy."

"My thanks," said Dunn. "When can we expect the lad with our meal?"

"I'll send him up straightaway. 'Tis a farthing if you'd like him to light the fire."

"Please." He paid the woman and closed the door behind her.

Mairi moved into the chamber, rubbing her arms. It was stark at best. The woman hadn't diminished the size of the bed. Pushed against the wall, it was barely the width of Dunn's shoulders. An old wooden table with two chairs sat near a small stone hearth. The room was no more inviting than servant's quarters.

Dunn used a flint to light a lamp on the table. "This will suffice for the night."

"Mm-hmm." Mairi strode to the window and looked down to the alley. Straight below, pigs wallowed in a sty, the mire akin to the moral impurity suddenly churning throughout her insides. No matter how much she wanted to be with Dunn, this charade didn't sit well with her. Things weren't the same as they'd been at his castle. Mayhap because they were on the run. It seemed like every time they were out and about, someone wanted to take advantage of her, or fight Dunn, or swindle them in some way.

"Apologies," he said in a low tone. "It was presumptuous of me to assume we would share." Moving behind her, he placed a hand on her shoulder—a big, warm, powerful hand. "I should sleep on the floor."

Mairi glanced to the hardwood. "I want..."

"What?"

She shook her head. Too many confusing emotions twisted her heart.

"Tell me what troubles you," he whispered.

"I want to be with you more than anything. I want to be your wife, but parading across England under the pretense of being joined in holy matrimony is akin to blasphemy." It made her feel dirty, and she ever so much wanted to be *righteous*, especially in her father's eyes.

"Lying does not sit well with me, either." Dunn slid his gentle hands around her waist, his breath caressing her neck. "If I could marry you this night, I would not hesitate."

A knock came at the door. "I have your tray, sir."

Mairi sighed. She should ask Dunn to wait until they were wed before she allowed him into her bed again. But the floor looked hard and uncomfortable, and he was injured as well.

He opened the door and ushered the lad inside. "Leave the tray on the table."

"Yes, sir. And the fire?"

"Aye, quickly now." Dunn held the chair for Mairi. "Perhaps you'll feel better after you've eaten."

As she sat, she nodded. But eating was the last thing on her mind. She'd waited days and days to be reunited with Dunn again, but not like this. She wanted everyone to be happy—mayhap even her father. She wanted a wedding with an enormous gathering of the clans. She didn't want to hide in a dingy room above an alehouse, pretending she was living in happily wedded bliss.

The Highlander sat in the chair opposite. He placed a plate with a steak and vegetables in front of her, then a tankard of ale, then broke the loaf of bread and put half on her plate. "Eat."

She picked up the bread and nibbled a bite. "I'm not very hungry."

After the lad lit the fire, he slipped out and Dunn bolted the door behind him. "We shouldn't be bothered again, though you ought to try to eat your fill. Who kens what the fare will be like when we're at sea."

The floorboards creaked as he moved back to the table. Rather than sit, he bent down and kissed her cheek. "Worry not, my love. Time has a way of softening the will of men. Even the will of hardened earls."

She grasped his fingers and kissed his palm. She closed her eyes, and a flood of emotion thrummed through her heart. When she'd fled London with Dunn, she'd been intent on running, driven to follow him out of the city. But now reality hit with the force of a blow between the eyes. "Tell me you love me," she whispered.

"I love you more than life." He cradled her head against his abdomen. "Are you worried about your da?"

"No..." That wasn't truthful. Taking a deep breath, she nodded. "Aye. I want him to accept us."

"I ken you do, but only he can overcome the hatred in his heart."

"Do you think he hates me?"

"Nay, how could a father hate a daughter as loving and bonny as you?" Dunn smoothed his hand up and down Mairi's back, easing the worry. "I am your family now. I will provide for you always."

"I want to be with you so much."

"Then take me."

"I want to, but things are not the same as they were when we shared intimacy at Eilean Donan." Mairi glanced from wall to wall. "This...this place cheapens the beauty of our love, and I never want that to happen."

He gave her a quizzical look. "Cheapens?"

She shook her head. "I must sound daft, but after all

we've been through this day, I need..." Her tongue tied. Goodness, she was so tired, she found no words to describe her feelings.

"You need to take a breath, as it were." Dunn's Adam's apple bobbed. "What we share *is* pure, divine. No one in all of Christendom can tear down our bond. Our love is greater than an ocean. It can withstand anything."

"Do you mean that?"

"You have my solemn oath, m'lady, and once given, it can never be rescinded." He slid into his seat. "I want to prove the depth of my love over and over. Let us remain chaste until we are wed."

The knot binding her heart loosened a little. But as her gaze slowly lowered from his smoldering eyes to the dark brown tuft of hair peeking above the V of his collar, the pull of desire swirled deep in her loins. But this time she must resist. "Chaste. It will not be easy but it will be right."

* * *

Dunn's hip ground into the unyielding floorboards. He tried to sleep while the day's events replayed in his mind over and over again. Why must Mairi's father be so obstinate? For the love of God, he'd forced them to flee London like common criminals. When would Cromartie realize his battle was lost? The man possessed everything, riches, lands, and good health. He stood as a favorite with the queen. In truth, Cromartie had been a more successful politician than most Scottish nobles during Anne's reign, even though his politics bobbed like a cork in the surf. Dunn had oft heard the earl avow his support of James Frances Edward Stuart to Seaforth, though Cromartie's actions indicated the opposite. When the queen was laid to rest and the topic of the succession came to a head, Dunn suspected Cromartie would turn his back on the Tory party and side with the Whigs.

Is that why he is so adamant about keeping Mairi and me apart?

The twist of Dunn's gut confirmed his misgivings. In fact, Dunn believed Cromartie had been relieved when Seaforth rescinded the betrothal. Somewhere in his political posturing, Cromartie had secretly become a Whig just like the Earl of Buchan, who appeared to be giving more than a wee bit of attention to Mairi at the ball.

That Cromartie was seeking an alliance with Mairi's hand had never been in question, but after the man's outrageous reaction at Castle Leod, the pieces of the puzzle were beginning to fall into place. When the time came, Gilroy didn't want his daughter to be aligned with the wrong party.

Dunn rolled to his back. He was Seaforth's man, and always would be. It had been thus since the Lords of the Isles ruled the Highlands. The thing Cromartie didn't realize was Dunn would go to any length to take care of Mairi, no matter any man's politics—and that included her father. In the future, they may need to take up arms for the Jacobite cause, but avoiding such conflict was exactly what he and Seaforth had tried so desperately to bring about. That is why they had visited James in Paris. If the exiled prince would convert to Protestantism, there would be no conflict. There would be no right or wrong.

On the bed above, Mairi sighed. Dunn rose to his elbow and watched her face. The glow from the fire made her pale skin look surreal. It illuminated the vibrancy of her red tresses as they glimmered with coppery flashes. If only he could reach out and run his fingers through the pure silk without waking her. Never in his life would he forget the softness of her hair, the suppleness of her flesh, the gentleness of her touch.

With her eyes closed, Her Ladyship's eyelashes played upon her cheeks. Across the bridge of her nose, a spray of faint freckles teased him. Lips like pink rosebuds, kissable lips begging for attention.

Aye, he wanted her more than he'd wanted anything in his life. He would wait to share her bed forever if need be. No woman had ever come to mean so much to him. Perhaps on her fifteenth birthday, he'd begun to adore her, but it wasn't until he nursed her back to health at Eilean Donan that he realized there could be no other for him. Together they would start a family, and the long-empty nursery at Eilean Donan would once again fill with laughter.

They were so close to leaving England's shores, he already smelled the peaty fires of home. On the morrow, he would take Mairi and begin the journey home. Happiness swelled in his chest—a feeling he hadn't experienced since Mairi had first declared her love.

Chapter Thirty

Dunn and Mairi left the inn at dawn and headed for the stable, which was a block away from the shore of the Thames. If he had blinked, Dunn would have missed two dragoons with muskets slung over their shoulders who raced through the cross street running parallel with the river. Dunn pulled Mairi into the shadows of the stable's open double doors. "Something's afoot."

"Do you think they're looking for us?"

"I aim to find out afore we attempt to board the ship." He inclined his head back toward the inn. "But first I'll see you safe."

He started out of the stable but stopped as two soldiers pounded on the door of the inn. "Change of plans."

"What now?" Mairi asked.

"Inside." He hastened to the loft ladder.

"Here to collect your horses, sir?" asked the stable hand, using a pitchfork to clean a stall.

"Aye." Dunn eyed the lad. "Are you friendly with the soldiers in town?"

The young man spat. "Afraid I cannot say I am."

Dunn patted Mairi's shoulder and gestured to the ladder. "Hide in the loft."

"Hide?" asked the lad.

After Mairi reached the top, Dunn sauntered toward the boy. "I aim to find out what those dragoons are on about afore we ride out into some sort of ambush. I trust those redcoats as much as I trust a thief."

"I don't trust them, either."

Dunn pulled a silver sovereign out of his sporran. "You'll keep mum about the lady in the loft?"

The boy licked his lips and grabbed the coin. "Yes, sir. Would there be anything else with which I can assist you, sir?"

Dunn glanced to the lad's breeches—he was a good deal smaller. "Where can I find a pair of trousers?"

Scratching his head, he shifted his gaze to the rear door. "Me mum hasn't yet brought in yesterday's washing. You might fit into a pair of Papa's. They're on the line."

"A guinea for the breeches. But do not give the coin to your ma until we are well away from here." Shaking his head, Dunn reached into his sporran. At this rate, the blasted thing would be empty before they sailed out of England. "Have our mounts saddled and ready to ride. I'll return in a quarter hour, no more."

Dunn strode to the loft ladder. "Are you set m'lady?"

Mairi popped her head into the gaping hole. "Ready to leave this place."

"Soon."

After swiping the breeches from the line and changing

in a stall, Dunn rolled his kilt and handed it to the lad, giving instructions to tie it to his saddle along with his sword. To add to his disguise, he borrowed a knitted workingman's cap from a peg on the wall, then twisted his sporran to the side, making it look like a Sassenach's purse, but he kept his dirk in its sheath on his belt. Straightening his leather doublet, he assumed a stiff Englishman's gait and headed for the harbor.

The dockyard was crawling with redcoats and busy with laborers. As soon as Dunn crossed the road to the pier, a dragoon backed right into him. "Out of my way," the man barked.

"'Pologies, sir," Dunn said, affecting a cockney accent. He walked to the rail and panned his gaze across the scene. He had to squint to see to the end of the pier, but a great deal of red swarmed around the skiffs rowing out to the transport Dunn and Mairi were planning to board. And if the black suit of clothes was any indication, the harbormaster was in the middle of it.

"Damnation!" Dunn swore under his breath.

But that wasn't the end of the commotion. Redcoats inspected fishing boats while their captains flailed their arms and complained about losing precious time. Good Lord, down the road, a dragoon shoved his bayonet into a cart filled with hay.

You'd think we murdered the queen herself.

To his right along a smaller pier, a two-masted brig was being boarded. That ship hadn't been in port last eve, and on closer inspection, the Saint Andrew's cross was flying atop her mast. Dunn slipped back to the stable and borrowed a barrow—one full of horse manure, thanks to the stableboy's hard work.

As he pushed the barrow along the footpath, no one

paid him mind. Even the nosy dragoons avoided coming too close. Dunn stopped on the pier beside the brig, where he was able to overhear the sailors' conversation. He pulled an old ceramic pipe out of his sporran, making a show of struggling to light it with a flint. Truth be told, the pipe was a talisman from his father and contained no tobacco. Dunn hated the rubbish.

"How could we be harboring a fugitive from Dartford? We sailed down from Edinburgh. Arrived only this morning," said a voice with a rolling Highland burr. "Check the ship's log. God's teeth, I must haste to offload this packing salt, we have a schedule to keep, mind you."

Footsteps clomped across the deck. "The hold's clear, corporal."

"Bloody oath it is," said the Scot.

Dunn cocked his ear toward the captain. The man's voice sounded familiar—almost like Kennan Cameron. But what would the Cameron heir be doing sailing shipments of packing salt around the coast? It had to be somebody else.

"It looks like you're clear," said the Englishman. "But do not tarry. Offload your cargo and set sail. I'll be watching this ship with keen interest."

Ballocks.

Footsteps resounded on the gangway as the band of redcoats disembarked.

Dunn looked up to meet the angry glare of a corporal. "Move along, ye worthless tramp."

"Just havin' a smoke, gov'nor." He tapped the pipe against the ship's hull to purchase time, then picked up the handles of the barrow, pretending to wheel it away until the redcoats moved on to the next ship tied to the wharf.

The crew on the brig continued offloading barrels of salt, stacking them alongside the road, where a horse and cart waited to take them elsewhere. Dunn moved in beside a kilted young man, someone he could easily overtake should a scuffle arise. "I need your help, laddie," he said in Gaelic.

The young man's eyes popped as he looked over his shoulder—but he understood all right. "Go away," he replied in the Celtic tongue.

"I'm taking a chance here—you can side with those yellow-livered dragoons, or you can play along. I'm Dunn MacRae, chieftain of Clan MacRae, and those bastards would sooner cut my throat than listen to the evidence from an innocent man."

"MacRae?" The lad's eyes filled with admiration. "The champion of Inverness?"

Dunn grinned, never so happy to have earned a name for himself. "The one and the same."

"Why did you not say so?"

Dunn flicked his fingers at the gangway. "Lead on."

He kept his head down as the lad led him aboard the ship while he looked for dragoons out of the corner of his eyes.

"Who the bloody hell are you?" asked a sailor.

Dunn removed his cap. "I'm MacRae. And your captain sounds like Kennan Cameron, if I'm nay mistaken."

"You'd be right." Cameron stepped into view and pattered down from the quarterdeck. "Good God, MacRae, where's Seaforth? Whenever there's trouble, he's most likely the cause."

"Not this time." Dunn shook Kennan's hand. "What in Hades are you doing sailing a brig? And on the eastern shores of England?"

"A favor to the Baronet of Sleat. He increased his fleet and needed a master to take the reins. The packing salt business is booming."

"Where to next?"

"Chatham is the last stop on this cruise. The hold's empty and we're sailing back to Skye for another load. Not fast enough, if you ask me."

"Can you accommodate a pair of stowaways?"

Kennan drew his eyebrows together. "Stowaways?"

"Is there somewhere we can talk?" Dunn might be a little careless when it came to announcing *his* name, but he certainly didn't want anyone in the crew to know Lady Mairi was accompanying him—not until they hit the open sea.

Kennan arched a knowing eyebrow. "Follow me."

* * *

Mairi watched as the lad from the stables led the horses away. Beside her, Dunn held up a woolen blanket. "Drape this over your head like an old matron."

She scrunched her nose, but did as he asked and looked up. "How do I look?"

He shook his head. "It won't do. You're too bonny."

"I beg your pardon? I'm standing here with a musty blanket over my head. I'd wager Mother Mary looked better riding the donkey into Bethlehem."

"That I would argue." Dunn pulled the edge of the blanket low over Mairi's brow and tucked her tresses under. "Now pinch it closed at your neck. If any of that hair blows about, we'll all be caught, and I'll most likely owe the Baronet of Sleat a new ship."

"The lad took the horses?"

"Aye, he's loading them into the hold. We'll walk." Dunn pressed on her shoulder. "Now stoop like an old woman."

Mairi curved her shoulders forward. "Like this?"

"Aye, and walk with a limp."

"My heavens, I might fall on my face. You've pulled the blanket so low I can't see, and now I'm to stoop and limp? I might as well be a blind beggar."

"I'll keep hold of your arm."

"You're not old and blind as well?"

"I'll stoop—and I already have a limp." He turned full circle, then picked up an old ax handle. "I'll use this as a walking stick."

"'Tis clear," said a young sailor from the stable door. "The redcoats are inspecting the boats down the other end of the harbor, but be alert, there are still plenty milling about."

"My thanks, laddie."

Clutching the blanket closed tightly, Mairi let Dunn lead her out onto the street, across to the pier, and along the planks, until they reached the gangway of a ship flying the Saint Andrew's cross. Her heart pounded as she looked up the gangway and saw a familiar face. Her best friend Janet Cameron's brother, Kennan. Goodness, she couldn't help but smile.

"Halt!" a voice boomed from the rear.

Curling her spine, Mairi chanced a backward glance. Curses, two soldiers sped toward them.

Dunn's fingers dug into her arm. "Keep going," he growled.

"Stop in the name of Her Majesty, Queen Anne!" the dragoon bellowed.

But Dunn forced Mairi onward. "It will not be as easy

for them to interfere if we are aboard," he whispered intently.

If only she could break into a run. "Must I keep limping?"

"You're doing fine, lass."

"If you do not stop this instant, I will be forced to shoot you in the back, sir!"

Mairi's foot hit the timbers of the deck. Kennan reached for her hand and pulled her to safety. "I beg your pardon, soldiers. What is it now? I've a schedule to keep, and due to the storm up north, I am already a day late."

"You said nothing about taking aboard passengers," the soldier shouted from the pier.

"I do not believe you asked. And do not toy with me. I am master and commander of this ship, and you have already tried my patience."

Both dragoons pointed their flintlocks at Kennan. "We will board your ship now, and conduct another search."

"Muskets!" Kennan bellowed. Within the blink of an eye, at least twenty sailors set to arms, their muskets pointed over the ship's rail. The master and commander signaled for the sailor to pull in the gangway. "It seems you're at quite a disadvantage, sir. Weigh anchor, lads!"

Chapter Thirty-One

*A*s they sailed out of the Thames and into the open sea, the clouds hovering over England opened to glorious sunshine. Mairi allowed herself to take a deep breath for the first time that day. Above, the enormous sails billowed with the brisk breeze as the ropes and booms creaked. Sailors busily attended to their tasks while she and Dunn stood beside Kennan near the helm.

Though the Cameron heir was only a year younger than MacRae, Kennan still had a boyish look about him. He raised a spyglass to his eye and searched up the Thames. "It looks as if the *Royal Sovereign* is not in pursuit."

"I'm certain such a grand warship has far better quarry to chase. The harbormaster said she was sailing across the channel to engage in battle."

Kennan lowered the spyglass and grinned. "Navigator, set a course for the western shores of Scotland."

"Aye, aye, sir."

Mairi clasped her hands beneath her chin. "Those words make my heart soar."

Kennan bowed and gestured aft. "Forgive me, m'lady. 'Tis time I showed you to your quarters."

Dunn held up his palm, giving the captain a knowing look. "May I have that honor? I have something I must discuss with Her Ladyship...ah...in private."

Mairi's mind ran the gamut of what he might say. The day was still young and they had already hidden from redcoats, dressed in disguises to board a ship and, lastly, engaged in a heated standoff between Scottish sailors and English soldiers. But now they were safe, and if Dunn had something to discuss, it must be important and the news had best be good. "At least no one fired their muskets on the pier."

"Thank the Lord for small mercies," Dunn said, leading her through the narrow corridor with his palm resting in the small of her back.

The ship swayed, making Mairi's footsteps awkward, as if she'd imbibed too much wine. Dunn opened the door aft and she stumbled inside. Giggling, she covered her mouth with her palm. "Forgive me. I'm afraid I haven't yet found my sea legs."

He smiled. Oh yes, she loved it when he smiled. "Not to worry. No one expects you to be floating like a swan."

Stepping farther inside, she took in the grandeur of the cabin. Straight ahead, a line of windows spanned the bow of the ship. In the center of the cabin, an ornate walnut table with matching chairs sat atop an Oriental rug. Starboard, a narrow box bed was built into the wall with cupboards on each end. And portside was a writing table with inkwell and quill. A bin filled with map scrolls stood beside it.

Mairi looked to Dunn. "This is the captain's cabin, is it not?"

"It is. Kennan has graciously offered it to you for the duration of this voyage."

"To me?" asked Mairi.

He cleared his throat and dipped his chin, giving her a sheepish look that said there was more to the story. "Och..." The big Highlander seemed oddly nervous as he raked his fingers through his hair. "I ken you wanted a wedding at the cathedral with a gathering of the clans."

Drawing a hand over her heart, she nodded.

"And I understand if you do not want to be hasty now."

"Now?"

He grasped her hand and dropped to one knee. Looking up to meet her gaze, the sunlight beaming through the window made his face dreamy. And then his jaw set with the fierce determination she'd come to know. "Kennan, as master of this ship, has agreed to marry us."

"Aboard this very brig?"

"Aye." Closing his eyes, he kissed her ruby ring and drew her fingers to his cheek. "I want to call you my wife more than I have ever wanted anything in my life. You are the only beam of sunshine in this brash Highlander's life, and I love you with every fiber of my being. I ken you want an enormous wedding, and I swear to you when we arrive home I will hold the biggest celebration Eilean Donan Castle has ever seen, but I ask you now to be my wife. To make our love holy in the eyes of God and to the crew that mans this vessel."

"Oh, Dunn, I want to marry you, too. I do not care if we are on a boat or in a wee chapel in the remotest part of the Highlands, I want to be yours forever." Her heart overflowed with joy as she laughed. "Even dressed in this dirty kirtle, I would proudly stand beside you and take my vows."

"I would marry you wearing nothing but rags. But I ken a lady as fine as my Lady Mairi would not want to face her groom on her wedding day unless she had a gown suitable for the occasion."

She knit her brows, a concoction of emotions swarming through her breast. "I would marry you in rags as well," she whispered. "I do not want to be like my father and place airs afore that which is truly important."

Dunn rose to his feet, and a deep chuckle rumbled from his chest as he pulled her into his arms. "With every passing day I love you more. But you'll not be attending your wedding in rags, lass." He cupped her face and kissed her.

"When is this wedding to take place?"

"This very day." He opened a cedar chest. "Kennan purchased this gown in Edinburgh for Janet. And I ken she would not think twice afore lending it to you for this special day."

Mairi gasped as she ran the blue silk between her fingertips. "'Tis a work of art." She held up the beading as it flickered in the light. "Such intricate detail."

"And the color of sky like your eyes." Dunn held it up to her shoulders. "The size is perfect."

Mairi glanced down with admiration. "'Tis funny. As we were growing up, Janet and I oft pretended we were twins."

"Then 'tis settled." He smiled broader than Mairi had ever seen. "I'll give you leave to dress. Ah...will you need assistance?"

"I think I can manage."

"Very well. I'll return in an hour."

"Do you think Kennan might have a hairbrush and pins?"

"Let me ask."

After the door shut behind Dunn, Mairi twirled across the floor, caring not about the sway of the ship. For today she would marry the man of her dreams. Her heart swirled and soared with each sweeping spin.

"Wheeeeeee!"

* * *

Dunn paced the deck at the bow of the brig, wiping his palms on his kilt. No matter how much the wind blew, his damned hands refused to stop perspiring. He pulled out his pocket watch and checked the time. *Fie*, only two minutes had passed since the last time he'd taken a look.

Kennan strolled toward him with a flask in hand. "Calm your nerves with a tot of whisky, my friend."

"I am not nervous," Dunn growled, grabbing the flask and sloshing some onto the deck.

"Could have fooled me." Kennan sniggered. "Must be the seasickness."

After taking a long swig, Dunn wiped his mouth with the back of his hand while a guttural sigh rumbled through his burning throat. "That did the trick. My thanks."

Kennan saluted with the flask. "Brought a cask of spirit down from Aberdeen. 'Tis from the Gordon stills."

"Och, the Gordons distill the best—do not cut corners with the aging." It was nice to engage in a bit of conversation while he waited . . . and waited.

I will wait for her forever.

Thankfully, forever never arrived. Instead, the door to

the officer's quarters opened. As planned, a sailor offered his elbow to Her Ladyship. A long, slender arm reached out from the doorway. Gooseflesh surged down Dunn's back as his bride stepped into the sun. God in heaven, she posed a radiant picture. Ethereal beams of light glowed around her, picking up the simmering highlights of her red curls. But Dunn's heart nearly hammered out of his chest when she looked across the deck and smiled.

It didn't matter if she wore a gown of blue with sparkling bobbles. Her genuine smile and the love in her eyes were all the assurance Dunn needed to fill him with everlasting happiness.

As Mairi started forward, Dunn hastened to her hand and assisted her toward the ship's bow. "You are nothing short of stunning."

A chuckle rolled from her throat. "I say, you are the most ruggedly alluring man in all of Britain."

"Not just the Highlands?" He led her to the foredeck, where the nose of the ship parted the seas.

"Nay, after my recent travels, I'd say I am an expert on the matter, and you are the most handsome man I have ever seen."

"And I am glad you are blind, m'lady."

She opened her mouth to protest, but Kennan stepped forward with a long silk cloth and a razor-sharp dagger. "Are you ready?"

"We are." Dunn offered his palm. Kennan took the blade and made a wee cut—one that would heal in a day or two, but deep enough for a line of red blood to seep through. Then he did the same to Her Ladyship.

"The union of a man and woman at sea is as sacred and holy as matrimony in God's church. And today your blood will combine. With this silken bond, I will make you one in the eyes of our heavenly Father." Kennan took their hands and pressed their palms together.

Dunn squeezed his fingers around Mairi's palm, so small compared to his. While Kennan wrapped the cloth around their hands, Dunn's throat thickened. He needed to protect her, to succor her, to love her. He would die for her.

While they stood facing each other with their hands joined, their blood mingling between them, Dunn gazed upon the only woman he would ever love. Kennan recited from the book of prayers, but the words were lost in the holiness of the moment. Had Dunn searched the world high and low, he would have found no better cathedral. The rush of the water breaking against the ship's hull, the call of the gulls, the flapping of the sails, and Lady Mairi gazing up at him with the beauty of a goddess made their wedding perfect—a day they would never forget.

"Those whom God hath joined together let no man put asunder," Kennan boomed while the crew applauded.

Dunn looked away for the first time. "Are we married?"

"You are," said the young man while he removed the binding. "Now kiss your bride."

Grinning so wide his face stretched, he dipped his chin and sealed their bond with a kiss—the first kiss of a new lifetime.

"Open a barrel of port wine for all!" shouted the ship's master.

Boisterous cheers resounded across the deck.

Dunn clutched Mairi's hands over his heart. "Kennan has offered to serve us a meal with the officers in his cabin...which would be your cabin at the moment. Do you mind, *mo leannan*?"

"Mind?" Happiness danced in her eyes as she gazed upward. "Mr. Cameron has taken us away from tyranny and has done us the great honor of presiding over our marriage. The least we can do is celebrate our good fortune with him."

He pulled her into his arms. "You are so fine to me, *wife*."

Chapter Thirty-Two

The festivities lasted until the sun set and the lanterns were lit in the master's cabin. And when at last the officers headed for their berths and left the couple alone, prickles of anticipation fired across Mairi's flesh. She stood across the table from Dunn, unable to draw her gaze from her husband's braw face. He licked his lips, his eyes growing darker by the moment. The day's beard had come in, making him look a wee bit dangerous, but she liked him that way.

"I want you, lass."

Blessed be the saints, she wanted him, too. So much. Her gaze shot to the small bed. "Will...will we fit?"

He stroked his fingers down his stubbled jaw. "I could shift the mattress to the floor."

She nodded eagerly.

Once he had the pallet arranged, he stood and faced her. "Are you willing to have me?"

Realizing she hadn't uttered a proper response when

he'd told her he wanted her, she took in a sharp breath and reached for his hands. "I've been anxious for the officers to take their leave. I have eager awaited this moment, trying ever so hard to be patient."

"I have as well. And now that it is here, for the first time in my life, I'm not certain how to proceed."

Mairi bit her lip, her hand moving to untie her bodice. She stepped forward as the neck fell open. "I believe we take it one lace at a time."

He chucked as he moved closer and released his belt buckle. "I like the way you think, m'lady." He let it drop to the deck. "But my garments are far easier to remove than yours."

Giving him a wicked grin, she reached for his tartan, unpinned the big brooch, and drew the wool from his shoulder. "Then I shall be rewarded by gazing upon you whilst you strip me bare." With a single flick of her wrist, she let the tartan fall. Her breathing became labored as she regarded his powerful body.

He began to shrug out of his doublet, but she stopped him. "Allow me."

He gave a bow. "My lady."

Mairi's desire mounted as she slowly peeled off the doublet, his shirt, and his shoes and rolled down his hose, careful not to aggravate his heel. With not a stitch of clothing, Dunn stood in the middle of the cabin, his shoulders square. Mairi's gaze meandered down his powerful chest, continued past the rippled muscles of his abdomen, and settled on his engorged erection. Unable to swallow, her tongue slipped over her lip as she stroked him. "You are magnificent."

The ship seemed to roll with Dunn's shudder. "Now you."

He took his time unlacing her bodice and stays. Still wearing her petticoat and chemise, he dipped his finger inside her neckline and lightly caressed the tops of her breasts—another shudder accompanied by the rocking of the ship, this time from Mairi.

With a tug on the bow, her petticoat whooshed to the floor. Then standing but a hand's breadth away, he slowly gathered her chemise in his fingers, inching it up to her ankles, her knees, her thighs. Mairi gasped when a rush of cool air swirled around her nether parts—though not nearly cool enough to quell the fire swirling within.

When at last they stood naked together for the first time as man and wife, Dunn held her at arm's length, his eyes filled with desire, smoldering and fixated only on her. "My God, you embody perfection."

With her inhalation, Mairi's breasts swelled with need. She could restrain herself no longer. "I must feel your skin against me."

He pulled her into his embrace and surrounded her with warmth. Sliding his hand up her spine, he cradled her head while his mouth claimed hers, wildly plunging his tongue inside, consuming her with a rush of frantic kisses.

Mairi's fingers sank into his powerful backside while her abdomen connected with his manhood. She rubbed her breasts against his chest, needing to be closer yet. He lifted her into his arms and coaxed her legs around him.

She gasped as her slick core slid over the tip of his erection. His thighs took her weight as he slipped deeper. Holding on for dear life, Mairi's breathing sped. Together they fused their bodies, completely absorbed in the love pulsing between them as, slowly, she took him into her core.

*   *   *

Too close to bursting, Dunn moved toward the pallet with Mairi in his arms. Everything about this woman heightened his need. Good God, he might come just by breathing in her scent. He kneeled and gently lowered her onto the soft bed. "I want it to be good for you, lass."

She pulled him over her. "Holding you in my embrace fills my soul with happiness."

Hovering over her, he started at her lips, then swirled kisses down her neck, along her shoulders. And finally kissed her breasts. Mairi arched up as he took her nipple into his mouth and suckled her. Forcing himself not to come, he continued lower, kissing her belly while his finger found her core and the slick button that would drive her wild. In and out he teased her, watching her buck, her eyes roll back. "Please, Dunn. I need you!"

Manna from heaven.

"And you will have me, *mo leannan*." His voice came out low, gravelly, and barely recognizable.

Dunn's breath stopped as she reached down and grasped him, guiding him to her entrance. While he slipped inside, he forced himself to clench his muscles to keep from exploding, but Mairi grabbed his buttocks and forced him deeper—forced him into ecstasy. Gripping the linens, he made ready for the charge. If Mairi dictated a ferocious tempo, he was not one to deny her demands. He let loose and thrust again and again and again.

"Faster!" she cried, her fingers digging in, showing him what she wanted.

Dunn gritted his teeth and sped the pace, his mind ravenous with passion. Higher and higher he soared until his vision blurred with the violence of his release. While he pulsed, Mairi arched up and shattered, calling his name, thrashing her head from side to side while her inner walls squeezed him.

Catching his breath, he dipped his chin and kissed her with the languid swirls of a satiated man. "You have charmed me body and soul, m'lady."

She chuckled wantonly. "You are mine for all of eternity."

"I am." He smoothed back her mane of wild hair and kissed her bonny ear. "You are so fine to me, Mairi."

"As you are to me, my love." She scrubbed her fingernails over the stubble along his jaw. "And I cannot wait to make love to you again."

"...and again," he teased.

She swirled her hips. "And again."

Chapter Thirty-Three

It took a fortnight to sail up the western coast of Britain—a fortnight of wedded bliss. Dunn and Mairi rarely left the cabin, spending most of the cruise on the wee pallet in each other's arms. Before the ship continued to the Isle of Skye, she dropped anchor in Loch Alsh at the confluence with Loch Duich. In close proximity to the very promontory where sat the bonniest castle in all Scotland, Eilean Donan.

How easily Mairi made the castle her home. All the servants welcomed her with knowing smiles, relieved not to carry on with the charade of her identity. As soon as she was settled, she and Dunn set to planning the gathering for after the harvest when the clan's crofters would be free to attend.

After organizing every last detail from the decorations to the food to the musicians, and after writing and sending out countless invitations, Mairi stood while Lilas finished pinning the ostrich feather atop an elaborate coiffure—

one fancy enough to make the ladies at court envious. Though Mairi missed Aela, Lilas was a close second for the role of lady's maid.

"You are the bonniest woman in all the Highlands, m'lady."

Mairi chuckled. "Have you met them all?"

Poor Lilas looked baffled. "Beg your pardon?"

"Thank you for the compliment." She patted the maid's hand. "You have worked miracles with my hair. 'Tis lovely."

"I'm glad you like it."

Dunn popped his head in from the adjoining door. "My word, must you grow more ravishing every time I see you?"

Standing, Mairi gestured toward the maid. "Blame Lilas. She has turned my hair into a work of art."

The lass blushed clear up to her linen coif.

"You are truly talented." Dunn gave Lilas a wee bow before returning his attention to his wife. "Are you nearly ready, my love? The guests are sure to start arriving soon."

Mairi patted her hair and looked in the mirror one last time before picking up her fan. "I cannot believe this day has come at long last."

Lilas glanced between them. "Is there anything else I can do for you, m'lady?"

"No, thank you." Mairi waved toward the door. "Go and enjoy your supper."

Dunn took her hands and regarded her from head to toe. "You really do look stunning."

"As do you. I will never grow tired of seeing you in full Highland dress. You do have quite masculine knees."

He laughed and wrapped her in his arms. "So now 'tis my knees that turn your head."

"Aye, and several other things which are covered up at the moment." She scraped her teeth across her bottom lip as his look grew dangerously rapturous. "I thought you said the guests would be here anon."

"I did."

"And you've taken care of the seating arrangements?"

"Aye, the Camerons and the Grants will be at opposite ends of the hall."

"Good." Mairi shook her head. "I cannot believe those two clans continue to feud. I love them both, and Janet Cameron is my best friend."

"And Robert Grant is mine—though Kennan did us a great service to which I will always be beholden."

"Indeed." Mairi took his hand while a bit of untimely melancholy made her throat thicken. She must ask once more. "Still nothing from Cromartie?"

"No word at all. No apologies. No regrets. Nothing."

Her lips disappeared into a thin line. She knew from the outset as soon as she left London with Dunn that her father was lost to her. But the truth didn't make her loss any easier to bear. "Well then," she said, holding her head high and summoning a smile. "We shall make merry and celebrate our nuptials with those who hold us dear."

"That we shall."

Together they proceeded to the banqueting hall to welcome their guests. Powerful clans had all replied favorably—MacKenzie septs from across Ross Shire, Robert Stewart of Appin, MacDonalds led by the Baronet of Sleat. MacIains, and though the Duke of Gordon had sent his regrets, neither the Camerons nor the Grants would miss the gathering, even though they were at odds.

* * *

By the time the guests were all announced, the feast was ready and spread out across the many tables Dunn had brought into the banqueting hall. He'd spared no expense, providing choice cuts of beef, lamb, and chicken. There was fine-milled bread for all, and he'd opened the best casks of wine and ale. And with so many apples yielded in the harvest, dessert would be his favorite, apple tart.

The musicians Mairi had hired from Inverness played softly—three fiddles, a flute, and a drum. And when the meal ended, the servants moved the tables for dancing. Mairi clapped as the pipers played an introduction to a Highland reel. "I hope your foot is completely healed, because I intend to dance all night."

"'Tis good as new," he said, taking her hand and leading her to the center of the floor. Laughter pealed through the air while the merrymakers made two lines, one for lads and one for lassies. Without the pomp, spirited Highland dancing was what he enjoyed most. For once Dunn didn't feel as if he needed to keep one eye out for enemies while he made merry. Tonight he swung his bride by the crook of her arm as together they threw their heads back and laughed.

When the set ended, Mairi and Dunn stayed for the next, watching Kennan escort Janet to the floor.

Mairi thrust out her hands. "Janet, my dearest. Did you ken your brother lent me your new gown on my wedding day?"

"Aye, he told me." Janet grasped the offered hands and kissed Her Ladyship on the cheek. "He even said how much bonnier you look in the dress than I do."

Mairi's jaw dropped as she looked to the master and commander of the ship that had taken them out of England. "He didn't."

"With all due respect," said Robert Grant with a Mac-Donald lass on his arm. "Though Lady Mairi is one of the most radiant matrons in the Highlands, I must say—"

"*Haud yer wheesht*," said Kennan, folding his arms and muscling in.

The two men faced each other in a showdown of brawn. The air grew charged with tension as Grant leaned in, his nose but an inch from Kennan's. "If I'd been able to finish, Cameron, I would have said your sister is as bonny as MacRae's wife. They're both bloody bonny."

"You have no cause to voice your opinion one way or another."

"That's enough, lads." Dunn hovered over both of them and lowered his voice. "Either you pull in your daggers and return to your corners, or I boot your arses outside the wall."

Arms still crossed, Kennan raised his chin. "I have no reason to quarrel."

"Neither have I," growled Grant, mirroring the Cameron heir's posture. "Yet."

"Och, if you pair could only see it, you men are both heroes in our eyes." Mairi flitted between them and gave each man a brimming tankard. "Laird Grant's army aided in Dunn's escape from my father's gaol cell, and Kennan Cameron sailed us away when the dragoons were closing in in Chatham. Without you brave and gallant Highlanders, I may not be wedded to the man of my dreams."

"Well put, m'lady." Filled with pride, Dunn bowed to his wife. "Musicians, play a tune for all to kick up their heels. For tonight we cast aside our differences and celebrate together as kin."

Mairi grasped his hand. "You dispatched that well."

"*We* dispatched that well. Bringing them ale and stroking their pride was nothing short of brilliant."

"I say MacRae and Lady Mairi are perfectly suited." A deep voice came from the passageway.

Dunn smiled. "Seaforth, I was just thinking the exact same thing. Welcome."

Reid stepped into the hall with his countess on his arm.

"I must agree," said Lady Seaforth.

"Aye." Ewen Cameron shouldered through the crowd. "It is a good match."

"Indeed," said Robert Grant, not to be outdone by Cameron. "There is no man better than the chieftain of Clan MacRae."

"I concur." The earl held up a hand. "Before I give the floor to our esteemed host, please allow me to present the couple with a wedding gift."

Dunn looked from Seaforth to Lady Audrey. "We are honored that you have blessed us with your presence."

"'Tis not enough." Reid pulled a document from inside his velvet doublet. "Duncan MacRae, more than once you tended me when I was on the brink of death. You planned and aided in my escape from Durham Gaol. On countless occasions you selflessly took up arms and rode beside me with your army. You have fought for me, risked your life for me, and pulled me from the mire. I owe you my life."

Dunn didn't often blush, but judging by the heat spreading across his face, he was certain he'd turned red.

Mairi grasped his hand, her eyes shining. "You are everyone's hero."

"But I am not finished, Lady Mairi," Seaforth continued, eying her. "I could not be happier that you have found the man of your dreams, Cousin. I highly approve of your choice, and will proudly stand in place of your father if ever you should need it."

"She will not," Dunn said with a wee growl.

"I thought not." Seaforth gave him a nudge, then presented him with the document. "This is the deed to Eilean Donan Castle. Your kin have held the keep on behalf of Clan MacKenzie for so many years, it is only fitting that with the joining of the House of MacRae and the House of MacKenzie I grant you title and lands."

For the briefest of moments, the back of Dunn's eyes stung. Mairi's brimmed with tears as she gasped. After a quick blink, he squared his shoulders and shook Seaforth's hand. "By God, I wish my father were here to see this. Thank you, m'lord. From the bottom of my heart, I thank you." Dunn turned to the guests and held the deed aloft. "Raise your glasses, to the Earl and Countess of Seaforth!"

Bless Mrs. Struan, she must have been paying attention, because a half-dozen stewards entered carrying trays filled with glasses of wine.

Seaforth took two and handed one to his Lady Audrey. "Please allow me to offer a toast in celebration of Dunn and Mairi as they embark on their journey of wedded bliss. May their worries be short, their happiness be long, and their children live to be healthy and happy. May the blessings of light from above shine upon you this day and forevermore. *Slàinte mhath!*"

"*Slàinte mhath!*" responded the guests most fervently.

As the music resumed, Dunn led Seaforth and Lady Audrey to the high table. "I thought you were on the Continent."

"Sailed into Inverness yesterday." The earl held a chair for his wife. "When Audrey met me at the pier and told me there was a celebration at Eilean Donan, we agreed it was an event neither of us wanted to miss."

"Thank you for coming." After helping Mairi sit, Dunn took a chair between Seaforth and his bride.

"We wouldn't have missed it for anything," said Audrey. "Lady Mairi, I've been ever so curious. How on earth did you wrest that dagger from your father?"

Mairi smiled—a wee bit sheepishly. "'Twas time to assert my will, I suppose."

Dunn winked. "It seems she has grown quite skilled with a wee dagger in her hand."

Reid gave a raucous chuckle. "Sounds as if she had a good teacher."

"Let us say I doubt she'll be cornered by dragoons anytime soon." Filled with joy, Dunn cupped Mairi's cheek and kissed her for all to see. For the rest of his days he would never tire of her kisses no matter the time of day or where they were or who was present.

Epilogue

Three years later

*I*t was a warm midsummer's day when Mairi sat on a plaid, watching Dunn take their son by the hand and wade into the pool at the Cavern of the Fairies. The water sparkled as the trees lightly rustled in the breeze. Now two years of age, Rabbie was the image of his da, fearless with dark, brooding blue eyes.

"Do not go in past your knees," Mairi warned.

The lad turned, looking affronted. "Rabbie swim with Da." He was so adorable, she almost laughed aloud.

"That's right." Dunn kept hold of the lad's hand. "But you must always listen to your mother, for she is wiser than both of us."

That made her chuckle. She'd learned so much from Dunn over the past few years; if she had grown wise, then it was because of her husband.

"Is the water cold?" she asked.

Dunn grinned. "Aye."

Rabbie shook his head and looked up at his father. "Nay. 'Tis nice. Come, Mummy."

"I think I shall stay here and slice the cheese so you'll have something to eat when you're finished playing."

Dunn took the lad under the arms, doused him in the water, and spun in circles. At the sound of her son's happy squeals, Mairi's heart soared with delight. She clapped and laughed, forgetting about the luncheon, almost ready to kick off her shoes and join them.

But her happiness turned to foreboding when Dunn stopped and looked in the direction of the rock shelf. "Ram?" Her husband carried Rabbie out of the water and set him on the plaid. "Is all well?"

The MacRae lieutenant dismounted and presented Mairi with a missive. "This arrived at the castle. I thought you'd want to see it straightaway, m'lady."

"My thanks." Mairi recognized the penmanship. "'Tis from my father."

Dunn sat beside her, his eyes wary. "What does it say?"

She'd written to her father to announce Rabbie's birth, and then on each of his two birthdays. But Cromartie had never honored her with a reply. She scanned the letter quickly, then cleared her throat. "I may as well read it aloud:

My dearest Daughter,

I have received your missives telling me about young Rabbie, and the parchment has grown tattered with my many rereadings. As I sit here alone in my study, I have spent a great deal of time reflecting on the decisions I've made in this life. I have but one regret, though I admit that single error has caused a hole in my heart that shall never be repaired.

I have pondered that which is truly important to an old man. After holding many esteemed positions for queen and country, nary a one of my accomplishments has mattered as much as clan and kin. I pushed you away and behaved badly, and for that I must ask your forgiveness. If you should ever find it in your heart to see me again, I want you to know that you and MacRae are welcome at Castle Leod. I want to see my grandson before I leave this world. I want to see you as well, Mairi. Bring that big husband of yours and I will treat him to a dram of fine whisky whilst I apologize for my past behavior.

Blessings to you and your growing family.

Your father,
The Earl of Cromartie"

Mairi folded the missive and wiped the tears from her eyes as Rabbie climbed into her lap.

Dunn smoothed a hand over her shoulder. "Well I'll be damned."

"Should we go to see him? I ken after everything he did, both of us were willing to wash our hands of him forever."

"Perhaps." He looked up to the rustling trees and sighed. "Time has a way of healing wounds. Though it might be better if we joined him at the next Highland gathering. Give him a chance to see how well we've flourished since he locked me in his gaol."

Mairi covered his hand with her fingers. "Can you ever forgive him for that?"

Dunn nuzzled in and kissed her cheek. "If you forgive him, then I can as well."

Rabbie clapped, threw back his head, and laughed as if the bairn knew how blessed they were and how magnificent the day.

Mairi took the hands of both her men and clutched them against her heart. "Well then, since we are in a magical place with news that has warmed our hearts, I think 'tis time to assuredly announce I am once again with child."

"You are?" Dunn's face beamed. "That is wonderful news!" He gave her another kiss, stood, and twirled Rabbie through the air. "Och, lad, ye'll have a wee sister soon!"

Author's Note

Thank you for joining me on Dunn and Mairi's romance. After writing this pair as supporting characters in *The Highland Guardian*, I was delighted when my editor suggested their story come next. As always with my historical romances, I take fictional situations and build characters and stories around the turmoil and politics of the times.

I styled Dunn after the heralded Duncan MacRae of Inverinate who was educated at the University of Edinburgh. A man of epic repute, he was renowned for his extraordinary physical strength as well as his poetic talent. He supported William (Reid) MacKenzie, Earl of Seaforth, and his "claymore" was once displayed in the Tower of London as "The Great Highlander's Sword." He married a Highland lass named Margaret MacKenzie, though I couldn't find anything regarding her parentage.

Because the MacRaes were a sept armigerous to the MacKenzies, at this point in history they did not have a laird or clan chief as I have put forth in this story. They bore arms for the MacKenzie line through the centuries and in medieval times were known as the "MacKenzie's shirt of mail."

Of note, in chapter 33, I indicated that Seaforth signed over the deed to Eilean Donan Castle to MacRae. This didn't actually happen. The MacRaes were the constables of Eilean Donan for centuries and maintained a close friendly relationship with the MacKenzies, though they only acknowledged the Seaforth line. The castle fell into ruin after the Jacobite uprising of 1745. In 1912, Colonel MacRae-Gilstrap acquired the ruins of Eilean Donan and restored it between 1920 and 1932 at the cost of £200,000. The castle is now considered the MacRae clan seat.

Mairi MacKenzie in this story is a fictitious character, though her father was (generally) styled after George MacKenzie, 1st Earl of Cromartie. George achieved great status in his lifetime. He did separate himself from the Seaforths and sided with the royalists, which, after the failure of the '45, proved to be in the favor of his familial line. Educated at St Andrews University and King's College, Aberdeen, he was an accomplished scholar and held many state positions under Queen Anne.

I hope you enjoyed reading this story as much as I enjoyed writing it. If you haven't read the preceding Lords of the Highlands or Highland Defender novels about Jacobite Highlanders, I suggest you peruse the books page on my website: amyjarecki.com.

Keep reading for a preview of

THE HIGHLAND RENEGADE

Available in early 2019

Chapter One

*T*he worn-in leathers of Robert's saddle groaned from years of use as he tapped his spurs into his horse's barrel. Eager to end his journey, he sat straighter, thinking of how he'd enjoy a hot meal, a tankard or three of ale, and a bath afore he invited a hearty Highland lass above the alehouse stairs. He could already feel the woman in his arms. Soft flesh, warm thighs wrapped around him, and breasts large enough to bury his face in.

"Mm," he growled to himself as he rode onward.

A westerly wind blew in from the sea, making the smokestacks of Inverlochy belch sideways. Above, the gray smoke disappeared into feathery wisps, mingling with low-hanging clouds. A light flickered in the distance, calling to him. Nearing the small trading village down below, Robert Grant, chieftain of Clan Grant, resisted digging in his heels and galloping for the alehouse. He had a mob of cattle to bring in first, and he wasn't about to lose one more head of prime beef.

Half his yearlings had been culled by poachers, namely those deceitful, lying Camerons. But no more. The remaining herd would bring in coin needed to buy more heifers and ensure a stronger yield when the cows next calved.

"Get back, ye beastie!" he hollered, cuing his mount to cut off a steer from departing from the mob. The healthy *coo* lowed and kicked its hind legs, tottering back to his ma.

At the front of the herd, Robert's man, Lewis Pratt, waved his hand, signaling his intent to follow the burn down the crag to the saleyard. Robert motioned his assent and rode around the flank of the herd to keep them on track. Weight lifted from his shoulders when they hit the dirt road and drove the cattle through the gates of a yard. He wasn't the first to arrive by far. Shaggy Highland coos brayed in yards and paddocks, all headed for the auction block. For it was Samhain, marking the end of the harvest and the biggest market days in Scotland.

After Lewis closed the gate, the Inverlochy factor scribbled into his book with an eagle's quill. He wore a mud-splattered suit of navy, and a brown periwig with a tricorn hat atop his head. "I counted one hundred and thirty-two, Mr. Grant."

"Agreed," said Robert, spying a herd two yards over that looked as if they might have been sired by his prized bull. "Can you tell me who that mob of steers belongs to?"

"The third paddock over?"

"Aye."

"That would be the Camerons' get."

"Bloody figures," Robert mumbled, catching Lewis's eye. "Take the men to the alehouse and buy them a round. I'll follow shortly."

Lewis gave a sober nod. "Aye, sir," he said before turning to Grant's men. "Stable the horses first, lads."

Robert stayed back to sign the factor's book accounting for his cattle. "How're things shaping up for Friday's sale?"

"Good all around. The cattle are fat and the harvest has been bountiful for once."

"Indeed? I reckon that's one thing the queen on her throne in London cannot take away from us."

Then man looked over his spectacles. "She's doing a bloody good job of trying. Word is English wool is selling for twice the price of Scottish in Carlisle."

"Miserable thieves." Robert watched a retinue of government dragoons ride past. "We're surrounded by them."

"Now more than usual. The colonel at Fort William has ordered an entire regiment of redcoats to Inverlochy to *keep order* for Samhain. As if we dastardly Highlanders would summon the fairies to play tricks and curse the English usurper."

"Aye?" Robert chuckled. "As unlucky and barren as the queen has been, I reckon a fairy curse would do her in."

"Today is not soon enough, if you ask me."

"Good day." Muck and mud squished beneath Robert's mount's hooves as horse and rider headed for the stable. Weariness spread through his limbs, but he'd be set to rights as soon as he ate a hearty meal—and then he'd prowl about for companionship of the female variety.

He rode through the big doors and into the dimly lit barn, the smell of hay a pleasant respite from the boggy, cattle-laden yards. He dismounted and wiped his eyes, helping them to adjust.

"Need a stall for this beauty?" asked a lad, reaching for the reins.

"Aye. And give the fella an extra ration of oats. He's earned it."

"Yes, sir."

As the boy led the horse away, Robert glanced up. *Christ.* Every muscle in his body clenched, his jaw twitched, and he balled his fists while hot ire raged from the base of his loins to the top of his head. The sudden burning throughout his chest could be nothing but pure, unadulterated anger. Janet Cameron, daughter of his nemesis, Ewen Cameron, stood but fifty paces away, right outside the tack room. Chin held high, she wore a maroon lady's riding costume, with ample skirts, trim of gold, and a lace neckcloth. Atop her golden tresses sat a black bonnet adorned with an enormous red plume. Complete with leather gloves, the ensemble must have cost a small fortune.

No wonder her father has resorted to thievery.

Robert glowered a moment too long, and the lady caught him staring. His stomach flew to his throat as if he'd leaped from a cliff and was plunging downward—or floating. God's blood, he'd seen the woman at countless fetes, and her bonny face never ceased to turn him into a deaf-mute. *Damnation.* His heart raced as he stood like a fool.

She arched her brows and quickly shifted her gaze away, but not before he looked into her eyes. Even at fifty paces, the intensity of the rich blue arrested him. Janet Cameron may be the daughter of one of Clan Grant's enemies, but she was a damned tempting sight to behold—though even looking twice at that woman was dangerous.

No, he would not be ensnared by a Cameron—or any woman, for that matter. These were perilous times with the Highlands infested with snoops and turncoats. Only the closest of kin were to be trusted. Robert had cattle to breed, crops to plant, and alliances to make to ensure his clan survived the reign of the English zealots to the south. Queen Anne's days were numbered, and when the time came, he would stand beside the true king. *It will be a glorious day, indeed, when James sails across the channel and claims his rightful place as king.*

Perhaps once things eased without a constant threat of war, Robert might consider taking a wife and starting a family. But such an endeavor was years away. At seven and twenty, he was still a young man and certainly not ready to settle down like so many of his friends had done. He would enjoy the life of a bachelor and answer to no one for a good deal longer.

"Come, Kennan. I'm hungry," Janet said, looking impatient.

Though her voice was smooth and sultry, Robert's hackles stood on end. He should have known her bloody brother was there.

The thief's heir himself stepped into the aisle. "All is in order, sister."

Robert girded his loins as he marched forward. "Hey there, Cameron, come to Inverlochy to sell my cattle, have ye?"

"Beg your pardon?"

"You ken as well as I, your da's using the same grazing lands as I am. My shepherd counted two hundred seventeen calves and, when he returned two days later, there were only one hundred fifty-one and no sign of dead."

Kennan thrust his fists into his hips. "And you believe they were stolen by my kin? You're daft."

"Cameron men were seen nearby. It only could have been they."

"With all due respect, Mr. Grant," Janet said, shouldering between the two men. "The Camerons are *not* thieves." The words were spoken with such surety, a more gullible man might have believed the lass.

Robert glanced downward, clenching his jaw and steeling his emotions from being overrun by her damnable cornflower-blue eyes. "So says who? Your da?" He snorted. "Mayhap he's a liar as well."

"Hold your tongue in front of a lady, ye maggot. How long have you been in the hills? Has the altitude addled your mind?" Kennan stepped closer. "Or is it your stench? Good God, Grant, ye smell worse than a swine's bog."

He did. He kent it as well. After a month of wrangling, Robert had no doubt he looked like a wild heathen. But he couldn't back away now, not even with the bonny lass watching. Taller than the Cameron heir, he stepped so close, Kennan was forced to crane his neck, their noses but a hair's breadth apart. "That's right, arsehole, deflect with insults. I would expect no less. You'd best pray we do not catch your men plucking the prime steers from my herd, else you'll be climbing the gallows whilst I stand back and laugh."

Kennan didn't flinch while both men slid their fingers over the hilts of their dirks. "I've no cause to quarrel with you, Grant. At least no' today. I hope you find your thieves. The Camerons have a keen interest as well. We lost numbers up near Brae Roy and reckoned it was Campbell poachers."

"Is that so?" Robert didn't believe it, though he trusted the Campbells even less than the Camerons.

"Aye." Kennan slapped his shoulder. "Good day. I've promised my sister a warm meal and I'm no' about to keep her waiting."

Robert gave a stiff nod, then tipped his bonnet to the lady. "Miss Janet."

Her eyes narrowed as she pursed her lips. Good thing, too. She might as well know now there was no love lost between their clans. Robert didn't care if she was the bonniest lass in the Highlands. She could keep her haughty airs *and* her beauty and marry a scoundrel to whom she was suited.

About the Author

Award-winning and Amazon All-Star author, Amy Jarecki likes to grab life, latch on, and reach for the stars. She's married to a mountain-biking pharmacist and has put four kids through college. She studies karate, ballet, yoga, and often you'll find her hiking Utah's Santa Clara Hills. Reinventing herself a number of times, Amy sang and danced with the Follies, was a ballet dancer, a plant manager, and an accountant for Arnott's Biscuits in Australia. After earning her MBA from Heriot-Watt University in Scotland, she dove into the world of Scottish historical romance and hasn't returned. Become a part of her world and learn more about Amy's books at amyjarecki.com.

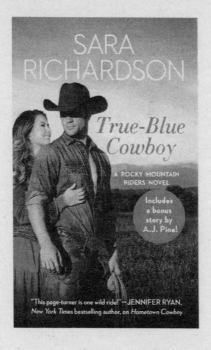

TRUE-BLUE COWBOY
By Sara Richardson

Everly Brooks is finally living her dream. There's just one problem: her new landlord. Mateo Torres is a handsome-as-hell bronc rider who oozes charm, melts hearts—and plans to kick Everly off the farm. But, when he comes to Everly with a deal she can't refuse, staying away from Mateo is not as easy as it seems.

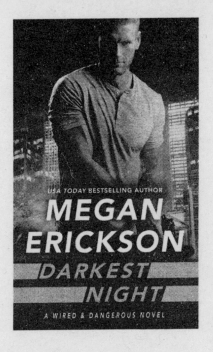

USA TODAY BESTSELLING AUTHOR
MEGAN ERICKSON
DARKEST NIGHT
A WIRED & DANGEROUS NOVEL

DARKEST NIGHT
By Megan Erickson

Bodyguard Jock Bosh has one job: Keep Fiona Madden safe. But with the attraction sizzling white-hot between them, that means keeping Fiona safe from *him*, too. When her enemies make their move and put Fiona and Jock in the line of fire, these two realize that there's more at stake than just their lives—they're risking their hearts, too.

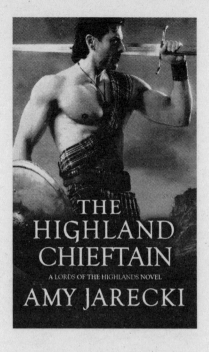

THE HIGHLAND CHIEFTAIN
By Amy Jarecki

After being jilted by her betrothed, Lady Mairi MacKenzie is humiliated and heartbroken—but she's not desperate. As the daughter of an earl, she won't give her hand to just anyone, and she isn't swayed by a last-minute proposal from Laird Duncan MacRae. Dunn may be a battle-hardened clansman, but he's always had a soft spot for Mairi. To win her heart, though, he will have to show her the tenderness in his own.

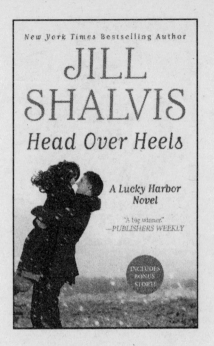

New York Times Bestselling Author
JILL SHALVIS
Head Over Heels

A Lucky Harbor Novel

"A big winner."
—PUBLISHERS WEEKLY

INCLUDES BONUS STORY!

HEAD OVER HEELS
By Jill Shalvis

Can this free-spirited rebel find a way to keep the peace with the straitlaced sheriff? It seems Chloe can't take a misstep without sinfully sexy Sawyer hot on her heels. But, with that rugged swagger and enigmatic smile, a girl can't help but beg to be handcuffed... Don't miss *Head Over Heels* from the *New York Times* bestselling Lucky Harbor series, now featuring the bonus story *Merry Christmas, Baby*!